WHEN THE HEART HEALS

HEARTS IN WINTER BOOK 3

SIMONE BEAUDELAIRE

This book is dedicated to those who struggle on in a world that doesn't recognize their value. Your bank account does not determine your value. You matter. You are loved.

PART I

CHAPTER 1

January 2001
Central High School

I don't like Alyssa Miller, Drew thought, scowling as he waited for the teacher to stop talking. His eyes skated over the object of his disapproval.

I suppose, objectively, that there's probably nothing wrong with the girl. She's certainly pretty enough, with a mane of silky, strawberry blonde hair, a heart-shaped face with turquoise eyes, soft rosebud lips, and a slender, waif-like figure. Not that I've been looking, of course.

No, there's just something about her personality that rubs me the wrong way. I can't put his finger on what it is exactly, but from early elementary, whenever we had class together (which was often, as they'd always attended the same school), we teased, made fun of, and generally tried as hard as possible to make each other miserable. And now, as seniors in high school, our stupid

A.P. English teacher is assigning us to work together on a major project that will count for a quarter of their semester grade.

It's bad luck really. How did the two of us – only us – both end up being absent on the day when groups were selected? And what a project it is: exploring theater, from Ancient Greece through the modern era, and our topic is the use of romance in plays. If there was one thing Drew did not want to talk to Alyssa about, it was romance.

"Mrs. Thompson, he begged, and his voice, he noticed, was no longer pitched for whining. The deep tone sounded collected and professional. *Good.* "Mrs. Thompson, can't I please with Adam and Jamal instead? I don't like romance. War is much more interesting to me, so I'll do a better job. You'll see. We'll have the best project in your class... in all your classes. I promise.

"I'm sorry, Drew." Mrs. Thompson said, her chins jiggling as she shook her head "But a group of three is too big for this project. I want you to work with Alyssa."

"I don't like her," he argued. Though his tone suggested calm, inwardly he raged. "She doesn't like me either. There's no way we can work together. It would be a disaster."

She closed one eye halfway, in that *oh please* look all teachers seemed to have. "Listen, Drew, sometimes in life, we have to work with people we don't like. Do you think I enjoy the company of every other teacher in this school? The real disaster would be if you two refused to do this project and got a bad grade for the whole semester. You're not changing groups. Make peace with it and get to work."

Muttering under his breath, Drew returned grumpily to the desk where Alyssa was sitting, along the wall under a large poster of a bear with paws over its face groaning about forgotten homework. *Mrs. Thompson seems to love those kinds of decorations. They dominate every wall of the whitewashed classroom.* "Sorry, Miller," he said in a sarcastic drawl. "No go. She won't let us switch."

"Shit," Alyssa whispered.

"No kidding," Drew agreed at normal volume. "Well, I don't know about you, but I'll be damned if I get a bad grade in this class. We'll have to make it work somehow."

She leaned her head back against the wall in defeat. "I guess. I need a scholarship pretty bad, so I have to keep my grades up, and pass the A.P. exam too."

Drew didn't respond. *I'd like a scholarship,* he thought, *but I probably won't need one. Dad can afford to send me to college if I live at home, but since my first pick is in town, that will be easy.* He turned his attention to his nemesis – now his project partner – and considered what the statement might mean about her. *I knew Alyssa was a little poor, but she always seemed all right.* It struck him how much worse off she suddenly looked. *Her clothes are shabbier than I recall, and that cheap makeup isn't doing her skin any favors.* A twinge of pity snaked its way through his insides. *Uh oh. Can't have that. It's too much fun teasing her. I don't want to give that up.*

She lifted her head and opened her eyes, suddenly determined. "Well, Peterson, let's brainstorm. What kind of project do you want to do?"

He shrugged, not yet finished being annoying. "I don't know. What do you think?"

She frowned at his obvious attempt to push the decision making back on her, but gamely stuck to the topic, suggesting, "A diorama? I think I have an old shoebox." She began to sketch on the notebook with a purple pen.

"Naw." He dismissed her thoughts with a wave, plucking the pen from her fingers. "That's pretty middle school. What about a commercial?"

"What kind of commercial?" she asked in a hard voice, narrowing her brilliant turquoise eyes.

He grinned at her annoyance. *She didn't appreciate the middle school comment.* Then he stopped teasing her and got down to business.

"Like, what if all our plays represent romantic getaways," he mimed quotation marks in the air, "each one with a caution, like those medicine commercials. We could talk about passionate Ancient Greece, where you can marry your mother, but the side effect could be gouging your eyes out, Venice, specializing in the interracial scene, like in Othello..."

"But you have to watch out for treacherous friends. Good idea." He could see Alyssa starting to get inspired. Her hard expression had softened, and her eyes were sparkling. "And how about a cruise, like in that Eugene O'Neill play, but you could end up..."

"In the zoo." They both laughed.

"I hate to say it, Peterson," she admitted, grabbing her pen out of his hand, "but you do sometimes come up with a good one. Let's do it."

"You know what would make it even better?" His enthusiasm sparked higher at his next clever inspiration.

"What?"

"If we recorded it on a video and played it for the class."

Alyssa got quiet, her smile inverting itself as the sparkle faded from her eyes.

"What's up, Miller?" he asked, wondering what had deflated her high spirits.

"Do you have a video camera?"

What a strange question. "No, but I think we can rent one."

"I can't afford it." Her pale cheeks turned pink.

It was a perfect opportunity to make fun of her, but for some reason, he didn't want to do it. *Teasing her about her dimple is one thing,* he reasoned to himself, *but Dad always told me not to be cruel to people. Making fun of this girl for being poor is ungentlemanly.* He refrained. "Well, the camera was my idea, so I'll take charge of renting it. How about if you work on the script?" *She is a good writer, that much I know. After all, we've been competing for top marks since we realized grades were something to fight over.*

It would have been a great opportunity for her to make a cutting comment to him, about buying his 'A', but she didn't. "That sounds fair," Alyssa said, and then, with a touch of intensity in her voice. "Thank you, Drew."

They never called each other by their first names, and he knew what she was trying to say, without really saying it... that she understood why he had said what he said, and she appreciated his kindness.

"You're welcome, Alyssa."

She gave him a little smile and leaned over the notebook to start working on the script. She kept running ideas past him the entire period, some that, even as she spoke them aloud, both could see wouldn't work. Others were so funny they had him roaring with laughter, to the point where the teacher had to tell him to calm down several times. He had never had so much fun in English class, at least not while working on his lesson, and it shocked the hell out of him. Stubbornly, he reminded himself, *everyone knows Alyssa's smart. That's not the problem, never has been, and I won't start liking her just because we have to work together.*

At last the bell rang.

"Alyssa, do you think you can finish the script this evening?" Drew requested as they gathered their books and pencil cases.

"Maybe. At least, I'll try," Alyssa replied. "See you tomorrow. I have to get to choir."

"Bye." He waved, friendly in a way that would have shocked him, had he taken the time to consider it.

As Drew made his way down the red and white tiled hallway, Dave and Jamal came up behind him, nudging him with their shoulders. "Looks like working with Alyssa is going to be okay after all," Dave commented.

"Yeah, you too seem almost like... friends," Jamal added.

"I'm not going to screw up my grade just because it's Alyssa," Drew shot back, trying to sound grumpy. "Come on. Physics. If we're late, Mr. Rodriguez will not be happy."

"Nerd athletes to class!" Dave shot one letterman-jacket sleeve into the air like some kind of dorky superhero.

"I'm looking forward to A&P this afternoon," Jamal added, scratching his head. "The cadaver lab is going to be so gross."

"Maybe if you're not planning to become a surgeon," Drew shot back. I need to be able to look at gross things and not get sick."

"True," Dave agreed. "I'm not sure why a future PT does. I'm going to stick with the outsides of people, thank you very much."

"We go because it's a class requirement, even for future engineers who are only taking A&P to stick together," Jamal reminded them. "So, let's get to *my* favorite class before we're late and we can debate the use of corpse gawking later."

The laughed. "Oh, by the way," Dave added as they neared the physics classroom, "I can't go to practice today. My mom's taking me to the orthodontist. Coach Berry already knows, but can you guys remind him?"

"Sure thing," Drew agreed. "Sorry to hear that though. I'd much rather work on my tackles than get my braces tightened."

Dave shrugged. "I want to be able to eat pizza on Friday after the game. It's better to get the pain over with early in the week."

They ducked into the classroom and took their seats, ready for another lesson. *We are a bunch of geeks. Good thing we play football and basketball, or we'd get beat up.* Mr. Rodriguez stepped up, the fluorescent lights shining on the bald top of his head and indicated the discussion question on the board.

Throughout the rest of the day, Drew found himself slightly distracted. A soft pink mouth turned up in a smile, a deeply dented cheek, and a pair of sparkling turquoise eyes kept lingering around the edges of his consciousness. He angrily tried to push the images away, but he couldn't do it.

By the next morning, he felt thoroughly grumpy and he wanted someone to blame for it. Alyssa provided a likely target, as it was her fault he was so distracted. He stomped into English class madder than he'd been the day before.

"Well, Miller, did you get the script finished?" He confronted her with a belligerent tone.

"I'm sorry, Drew," she said softly, "it's not quite done."

"Why the hell not?" he all but howled. Mrs. Thompson gave him a warning look from across the room.

"I had choir practice after school and then I had to work," she explained, chewing on her lower lip. "I'll finish it at lunch, I promise. Would you like to see what I've already done?"

Odd, normally she would have fought back. Today she's answering softly. "Work?" he asked, still feeling aggressive but lowering his volume a bit. He placed his hands on his hips and glared, demanding an explanation.

She blushed, her gaze skating away from his, and she fiddled with the end of her hair. "I'm a cashier at Sophie's Groceries most evenings. Last night I was scheduled from 5:00 to 10:00, but they kept me until 11:30. Then I still had homework due today in two other classes."

No wonder she had such dark circles under her eyes. The fight went out of Drew. "Why didn't you just tell them you had to go home?" he suggested. "Legally I don't think they can keep you so late on a school night."

"We need the money."

We is a strange thing to say. Every other high school student he knew who worked did it to save money to buy a car, or a prom dress, or save for college. *I wonder who exactly is spending Alyssa's grocery cashier paycheck.* But they weren't friends, and it was none of his business, and so he let it go. "Are you working today?" he asked, returning the conversation to safer territory.

"No, I'm off today. I still have rehearsal though." She tugged on a strand of strawberry blond hair.

"Until when?" he pushed.

"Until 4:30."

He nodded. "Okay, I have basketball practice until about then. Can we get together after that and finish the script?"

She shook her head. "I have to go home afterwards. My parents are expecting me."

Drew sighed, beginning to feel exasperated again. "Call them and let them know."

"We don't have a phone at the moment," she admitted her face flushing a dark red color.

He stared, appalled. *Who doesn't have a phone?* It took a moment of him opening and closing his mouth like a hooked fish before his thoughts could coalesce into an answer. "Okay, how about this? I'll go home with you and we can work on the project together at your place. I can see you don't like that, but listen, Allie, we've got to work on it. I promise to be nice, no matter what, okay?"

"Okay," Alyssa said, gnawing on her thumbnail, her nerves plainly displayed.

They spent the rest of the period working on the script together.

After practice, a freshly showered Drew, his hair still wet despite the biting January cold, located Alyssa in the choir room and followed her to her car.

The crusty old family sedan in the final stages of decomposition, heavily rusted, did not surprise him at all. *Hope it runs,* he thought with a frown, eyeing the decaying exterior as she opened the driver door with an audible groan of metal, but when she turned the key, it started right up and purred. *Someone's taken good care of it... at least of the mechanical parts.* He felt a little bad, following her in his almost new Trans Am. He felt even worse when he parked in front of her... home.

Alyssa lived in a mobile home, in a seedy trailer park on the east side of town. Drew's neighborhood was only a few blocks away, but for all the close proximity, it could have been another planet. Others of the same sort surrounded the pretty, spacious red-brick rambler he shared with his dad; large lots, manicured lawns, all well-kept and clean. The Millers' mobile home was old but tidy, with no junk in the yard.

Many of the neighbors seemed less fastidious. Broken toys, empty cans, and cigarette butts lay strewn everywhere, and across the street, a man with a huge beer gut sat on a broken-down folding chair, in a dirty tank top and unbuttoned flannel shirt, smoking something that neither looked nor smelled like a cigarette. The man eyed Alyssa with unwarranted interest. She shivered, and Drew deliberately stepped close to her and put his arm around her waist, making them look like a couple. He gave the pothead a hard look and escorted Alyssa into the house.

Huh. It's not as bad as I expected, he thought, considering the mobile home. While made of cheap materials, someone had taken obvious care to make the place look nice. A comfortable sofa faced a small television in the living room, and the end table had a bouquet of plastic flowers in a pretty vase. The kitchen sparkled. The room smelled fresh.

Alyssa grew a little pink in the face as Drew scrutinized her home. He still had his arm around her, and she hadn't shaken it off yet.

"Nice place," he said at last.

She reacted strangely, flinching as though he'd offered a blow rather than a compliment, then her eyes widened, and she stammered, "Th... thank you. Shall we get to work?"

"Sure." He walked her to the kitchen table, at last releasing her slender waist, and they spread out their homework.

A few minutes later, a thin, middle-aged woman with a sad expression on her face ambled out of one of the bedrooms. Drew stood as she entered.

"Hello, Alyssa," she said, giving her daughter a hug.

"Hi, Mom." She kissed the woman on the cheek and smoothed a strand of fading light brown hair from her forehead.

"Who's your friend?"

"This is Andrew Peterson. We're doing a school project together."

Mrs. Miller's eyes narrowed a bit at the mention of his name. "Oh. Nice to meet you, Andrew."

She must remember... all the trouble I've had with Alyssa, he thought, but since she was observing the protocols, he could do the same. "Nice to meet you too, ma'am."

He shook her hand politely. She gave him a sad-eyed smile and went back the way she had come.

A thousand half-formed questions crowded into Drew's mind, all awkward and none his business. He kept them to himself.

They worked for a couple of hours, finishing the script

together and practicing their lines so they could say them smoothly.

"Allie, when do you have your next day off from work, so we can finish this?" he asked, as he pulled on his letterman jacket and gloves.

She thought for a moment, one finger tangling in the bottom of her strawberry blond ponytail. "Well, I work tomorrow and Friday until close, and I'm opening Saturday, but I should be off Saturday afternoon, say about four. Would that work for you?"

Uh oh, so much for my date. Marcie will understand though. It's school. She'll understand, but she won't like it, he amended. Drew felt a profound sense of relief at being able to put it off. "Sure, that would be fine. Listen, I have to go. Dad's expecting me for dinner."

She smiled at him. "Okay. See you in class tomorrow."

Why have I never noticed what a pretty smile Alyssa has? Maybe because we used to frown at each other all the time? Shaking off the unwanted thought, he said, "See you. Thanks for inviting me."

"Thanks for your help." Alyssa rose.

Drew glanced out the window. "Hey, don't walk me out, okay? That guy's still there and I don't like the way he looked at you."

She shivered. "He freaks me out."

"Keep your distance from him."

"Right."

Drew walked out to his car. He gritted his teeth and growled. Someone had dragged a key over the cherry red paint. *That figures. Poor Allie, having to live in this junk heap.* Rolling his eyes in disgust, he drove home, still thinking about her. *It's amazing how being polite to someone changes the entire nature of their relationship and my own feelings about her.* Working with her was almost like working with a friend, and he suddenly felt protective as well. *Marcie isn't going to like this.*

～

Saturday afternoon, Drew picked Alyssa up and drove her to his house, so they could finish on the project. As Alyssa got out of his car, the scratch marks on his door captured her attention. "Drew, someone keyed you."

"I know." He shrugged. She didn't need to know how he'd kicked the hell out of the punching bag he and Dad had hung in the basement. *It wasn't her fault.*

"Was that on Wednesday?" she asked hesitantly.

"I think so," he admitted.

"I'm sorry." She touched his arm with one bare hand. Her fingers looked cold. "If you have to come over again, let's leave your car at school, okay? It kind of stands out in my neighborhood."

He patted her hand, finding her fingers cold as he'd expected. *It's about 12 degrees out here. Where are her gloves?* "That's a good idea, but don't worry about it, Allie. It's not your fault."

Without thought, he slipped his arm around her waist as he walked her into the house and down the hallway to the den. He had placed the rented video camera on the coffee table and rearranged the brown leather furniture, pushing it up against the walls to create an open area in the center for their commercial set. "Right. Okay, let's run through our script one more time. I want to be sure I've really got it all down before we turn on the camera."

"Sure."

They practiced a while, and then set up the camera on its tripod and got to work. It took a few tries, but they eventually got a video they were proud of. Then Alyssa helped Drew move the furniture into its usual configuration around the entertainment center. At that point, Drew's dad came in.

"Hey, Dad. This is Alyssa. Allie, my dad, James Peterson."

"Hello, Alyssa," James replied, his pale blue eyes shining with mirth at the mention of her name. *I'm going to have to answer some questions later, I see.* Then his father continued. "Hey, would you two like some banana bread?"

"Sure, Dad," Drew agreed eagerly, his mouth watering at the thought of his dad's expert baking. "You know I'm always hungry."

"Yes, please."

What's that note in Alyssa's voice? Drew turned to study her and found a strange, manic expression on her face. She rubbed her lip with the back of her hand.

James returned with a plate laden with four thick slices of the bread. Alyssa grabbed a piece and took a bite. Her eyes, just before they slid closed, took on a wild, wolfish expression. She trembled as she chewed.

He finished his slice and deliberately pushed the other two towards her without a word. Then he got up and left the room. When he returned with a tall glass of milk, the plate was empty of every crumb. He sat down beside her on the sofa and handed her the milk. She accepted and downed it quickly, setting the glass on a coaster. Then she looked at Drew, blushing furiously. He held out his hand to her, and she took it. He pulled her against him, hugging her tight. She didn't fight, she just leaned her cheek against his shirt. Her hands rested on his chest.

"When did you eat last?" he asked gently.

"At school," she replied, her voice strained.

"Lunch yesterday?" he asked, dismayed.

"Yes," she mumbled into his shirt.

"Why?"

She lifted her head at last. "It's pretty normal."

He looked into her eyes and saw the strain she had been living under. *School, work, no food. Alyssa's on the brink.* "Oh my God. I'm sorry I've been so mean to you. I had no idea."

She tried to smile. "I've been mean to you, too. It was stupid, wasn't it?"

"It was," he agreed. "Let's not do it anymore."

"Okay."

Alyssa's tenuous control over her emotions slipped, and the longer Drew held her, the harder it became to hold on. When she felt his hand sliding through her hair, caressing her, she lost it completely. Try though she might, she couldn't hold in her sobs. He sat with his arms around her, petting her back and hair while she cried.

At last, the storm passed. Alyssa wanted to be embarrassed, but Drew wouldn't allow it. He handed her a tissue and asked, his voice filled with concern, "Is there anything I can do?"

Alyssa shook her head and blew her nose.

"Can you tell me what's going on? Is anyone... hurting you?"

Who is this boy with the gentle eyes? I think I preferred mean Drew. At least I understood him. "No. I'm not being abused. I'm fine."

"That's a lie. You're not fine at all," he said gently, wiping her cheeks with his thumbs.

She shook her head. "I'll get through. Sorry, but I don't want to talk about it. No one can help, so what's the point?"

Drew nodded. Then he did something she had never expected. He pressed the back of his hand against her cheek. She leaned into the soft touch that seemed to awaken warmth that thawed her frozen spirit. He stroked her skin for a moment, and then turned his hand over, his fingers on one side of her jaw, his thumb on the other, and he tilted her face up, so he could look into her eyes. She could see the hunger in those emerald depths. It startled her almost as much as when, a moment later, he leaned forward and touched his mouth gently to hers.

The couple shared a long sweet, innocent kiss. He made no attempt to penetrate her mouth. *Who would have guessed, after all these years of animosity that I would be here, now, with Drew Peterson, and kissing him, of all things?* And yet, it was the nicest kiss she had ever had. Granted her opportunities had been somewhat limited, but she did not completely lack experience. Then she remembered something important and pulled back. "Drew, don't."

"What? Why?" He appeared bewildered.

She glared at him. "You're playing with me."

"I'm not," he protested.

The sun shone through the window, accentuating the ruddy strands that threaded through his light brown hair. *Did I know he's this attractive? Until recently his face represented trouble.* Trouble it, seemed, had not finished with Alyssa. "Yes, you are. What is this, take advantage of the poor girl? She'll be grateful for the attention? You have a girlfriend," she reminded him, furious.

Understanding dawned. He stroked her cheek again as he explained in a soft, thoughtful voice, "It's not like that. And I don't have a girlfriend, not anymore. We broke up last week."

"What?" *Beautiful Marcie? The cheerleader with the big eyes and bigger boobs? Who would break up with her?* "Why?"

"Because of you."

She lowered her eyebrows. "What do you mean?"

"I had to cancel a date with her to work with you today. She took it the wrong way."

Ah, that makes sense. Marcie has always been... touchy. "But once she sees the video, she'll understand it was just schoolwork."

Drew shook his head. "No, Allie, it's over between Marcie and me. We weren't getting along well anyway, and it was past time."

"But... but..." Alyssa spluttered, "she's crazy about you. I thought you two might be the ones to prove high school relationships can work out."

His expression turned rueful. "I don't think she was crazy about me so much as about being with an athlete. She really didn't care much about what I wanted or felt."

Alyssa looked at him quizzically.

"Okay, look, I'll tell you, but only if you promise never to say a word about it to anyone. I don't want people spreading rumors about Marcie, okay?"

Drew wants to confide in me? He dumped Marcie but doesn't want to spread rumors? Wow, what a gentleman. "Sure. I know how to keep things private."

"She wanted more than I was willing to give." He flushed.

"More what?" Alyssa asked, struggling to understand.

"More physical." Drew was really blushing now.

Alyssa's eyes widened. "Really? A high school boy not willing to... get physical? How strange."

Drew shrugged. "It's not a great mystery. My dad raised me to be a gentleman, and one thing that means a lot to me is treating my girl right. It's okay to date someone, but I would never go to bed with her if I didn't love her. I don't love Marcie."

Alyssa blinked. *What teenage boy thinks like that?* "Wow.

That's amazing, Drew. I'm impressed. Not too many guys would turn down an offer like that."

"Well, that's just how it is."

"So, you've never..." Her cheeks burned. *What did you ask that for?*

His face remained red, but he replied in a matter-of-fact tone, "Nope. Not yet. I'm not ready."

Shaking her head at her own nosiness, she hastened to reassure him. "Me either. You're not the only one, Drew."

"Thanks, Allie." He grinned lopsidedly, making her stomach flutter. "So, at any rate, you can see I'm not playing games with you. Marcie and I are through, and I... well, suddenly I seem to like you. If you don't like me, could you please tell me, so I can stop pursuing you?"

"Is that what you're doing?" Alyssa's heart gave a wild thump and commenced to pounding.

"Yes."

"Wow." She gulped. *What am I supposed to do about this?* She felt a bit lightheaded. *It's more than I can take in all at once.* "Okay, um, can I think about this a couple of days?"

"Of course." He smiled shyly.

How often did I make fun of those braces he just had removed? Now he has a perfect, movie star smile. She blinked. *Don't get star struck. He's still the same Drew Peterson who made your life miserable since kindergarten.* Confused, Alyssa blurted, "I need to go home."

"Okay, but before you do, let me make you some sandwiches, okay?"

Alyssa's mouth watered, but her excitement gave way to shame. "No thanks, Drew. I don't want any charity."

He thought for a moment. She could practically see the gears turning in his brain. "It's not charity. We bought too much lunchmeat at the store, and we won't be able to use it up before it spoils. You would be doing us a favor by taking it."

She gave him a long look. *Sure, Peterson. What happened to using all that creativity and intelligence to be annoying?* But the lure of food could not be denied, nor could the excuse that spared her pride. "All right."

He took her hand in his and led her into the kitchen. *Whoa. This room is at least three times the size of ours, and just look at those granite countertops and wood cabinets.* The longer she lingered in Drew's stylish home, the more uncomfortable she felt.

Drew pulled out a loaf of bread and opened the fridge. She could see he hadn't been lying. The meat drawer was piled with plastic tubs of lunchmeat, way too much for a small family like his. *Way to go, Drew. I can almost accept it's not charity.*

Drew made Alyssa enough sandwiches for three people for two days, along with carrot and celery sticks and apples. He piled the food into brown lunch bags and escorted her to the car.

They drove in silence, Alyssa digesting this new side of Drew, wondering what to make of it all.

Alyssa is so pretty, Drew thought. *It's sad she has to live in poverty so deep she doesn't have enough to eat, and no one knew. If she'd let me, I'll make an effort to change that. But I have to watch out for that stubborn pride of hers.*

At her house, he noticed the scary man sitting on his chair again, this time swilling cheap beer. A six pack, half gone, sat at his feet, and empty cans littered the patchy snow. *Disgusting. This is no environment for a teenage girl to grow up in. No environment for anyone, really.* Drew walked Alyssa to her door. On the step, he turned to her. "Think about what I said."

"As if I could think about anything else," she replied. Her cheeks flushed with the cold and her lips looked nearly blue. He needed to get her inside. But first... "There's something else."

"What's that, Drew?"

"This." He pulled her into his arms and kissed her again... and again... and again. And then he pushed her through the door of her house and vaulted into his car.

CHAPTER 2

*B*y the time the tardy bell rang for English class Monday morning, Drew had about lost his mind waiting to see Alyssa. He knew she'd had no way of contacting him over the weekend, but he didn't like it. He wanted the answer to his question, and he had another one to ask her.

She walked into the room. Drew's heart thumped even as he narrowed his eyes, studying her. *She looks different. What is it?* Something about her appearance seemed... subdued. It gradually dawned on him that she wasn't wearing any makeup at all. *She can certainly pull it off; her natural face is pretty enough, but makeup and high school go hand in hand for most girls.* She slipped into the desk next to his.

"Do you have the video?" she asked.

"Yup."

"Good."

"Allie, about what we were saying over the weekend..."

"Hello, class," Mrs. Thompson said, rising from her desk with an audible popping of knees and hips and waddling to the board. "I hope all of you have prepared your projects and presentations for today."

"Talk to me at lunch," Alyssa whispered. Drew nodded. There would be no time for further conversations. He passed the video cassette to the teacher and returned to his seat, shifting it subtly to move closer to Alyssa.

Mrs. Thompson squeezed into one of the desks near the front of the room, which left Alyssa and Drew unobserved in the back. He reached over and took her hand in his. She let him, stroking the side of his index finger with her thumb. The presentations began: an assortment of dioramas, skits and posters. Last came Drew and Alyssa's video, which the class found highly amusing. Mrs. Thompson tried to conceal her laughter under a cough, a sneeze, but eventually, a porcine snort erupted from her nose, and she began to chortle along with the rest. Drew grinned and Alyssa seemed to glow from within. *We did a good job,* he thought. Her expression reflected his sentiment. The bell rang, and the class packed up their materials and prepared to depart.

"Drew, Alyssa, please come here," Mrs. Thompson said softly. They went, still holding hands.

"Well done, you two. I see you've worked out your differences." She indicated their interlaced fingers with a nod of her permed black hair.

"Yes, ma'am," Drew said. "Thank you for making us work together."

She wrinkled her nose at them. "Of course. See you tomorrow."

Drew walked Alyssa to choir and then had to hurry to physics. He barely made it before the bell and had the hardest time concentrating, even though he liked the class. The hour crept by.

At last the bell rang. He made his way to his locker, pulled out his lunch and headed to the cafeteria. Taking a seat at a round plastic table in a little-used corner of the expansive, echoing room, through which hundreds of adolescent voices currently roared, he looked around for Alyssa. She stood in the lunch line, but he caught her eye and she waved at him. A little half smile turned her cheek into a crater. *That dimple is really cute. I bet she hates it.* A few minutes later, she slid onto the bench next to him with a tray of something mysterious and goopy that smelled unpleasant.

"What is that?" he asked, disgusted. *There's a reason I bring my lunch each day.*

Alyssa shrugged and began eating it. Clearly, it made no difference to her whether it tasted appealing. He pulled out his sandwich, a banana and a bottle of water.

"So, Alyssa," he said casually, as he peeled back the plastic bag to eat his ham and Swiss, "what do you think? Am I good enough to be your boyfriend, or what?"

She blushed, swallowed, and took a sip of milk. "You're good enough, Drew. More than good enough."

"Good, because I'd like to take you to prom."

The endearing pink in her cheeks intensified until it looked almost painful. "I... I don't know what to say. Okay, I wasn't really finished. You're good enough, certainly. You're actually terrific, now you're not acting like a butthead anymore, but I don't have time for a boyfriend. I work a lot, and when I'm not working, I'm doing homework or going to choir practice."

That argument won't sway me. "Well, I have homework too. Why couldn't we do it together?"

Alyssa's eyebrows drew together. She popped some wrinkled grapes into her mouth, chewed, and swallowed before answering. "We could, but why would you want to?"

He answered honestly, with no joking. "I like you, Allie. I know, it shocks the hell out of me too, but can't we just try it? See how it goes?"

She shook her head. "We'd better not. You'll only break my heart."

"Hmmm. Sounds like you like me too." He winked at her.

The faint hint of roses in her cheeks bloomed to full flower. "Well yes. I guess I do. But it's not a good enough reason."

He chuckled. *She's grasping at straws.* "What other reason is there? I'm not proposing marriage, just asking you out. It happens all the time. I bet you've been on a few dates before."

"One." She shuddered.

"What happened?"

"Icky Sam Watson took me to the movies and tried to grope me. He put his tongue in my mouth. It was disgusting."

Drew scanned the room until he found the boy in question. *Greasy black hair and pimples, with one finger up his nose.* "Ugh. Sorry."

"It's okay. I made such a fuss they asked us to leave. I've never been so glad to walk home in my life."

Drew's neck shot out in her direction. "What? Walk? You don't live close to the movie theater." *How did I miss so much?*

Alyssa shrugged. "At any rate, I can't go to prom. We can study together sometimes, as friends, if you want, but dating just won't work. We're too different."

I don't agree with that either. "I don't think we're really all that different. We're both smart, we both know what we want in life, and during the project, we found out we're pretty compatible. Okay, so I can see that your family doesn't have a lot of money, but it's not a problem."

"It is to me," she retorted. "You're rich, Drew. You can't imagine what it's like to be poor."

"We're not rich by a long shot, Allie," he insisted. "Just middle class."

He noted a hint of despair in her ocean-colored eyes. "You live in a house with a basement. You drive a nice car. I bet all your clothes were new this year. Compared to me, you're like King Midas. I would as soon try to date a movie star." Despite her firm tone, her eyes looked sad. *She does want to go out with me, but she doesn't think it would work. She's giving up the idea before she even gives it a try. Now that just isn't okay.*

"Allie," he said gently, trying to think of how to convince her, "I know what you're saying is true, but money doesn't make people better or worse than each other. You're just as valuable as I am, and it has nothing to do with your family's income or the kind of house you live in. It's you yourself, Alyssa. You're an amazing girl. I like you a lot. Can we please just try to be together?"

He could see the longing in her expression. He glanced around the room, and, having discerned no principals were looking, kissed her quickly on the mouth.

"I really want to, Drew," she said at last, eyes swimming with moisture.

"Then just do it," he urged. "Say yes, Allie."

She closed her eyes. "Yes."

"Good girl. Now about the prom?"

"That I can't do." She shook her head vigorously from side to side.

"Why?" he demanded.

"I don't want to go to prom." She crossed her arms over her chest and frowned.

"Is that true or is the real reason because you don't have anything to wear?" he guessed.

"The latter." She blushed.

"I'll see what I can do about that."

"No, Drew." She pressed her hands to her cheeks. The redness, which had begun to fade, returned full force. "It's too embarrassing."

"Don't be embarrassed," he urged. "I want to spoil you a little. You need it. You're under a lot of stress, aren't you?"

"Yes," she admitted, nibbling her lip.

"Care to tell me what it is?" he asked.

She seemed to withdraw from him. "It's a long story."

"We have the rest of lunch."

She considered him for a moment. "Well, fine." Her hand slid into his, and she took another bite of her mysterious lunch, chewing thoughtfully. Drew ate his banana while he waited. "We've never been very well off, you know, but the last few months have been especially hard. My dad is a mechanic, at this really small family-owned shop. Because they have a tiny number of employees, they can get away with not paying my dad much, and his insurance is piss poor. Mom's a secretary and while her insurance is better, her pay is low, but between the two of them we always did okay, until last October."

She stopped speaking, her eyes scanning something Drew couldn't see. "What happened in October?" he prompted.

She gulped, sniffled, and forced herself to go on in a voice that wavered on every word. "Well, my dad hadn't been feeling well for a while. He finally went to the doctor and found out that he... has cancer."

Drew closed his eyes. "Oh jeez, really?"

"Yes. The bad, scary kind. He's been on chemo and radiation since then, but he needs surgery, and his insurance doesn't want to pay for it. They'll only cover this tiny percentage, but if he doesn't have the surgery..." She paused, swallowing hard.

"He'll die?" He pronounced the brutal words in his softest, gentlest voice. Alyssa flinched and then nodded. "I'm so sorry."

"The thing is, Drew, if he doesn't have the operation, well, there's no doubt what will happen, but even if he does, there are no guarantees. His life expectancy with this condition is five years, even if all their procedures are successful. He isn't sure he wants to bother."

"Five years makes a big difference. He should do it," Drew said firmly.

"I know, but it's his decision, not mine. Oh, Drew, what will I do without my daddy?" A tear rolled down Alyssa's cheek. He hugged her fiercely. She stayed in his arms for several long moments. The front of his shirt grew wetter and wetter, but he didn't care.

"Drew, Alyssa, what are you doing?" The assistant principal, Dr. Rhodes, appeared beside them, her expression displeased.

"Sorry, Dr. Rhodes. This isn't really a public display of affection. Allie's going through a hard time. She needed a hug."

Alyssa lifted her head. The principal looked at her red face and tear-swollen eyes and walked away, shaking her head.

"Come on, sweetheart, let's get out of here and go outside. You could probably use some fresh air."

Alyssa gulped the last of her milk and grabbed her roll before dumping her tray. He took her free hand and walked her out to the courtyard. She munched the roll as they went along.

Outside, the biting January wind whistled down the walkway and nipped at the couple, finding its way right through Alyssa's thin coat until she started shivering. Drew took off his letterman jacket and draped it over her shoulders. She snuggled into it, turning her face into the wool of the shoulder as though savoring the scent of his cologne. His heart clenched. *Marcie wore my jacket more than once. She loved it but seeing her in it never affected me this way. Wow.*

Drew walked Alyssa to a part of the courtyard that wasn't visible from either the cafeteria or the hallway. It was a favorite make-out spot, so teachers patrolled it regularly. *We might get caught, but I've never seen a girl so in need of a kiss in his life. I'll risk it.*

Alyssa knew this sheltered corner, behind the support pillar of the partial roof that protected the courtyard in bad weather, but she had never been in it, only walked by and seen couples holding each other close there. *Now it's my turn.* Nerves fluttered in her belly. Drew pulled her against his body, adding his warmth to hers and lowered his head to whisper in her ear. "I'm so sorry, Allie. I'll be here for you, no matter what."

Tears blurred her vision again. "Thank you, Drew."

He lifted her chin and pressed his mouth to hers again in a delicious, tender kiss. It felt soft and sweet and lovely. This time, though, he lifted his head after a disappointingly short time.

"Allie? Remember when you told me about your date with Sam?"

She nodded.

"Was it him you disliked, or the fact that he put his tongue in your mouth?"

Oh dear. I wonder where this question is headed. "Both, why?"

"Because I want to put mine in there."

Her eyes widened. *That's what I thought. But is this what I want? Well if it isn't, why is my stomach fluttering in half-nervous excitement?*

"Will you let me try it?" he pressed.

She peeked out but found no teachers around. "Okay, I guess."

"Open a little."

Okay, Allie. This is high school. You shouldn't graduate without at least one decent French kiss... I hope it's decent. Half-excited, half fearing she'd find it revolting, she parted her lips slightly and he lowered his mouth again. This time Drew tasted her, first on her lips, and then by sliding his tongue gently between them, touching hers.

Alyssa gasped at the startling, pleasurable sensation. Drew's kiss felt wet, but not disgusting. *I actually kind of like it.* As Drew's tongue swirled and played, Alyssa found the sensation growing in appeal from neutral to exciting. She allowed her own tongue to touch his and was rewarded with a tingle of arousal low in her belly. *Oh, my.*

Her arms snaked around his neck, holding him firmly against her. *Is this really the same Drew I've known all these years? How can it be so?* And yet his delicious taste and tempting caresses pleased her more than she would ever have imagined anyone being able to do. *Could it be that we fought to disguise how much we like each other?*

Drew kissed Alyssa for a long time, and then, apparently deciding they had tempted fate enough, walked her out of the hidden spot, his hand in hers, and strolled back towards the entrance of the building. His lips curved up in a satisfied grin, and she knew she had a goofy, dreamy expression on her face. *Oh well. It isn't every day a girl gets to make out with one of the hottest, most popular boys in school.*

"I knew it," an angry female voice growled behind them. Both turned. Marcie Lamar glared at them, her dark hair practically vibrating with fury. "You're a liar, Drew. You told me that us breaking up had nothing to do with Alyssa."

"It didn't," he replied calmly. "We have different values, Marcie. We didn't belong together. I'm sorry if that upset you."

"You asshole," the little brunette snarled.

"Hey, leave him alone," Alyssa interjected. *Marcie can be disappointed, but there's no need for name-calling.*

"Shut up, Alyssa," Marci snapped. "You're so poor you think a flush toilet is a luxury. Do you think it's like Cinderella, bitch? The handsome prince will come and rescue you? Forget it. He'll just break your heart too. I hope he hurts you real bad."

She turned and stormed away.

"Wow," Alyssa said. "Are you sure she wasn't in love with you?"

Drew shrugged, seeming unconcerned with all the insults Marcie had just heaped on him. "I'm sure. And even if she was, there was no future there. It wasn't working. I couldn't pretend anymore."

Alyssa squeezed his hand. The bell rang, and they headed off to class.

That evening, Drew sought out his dad.

He found James in the kitchen, breading chicken breasts for their dinner. Drew grabbed some lettuce from the fridge and started chopping it for salad.

"Dad?"

James lifted his head from the slimy mess on the cutting board and met Drew's eyes, giving him his full attention. "Yes, son?"

One thing I've always appreciated about Dad. No matter what's going on, he always makes time to listen. "Can I borrow some money from you?"

James lowered one eyebrow. "What for? Is your allowance spent?"

"No, but I need more than that." Drew set the knife down. *Can't chop while looking away. I need my fingers, so I can perform surgery someday... and for that shark dissection next week.*

"Why?" His dad's eyebrows drew together.

Drew took a deep breath and explained. "I'm taking a really special girl to the prom, but she doesn't have money to buy a dress. I want to help her out."

"What happened to Marcie?" James gave his son a quizzical look before returning to his raw chicken and bowls of breading ingredients.

"We broke up," Drew explained, and then, before his dad could ask, added, "We didn't have the same values."

James stilled his busy movements. The chicken he held dripped buttermilk back into the bowl. "So, who are you going with then?"

"Alyssa. Do you remember her? She came and worked on a project here last week."

"Yes, I remember," James said. His tone left Drew with no doubt that the promised interrogation was about to begin. "Is this the same Alyssa I made you apologize to in the fourth grade for putting gum in her hair?"

"Yes," Drew admitted. The memory twisted his heart. *How much strain was the family under back then?*

"The one whose mother called me in the sixth grade and complained you were bullying her?" James pressed.

"Yes." Drew felt sulky. *Do I have to remember what a jerk I was? Isn't it enough to realize I was wrong?*

"What happened?" James asked at last.

Drew blew out between his lips, making a noise like a displeased horse. "I got to know her."

James smiled, and more than a hint of paternal pride shone in it. "Ah. So, she can't afford a dress?"

Surely telling Dad isn't the same as spreading rumors. I'm in over my head with this one. "They can't even afford a phone. Her dad is sick, and she's working all the time. She deserves to have a special evening, and I want to give it to her."

James returned to his chicken in silence, dipping the wet meat into a bowl of bread crumbs and shredded Parmesan. At last, he spoke. "Son, do you have any idea what prom dresses cost?"

"Not really."

"I'll give you $100.00. You have to figure out the rest."

That should be enough, right? "Okay. I'll pay you back, Dad. I promise."

"Yes, you will," James agreed. "This weekend, you're going to clean out the basement *and* the garage."

It was a big job, but Drew smiled. "Sure. I can do that."

James set the breaded chicken onto a rack, which had been placed on a baking sheet. Four other pieces waited. He returned to the bowl of buttermilk and retrieved another strip. "She must be a very special girl," he said in a neutral voice.

"She is." Drew pondered before voicing his most terrifying, heady thought out loud. "I think I might be falling for her."

"Take it easy, son. Girls who are in the midst of hard times can be awfully susceptible." James added a telling glance to the statement before dipping the chicken breast into the breading. Bits of dry bread and cheese clung to his fingers.

"Dad, I didn't sleep with Marcie, even though she offered right out. Alyssa isn't like that. I promise I won't take advantage," Drew vowed. *Knowing what I know now, I realize that would be a bastard thing to do, even if I wanted to – which I kinda do.*

His announcement got James' full attention. "You're a good guy, Drew." His voice caught.

Oops, took the feelings a bit too far. "No offense, Dad, but don't hug me when you've got chicken-juice, buttermilk, bread-crumb, monster hands."

James waggled his dirty fingers at his son, and they both laughed. *I am so lucky to have a dad as great as this. It almost makes up for not having a mom.*

CHAPTER 3

*F*or the next week, Drew dedicated himself to spending as much time as possible with Alyssa. It stunned him how wrong he had been about her. Now that she had her guard down, she was actually great to be with; friendly, funny, and not at all shallow or ditzy. He could tell if she was under less stress, she would be devastatingly beautiful. Even as it was, with her natural sparkle diminished, her loveliness distracted him beyond reason. He really was falling for her.

On Saturday afternoon, he picked her up to take her shopping. As he drove under the naked oak and maple trees, turning carefully on the slippery pavement, he pondered how much his feelings had changed, about so very many things.

I remember when Marcie and I got together. She's pretty and has that sexy figure. When she started staring and winking at me, I felt flattered, and at the time, it seemed like reason enough to give it a try. After about four months of heady kisses and wet dreams, I slowly realized she made me uncomfortable. She makes cutting remarks about a lot of things that matter to me, like the Catholic Church, getting good grades, and family. She's also rude to her mother. Her pressuring me to have sex was the last straw. I would have broken up with her anyway, even if someone better hadn't come along. Now Alyssa, on the other hand, is a different sort, someone I can respect.

He parked in front of her mobile home and walked up to the door. Mrs. Miller answered his knock, looking exhausted. He shook her hand politely. She stepped outside and shut the door behind her. "Hello, Drew. Good to see you. How are you doing?"

"I'm well, thank you. And you? How are you holding up, ma'am?"

"As well as can be expected, thank you for asking," she began, and her face grew so sad, he feared she might burst into tears. Then her expression hardened. "Listen, Alyssa is just finishing up in the shower and will be out in a moment, but talk to me, would you? Why are you doing this?"

Drew blinked. "Doing what? Taking her out?"

"Yes, and buying her things, and giving her food. This is not a soup kitchen."

Such pride. Just like Alyssa. I wonder why it's so hard for them to admit they need a little help. Maybe Dad will get it. I'll ask him later. He weighed his words carefully. "I realize that, ma'am. I mean no disrespect, I swear. The thing is, I like Alyssa a whole lot. She's a classy girl and really special. I like seeing her smile, and with everything that's been going on, that smile has gotten pretty rare. I wish there was more I could do to help, not because I feel sorry for you guys, but because I want to make Allie happy."

Mrs. Miller's eyes grew misty again. "I wish I could give her the senior year she deserves; a nice car, a prom dress, and free time to enjoy with a handsome boy."

He smiled sadly. "I understand. Life sometimes gives us things we don't want."

Her gaze and voice hardened again. *Oops, she thinks I'm pitying her.* "What do you know about it?" Mrs. Miller snapped, confirming his suspicion.

He answered with brutal honesty. "My mother left when I was five and I never saw her again. I do understand a little."

His words calmed her. The edges of her rough strength seemed frazzled, as though she might crack and shatter at any moment. "I see. Well, you be sure and treat Alyssa with respect."

Of course. "I promise."

She gave him a long look and went back into the house, returning with her daughter in tow. "Have a good time, honey, and get something really pretty."

"Ma'am," Drew interjected, "would it be all right if I took Allie to dinner and a movie after we finish shopping?"

She considered. "Yes, as long as you get her home at a decent hour. She's due back to work tomorrow at 6:00."

Drew glanced at his watch. "Well, it's 2:10 right now. I think I can get her home by eight or so."

"Let's say no later than nine," Mrs. Miller suggested.

"Great. Thank you." He slid his hand into Alyssa's and walked her to the car, opening the door for her, the way his father had always insisted he do. She gave him a shy smile that proved the value of such a simple gesture. His next act, though less courtly, had a more practical purpose. He climbed into the driver's seat and opened the glove box, pulling out a plastic bag and handing it to her. Inside, a pair of warm knitted black gloves and a matching hat with a black and gold rose on it awaited her chilly head and hands.

"Drew, what's this?" She gave him the same look her mother had, the one that refused even the most necessary gifts if they felt like charity.

"You look cold," he stated bluntly. "I'm shivering just looking at you." He feigned a frozen shudder.

She leaned over and kissed him on the cheek. "You keep me warm enough."

He played his gift off as a joke. "I know, but if we walk around with your hands in my coat pockets, we're going to get detention."

Alyssa laughed and tugged the cozy garments on. Just as he'd suspected, she looked great in black. The hat contrasted with her golden-red hair and pale skin and made her ocean-colored eyes sparkle. *Or maybe it's her smile that does that.* He touched his lips gently to hers and started the ignition. "Do you have any stores you like to shop at?"

"Yes, actually I do. There's a great consignment shop downtown."

Used clothing? What an odd choice. "What about the mall?"

She pursed her lips. "Those places are expensive, and honestly, the quality isn't great. You get a lot more for your money second hand. Besides, it's a really high-class consignment shop, not some trashy thrift store. I used to shop there all the time. I mean really, if some rich girl already wore the dress once, it doesn't matter to me."

"I suppose." He had the hundred dollars in his pocket and would be earning it tomorrow, organizing the piles of junk he and his dad never got around to. *Most likely, it won't be enough to get something at the mall, though, if those dresses are as expensive as she says.*

He drove her downtown and parked along a street lined with angled spaces. Typical of a Saturday in the city, the crowd had long since gathered, clustering in the chilly streets and ducking past each other without making eye contact. Cars whizzed by, showering the pedestrians with slush. He wrapped his arm around Alyssa's waist, sharing his warmth with her, and wishing he could do more. *She needs so much... a warm coat, food, makeup. Simple things, things parents buy for their children, but she has none of them. In fact, I suspect she's providing for her parents rather than them for her.* It bothered him to think that. *She wouldn't appreciate me saying it though, so I'll keep my opinion to myself.*

They stepped through a heavy glass door into the consignment store, and Drew realized Alyssa was right. The owners had gone to a great deal of trouble to make it look pretty, putting up silver and white striped wallpaper, laying cream colored tile on the floor, and hanging reproductions of impressionist paintings on the walls. The clothing had been neatly organized by size and category. Off to one side, a whole rack of prom dresses hung, waiting to be investigated. Alyssa led him straight to it.

Circling the rack to the size medium section, she began looking through the dresses. He watched her shop, grinning at her pleased expression. *She's choosy,* he realized, as she pushed dress after dress aside without a second glance.

"Is it hard to find clothes?" he blurted, not really thinking the question through.

She looked up at him quizzically.

Drew's face heated. *Make sense, man!* "I mean, with your coloring. Is it hard to find things to compliment it?"

Understanding dawned with a shy smile. "Yeah, most clothes aren't made with redheads in mind."

She pulled a turquoise dress off the rack and draped it over her arm. Drew unobtrusively glanced at the price tags of a couple of dresses on the other side of the rack and grinned to see he would have some money left over.

"Let me know when you're ready to try things on, okay?" he said as he wandered towards the outerwear.

There he selected a warm but inexpensive black jacket with faux fur accents on the hood and sleeves. He had seen several other girls at school wearing coats just like it. He carried it to the counter and asked the cashier to set it aside for him.

"Drew," Alyssa called, "I'm ready."

He walked over to the fitting room as Alyssa emerged in the turquoise dress. The color looked exquisite on her, calling attention to her turquoise eyes and setting them sparkling. However, Drew could see that someone heavy had squeezed herself into this dress and stretched it out terribly around the middle. It sagged on Alyssa's slim frame.

She held a hand over her mouth to conceal her laughter. "Well, that sometimes happens. Never mind." She ducked back into the room and tried again. This time the dress – a long black sheath with a thigh-high slit and glittering black sequins on the low-cut bodice – hugged her slender curves like a second skin.

"Hmmm," Drew said. "It looks great on you, but if you wear it, I'm going to get into about a hundred fights. Let's keep it as a last resort, okay? I don't feel like getting beat up."

Alyssa kissed him, beaming at the compliment, before sneaking back behind the curtain to try on the next dress.

While Alyssa changed, Drew stepped out of view and adjusted himself uncomfortably. Just because he wasn't ready to become intimate with someone, didn't mean he lacked normal teenage male hormones, especially where Alyssa was concerned.

"Drew, where are you?" she called.

"Right here, Allie." He returned, pulling his letterman jacket lower around his hips. The vision in scarlet standing before the curtain stopped movement and breath in one. *Now, this dress is perfect.* The shimmering satiny red sparkled with a hint of gold. It was sleeveless but had thick shoulder straps. The neckline came straight down past her collarbones and turned sharply at an angle, making a V between her delicate breasts, low enough to be enticing, but not enough to be sleazy. The long bodice came to a point, front and back, with several vertical seams that made her figure appear even more of an hourglass. Below, the smooth skirt skimmed her hips before floating around her to the floor.

"Beautiful," he said, his eyes glowing. Then he simply had no choice but to gather her up and kiss her.

"I like it," she told him.

He lifted the tag and nodded to see the dress only cost $50.00. *I have enough to buy the dress and the coat, with a little left over. Perfect.*

Alyssa changed back into her jeans and sweater and handed him the garment over the fitting room curtain. He took it to the front and paid for both items.

When she emerged, he tenderly wrapped the warm jacket around her and zipped it up. Her eyes grew shiny. "Thank you, Drew," she said softly.

"Anything for you, Allie." He hugged her, and, scooping up the garment bag from the counter, walked her back out to his car. Instead of loading her inside, he spread out the dress on the back seat, so it wouldn't wrinkle and turned, escorting her down the street, asking, "Allie, are you making a stand against makeup these days?"

She sighed. "No. I'm out."

"That's what I thought. Now listen, your skin is so pretty, you don't need any powder or blush or anything, but how about something to bring out your eyes?"

"That would be very sweet," she said, and the waver in her voice told him she had nearly reached the limits of her composure.

"Good." He brought her into a drugstore on the corner. With the last of his borrowed money, he paid for her selections

SIMONE BEAUDELAIRE

of two eyeliner pencils, a tube of mascara, a palette of eyeshadow in multiple shades, and a red gold lip gloss.

She scooted back to the Trans Am and pulled down the mirror, quickly decorating her eyes with brown shadow and eyeliner and painting her lashes with the mascara. "Allie, don't," he said as she attempted to open the lip gloss.

"Why?" she made a face at him.

"I don't want to wear it."

Her scrunched lips and wrinkled nose gave way to a puzzled expression.

"If you put it on, I'll have it on too, in about thirty seconds," he explained.

Alyssa blushed and dropped the little tube back into the bag.

He continued. "Okay, well, here's the thing. I had to borrow money from my dad for today, and it's gone. I still have my allowance, but it's the end of the month, and I'm a little short on funds right now. I have enough for dinner or for a movie but not both. Which do you prefer? If you want to go to a movie, we can eat at my house."

"I think a movie would be nice," she said softly, and he could almost see visions of kisses in the dark flashing through her mind, if that nervous, excited expression provided any indication.

He took a guess. "Are you hungry? We can eat first if you like."

That hated flash of desperation darkened her face. "Yes."

Drew nodded and drove back to his house. Dad had gone to the grocery store, as he normally did on Saturdays, and Drew intended to take advantage of that. *But first, some food. I don't want Alyssa to be hungry, and from the look on her face, she hasn't eaten recently.* He walked her to the eat-in kitchen and urged her to sit at the rectangular pine table while he rummaged around, trying to assemble a simple meal.

He found last night's leftovers – a pot of homemade chili – in the fridge and he scooped out a generous portion into a deep white bowl. *Perfect. Freshly made but not with a particular use in mind.* Alyssa, poor girl, practically shook as the warm spicy aroma floated out of the microwave. He set a glass of milk and the dish in front of her, plunked a spoonful of sour cream on it, and then excused himself, saying he needed to use the restroom.

He took his time and felt no surprise, when he returned, to see both the bowl and glass empty. Without a word, he buttered some French bread and handed it to her. Now that she had satisfied the sharpest hunger pangs, she was able to nibble the bread daintily. *Poor Alyssa. Her desire to be mannerly and polite is impossible to meet when her basic necessities are so lacking.* He pictured her, years down the road, living happily in a cozy little house, making dinner and eating it because it was dinner time, not because she was starving. *She'll have a little money to buy herself a pretty outfit if she wants it, and all her needs will be met.* Someday, he would be able to provide these things for her, and it surprised him how much he wanted to. *I want to be a doctor because it's interesting. Did I ever think about how I would use the money, or just having it?* Pleasing and spoiling this deserving girl made his goal even more appealing.

The bread was gone, and Alyssa no longer looked ravenous, so he scooped up her hand and led her to his bedroom.

She looked around at the basketball posters, the messy, half-closed dresser with shirtsleeves and pants legs hanging out, and the closed door, and then returned to him. "Drew?" she questioned nervously.

"Yes?"

"Why are we here?" Her golden eyebrows drew together, and her lower lip found its way between her teeth.

"I wanted to talk to you."

The announcement seemed to generate more anxiety. "Talk as in have a conversation, or what most teenagers mean when they say 'talk'?"

"Both."

She swallowed. "Drew, I really like you a lot, but I'm not..."

He hushed her with a fingertip to her lips, and then smoothed an errant strawberry strand off her forehead. "I know, Allie," he said, reassuring her with a speaking look. "You know I'm not ready for that either. I just want a little taste. Stop me if you feel uncomfortable, okay?"

"Okay." She already looked uncomfortable.

He sat on the edge of the bed and held out his hand to her. She sat nervously beside him.

He stroked her cheek. "Hey, we've been kissing all day. What's the big deal?"

"I don't know." She shuffled the toes of her worn sneakers in the carpet. "I feel like something big is about to happen."

"It might," he teased. "Who knows? But I won't take advantage of you. At least, not very much."

He slid his arms around her and laid his mouth on hers.

Drew took his time kissing Alyssa. He spent forever just holding her, mouth to mouth, letting her get comfortable with his embrace. Once her body relaxed and her arms slid around his neck, he began to taste her with the tip of his tongue.

"Open, sweet girl," he murmured, and she obeyed. He slid his tongue into her mouth for a deep, passionate exploration.

Alyssa let him, passively receiving the pleasure he gave her, too shy to respond. He delicately licked her mouth, teasing her tongue with his until she had to move, to touch back. He retreated, she followed, sliding her tongue into his mouth now, tasting him. Suddenly the kiss turned hot, too hot. Alyssa clutched Drew tighter and kissed him hard, her slender curves pressed against his chest. Sense faded. His hands itched to touch her as her resistance melted...

And then a knock on the bedroom door interrupted their passionate embrace. Alyssa gasped and jumped to her feet. Drew stood up beside her. "Hi, Dad," he said, trying to sound calm despite his pounding heart.

James regarded him with a less than pleased expression. "Talk to me, Andrew," James ordered his son in a tone that didn't bode well for the conversation. "Alyssa, guests need to stay out of the bedrooms. You may not have known, but please remember in the future."

"Yes, sir," Alyssa whispered, her face pink, and she scuttled down the hall like a startled rabbit.

James turned back to Drew, his frown terrifying. "Well, son, explain yourself."

"Explain what?" Drew demanded, attempting to defend his behavior. "It was just a kiss."

"In your bedroom? I don't have to tell you that's inappropriate."

Drew screwed his lips to one side. "Maybe so, but don't make more of it than it was."

James narrowed his eyes and nailed his son with a look that threatened dire consequences if he didn't change his tone. "What it was, son, was much too passionate for someone who is still in high school, especially when the girl in question is in a rather delicate state. You're going to overwhelm her."

Okay, belligerence isn't working. Drew tried for honesty. "Dad, I think I love her."

Something dark and sad flashed behind James' blue eyes. "I've never heard you say that about a girl before."

I've never felt it before. "Allie's special."

James exhaled noisily. "Yes, I know. I expect you to treat her as such."

"I was. You don't know how much she needed that."

James' softening expression hardened again, his scowl growing more imposing than ever. "That kind of thinking will get you into trouble, son. Please don't argue. Just listen. I understand that you care for this girl. That's fine, but don't let your affection for her overcome your common sense. It won't do either of you any good. If you really do love her, you'll want what's best for her, and the best thing is not to get overcommitted in high school. You know how many years of school you have left. What is she supposed to do in the meanwhile?"

Dad always asks the hardest questions. "I don't know," he admitted with a sigh. "I just wish there was something I could do to help her. Her life is so hard."

James didn't give an inch. "So be her friend, have fun with her, feed her – I know you've been doing that – but don't make her fall in love with you when both of you are so young and neither of you is ready for it."

Good advice. Dad never gives anything else, but I'm not sure I'll be able to take it. Something told him this relationship would be worth all the time it would take for them both to be ready. But Drew didn't want to argue, so he just nodded.

"No girls in your bedroom. Especially not that one." James' voice, hard as stone, chipped away at Drew in a manner he couldn't remember ever hearing before.

"Yes, sir." Drew sighed. Rising, he walked slowly down the hallway, thinking about what his father had said. *Well, movies are fun, and in the dark, I can hold Alyssa's hand and kiss her some more. It's a public place and we won't be able to go too far. One thing Dad's right about; kissing on a bed in private is too much.*

CHAPTER 4

*P*rom night finally arrived. Alyssa stood in the small white plastic bathroom of her home, in her red dress and the black heels she wore to choir concerts. She had her makeup on and it looked pretty, but her hair refused to coalesce into the mature, sophisticated style she wanted.

"Is anything wrong, Alyssa?" her mother asked from the doorway.

"Not really, Mom. I'm just not having much success with this rat's nest." She tugged on a strawberry blond strand.

"What are you trying to do?" Beth asked.

"I don't know," Alyssa whined. "Something elegant. It's my senior prom. I want to look nice."

"You do look nice, darling," Beth informed her, regarding her dress with a wistful smile. "If you don't know what you want your hair to do, how can you do it?"

"A good question," Alyssa conceded. "What do you think would go with this outfit?"

"A ponytail," her mother said, beaming.

Alyssa made a face. "How ordinary."

Mrs. Miller gave a wry half-smile. Her cheek dented in a dimple that matched her daughter's. The grin held no mirth. "No, listen. Let me help you. I saw this in a magazine on a girl who looked a lot like you."

Alyssa felt a twinge. *With all Mom's going through, there's no call to be sarcastic. Let her try to help.* "Okay, show me."

Beth lifted the already-heated curling iron and ran it through her daughter's hair repeatedly, until every strand hung perfectly straight. She separated out most of the front, parting it low on the side and brushing it forward. The back she pulled into a smooth ponytail, secured with a simple red elastic. Then she turned to the section she had left out. She swept the larger portion low across Alyssa's forehead, pinning it behind her ear and then smoothing it up around the ponytail, hiding the band. She pinned it into place. The smaller section she curved around the other side and repeated the process until all Alyssa's hair had been secured. A quick blast of hairspray completed the look.

"There. What do you think of that?" Beth asked, looking pleased with herself.

"Wow, Mom. It's perfect." Alyssa stared in the mirror, amazed.

"Yes. You look like a model." Beth stroked the sleek column of hair.

"I'm too short to be a model," she joked.

"You look like an angel then," Beth insisted. "I'm sure Drew will think so."

Alyssa smiled but didn't answer.

"Alyssa..." Her mother paused, seemingly not sure how to say what she wanted.

"What is it, Mom?"

Beth tugged on a strand of her own fading hair. "I know

this boy means a lot to you, and I'm glad for you to have a special friend, but please, don't go too far tonight."

Alyssa blinked at her mother but didn't speak.

"Apart from the fact that you deserve better, if you were to... get pregnant, it would be a disaster for the whole family."

Goodness. Mom and I can talk about anything, but I didn't expect this. "Don't worry, Mom. Drew isn't like that."

"All boys are like that," Beth replied sourly, a vision of MTV seeming to play before her eyes.

"Not really," Alyssa insisted, her cheeks heating. "Listen, he broke up with his last girlfriend because she wanted to, and he didn't. I really like Drew, but we've already talked about this. We're not ready and that isn't going to change just because it's prom. I swear I'm not going to sleep with him."

"Well good." Alyssa's mother hugged her tight, crushing a wrinkle into the pristine fabric. "You're such a good girl, darling. Now go and have fun, just not too much."

Alyssa grinned through her blush. "I promise."

A knock sounded at the door, and Beth went to let Drew in, Alyssa trailing after her. The sight of her date pulled a gasp from her. *He looks so sharp in his suit, with his auburn hair neatly trimmed.*

"Hello, Andrew," her mother said, eying his attractive attire with approval.

"Mrs. Miller." He handed a bouquet of tulips to Alyssa's mother.

She beamed, and for a moment the image of a worn-out, middle-aged woman gave way to a flash of the sparkling girl she had once been, before hardscrabble life and too much stress had drained her. "How sweet. Thank you. Won't you come in?"

He stepped into the living room. "Oh, Allie, look at you. You're beautiful." His green eyes glowed as he looked her up and down. "I have something for you." He presented a corsage of white and yellow roses, which complimented Alyssa's dress. He carefully pinned them high on one shoulder and gave her a gentle hug.

The warmth of his embrace brought tears to her eyes. "Thank you, Drew." She bit her lip. "Would you like to meet my dad?"

"Yes, of course," he replied easily, as though the request had little import.

She took him by the hand and led him back into the normally unused third bedroom. "Daddy?"

"Yes, princess?" A pinched and mournful-sounding voice whispered through the darkness.

"I want you to meet someone," she said, her tone wavering. *Hold it together, Alyssa.* "Can I please turn on the light?"

"Of course."

Alyssa flipped the switch to reveal a hospital bed with a man lying on it. David Miller had been a mechanic all of his life and had the physique to prove it. Wiry and suntanned, his face heavily lined, he looked like a man who worked with his hands. He also looked more than half dead. Despite the small pharmacy of medications on the bedside table, he was not completely able to conceal his pain. It tortured her heart to see him so sick.

It's difficult to look at him, Drew thought. *Good thing Dad's healthy as an ox.*

"So, Alyssa. Who is this?" Alyssa's father rasped.

"This is my boyfriend. His name is Drew. We're going to the prom tonight. Drew, this is my dad, David Miller."

"Pleased to meet you, sir." He walked to the bed and offered his hand. David took it, his grip weak and unsteady, and pumped once. Then, as though the effort had been too much for him, his hand flopped back onto the bed.

"Glad to meet you, Drew," he said his tone hollow. It sounded like a once-booming voice that had lost its strength. "Take good care of my little girl. She's my only legacy."

A long look passed between the two men.

"I promise," Drew said at last.

David slowly turned to face Alyssa. "Go and have fun, princess."

"Goodbye, Daddy. I love you." She blew him a kiss.

"Love you too," David said. Laboriously, he rolled onto his side, effectively ending the conversation. Alyssa switched off the light.

Drew wrapped his arm around Alyssa's waist and walked her out of the room. She pulled on the coat and gloves Drew had bought her, but not the hat.

"Aren't you going to be cold?" he asked, indicating her bare head.

"It's worth it," she replied, smiling while her eyes sparkled with unshed tears. "I can't stand to mess up my hair."

"All right then." He walked her out to his car, listening to her sniffle. Before he opened her door, he lowered his lips to hers for a long, sweet kiss. "Remember, Allie, you're not alone," he told her softly, as she climbed into the car.

Alyssa remained silent as they drove to the high school. Drew held her hand. She appreciated the comfort of his touch. Parking in the overcrowded student lot, he opened the door of her car, helping her to her feet.

After leaving their outerwear in coat check, they joined a long line of chatting students who waited to have their pictures taken. Alyssa still didn't say a word. She stood in the milling crowd of formally dressed seniors, under a series of arches hung with purple and white balloons and gold ribbons. Drew slipped his arms around her and she leaned on him, drawing strength from his presence.

Finally, they entered the gym, which had been decorated with more balloons and ribbons, interspersed with paper flowers, just as a slow song began to play.

Alyssa wasn't ready to let go of Drew yet, so they turned the long hug into a dance, swaying together. She laid her head on his shoulder and listened to Boyz II Men sing "The End of the Road." The appropriateness of the lyrics brought tears to her eyes.

"What's wrong, Allie?" he asked, as one tear escaped.

He's just too sweet. I'll never know where this nice Drew came from, but I'm sure glad he did. "Nothing."

"Never lie to me. I can tell something's wrong. Please talk to me," Drew urged. He released her waist with one hand and lifted her chin.

Alyssa drew in a deep breath. "My dad's having the surgery."

"That's good, isn't it?" Drew asked.

"Yes. He might live longer that way. On the other hand, he might not wake up from it." She squeezed her eyes shut to prevent more tears escaping.

"Sweetheart, either option is better than the way he is now," he said it as gently as he could. His expression spoke of such tender sympathy, as though he wanted to protect her from the world.

Alyssa stifled a sob. "I know. That's why he agreed to it."

"So then, what's the problem? Are you scared for him?"

She took several deep breaths, composing herself. "Kind of, but like you say, he's better off with the surgery no matter the outcome." Her voice broke. "The thing is, it costs a lot of money. It's going to take mom's whole paycheck just to cover the medical bills. Once I graduate, I'll have to work full time, maybe two jobs, just to pay the rent on our home and the groceries, and the car insurance. I won't be able to go to college."

Drew's eyebrows came together. The skin of his face drew tight against the bones, showing his anger. "Allie, you have to go to college. How can you even think about not going?"

"Family is more important," she insisted, "and we can't pay for it anyway."

"What about scholarships, grants, loans?" he exclaimed.

"All meaningless if I have no time to attend class," she pointed out.

"It's not right of them to ask this of you." She could hear his molars grinding.

She sniffled. "No one asked, it just has to be. Are you really saying college is more important than my dad's life?"

His face relaxed. "Of course not. God, what a mess."

"I know." In the most comforting place in Allie's world, her boyfriend's arms, she dared to speak the awful truth. "The really bad part is, I'm kind of mad about it. I wish I *could* go to college. I wanted to study music, teach elementary school. I guess I'll just be a grocery store cashier. It could be worse. At least I'm pretty good at it."

"I can't help but think there must be a solution that lets you do both, somehow." Drew studied her face as though the answer to her question lay in her eyes. "Isn't there anything I can do?"

If only. "Not unless you have a couple hundred thousand dollars lying around somewhere."

He hugged her tighter. "My dad's right. Getting so deeply involved with someone is difficult when you're too young to do anything significant for that person. I want to take you away from all this."

She smiled sadly. "You are. I'm glad to be here tonight. You're so sweet, Drew."

"It's not sweetness, Allie. I want to be with you," he told her.

"Why?" she demanded. "I never have understood why."

"Because I love you." He said it calmly, without drama, as though it were like any other fact.

Alyssa closed her eyes and let the words wash over her. *Drew loves me.* Her lips turned up, with more sincerity this time. He pressed his lips to her dimple. "I love you too," she told him softly.

Alyssa's future looked none too bright, and it was closing in on her with alarming speed. But at least for tonight, she had the love of a bright and beautiful boy, the kind of boy who would go places and do things and take her memory with him. It wouldn't last. She knew it for a fact. *He's as high above me as a star. I won't try to hold him, but I will never forget how we touched. It has to be enough.*

PART II

CHAPTER 5

April 2009
Memorial Hospital

"Miss, can you hear me? If you can hear me, squeeze my hand." The voice faded into a garbled and unintelligible hodgepodge of sounds. Alyssa groaned. Lights flashed outside her closed eyelids.

"Open your eyes, miss. Stay with us. Don't go back to sleep."

I'm sleeping? How can I be sleeping? She could hear people talking... and understand some of it. *Sleep sounds good though. My head hurts. So does my leg. If I can sleep, it will stop hurting.*

"We're losing her."

"Let me do it." This voice sounded familiar. "Allie, can you hear me?"

"Do you know this girl?"

"We went to high school together."

"What's her name? She didn't have ID on her."

"Alyssa Miller. Allie, open your eyes, sweetheart. Wake up."

Through the confusing mélange of voices, a single idea crystallized. "Drew?" Her voice sounded strange, slurred and croaking.

"Yes Allie, it's me. Open your eyes."

"Can't," she moaned.

"Yes, you can. Try."

Alyssa's eyelids felt like ten-pound weights, but she managed to force them open. She looked up into a bright light, very bright. It hurt her eyes. "Owww," she moaned, squinting. The light moved away from her face.

"Is that better?" She looked again, and Drew's face loomed, fuzzy and indistinct. He had matured, his face thinner and more handsome than ever because of it, but the piercing green eyes remained the same.

"Hurts," she whined.

"I know. We'll get you something for the pain soon, but we need to know you're okay first. You've been unconscious for a while."

"Where?"

"You're at the hospital."

"Hos... what? What happened?" The words slurred so badly, she almost couldn't recognize them herself.

"You were in a wreck."

"Wreck?" *Why does nothing make sense?*

"Yes, Allie. A car accident. A driver ran a red light and T-boned your car."

"My leg. It hurts"

"You have a broken femur. We're going to take care of you. Don't worry, Allie, I'm here." His hand slipped into hers, warm and familiar, and she instantly felt better. She squeezed his hand. The room came more into focus, but there was not much to see: glaring white walls and bright lights reflecting off the chrome on the gurneys, and the stainless steel of instrument tables. She returned her gaze to Drew. The sight of those kind green eyes soothed her.

"Drew?"

"Yes. I'm here. Try to wake up the rest of the way. Does anything else hurt?"

"My head." One hand seemed to float up in the direction of the splitting pain just above her left eye. Her motion was arrested, and she focused to see he had captured her fingertips.

He laid her arm back down on the bed and patted it gently. "You hit it on the steering wheel. That old clunk didn't have an airbag. Thank God you were wearing your seatbelt. We need to see if you have a concussion before we give you any medication."

"How?"

"This is my friend, Dr. Turner. He's going to shine a little light in your eyes. Hold on to me, sweetheart." A light flared, painfully bright, and Alyssa groaned.

"Her pupils look normal so far," another voice cut in, but Alyssa didn't turn. "That's good, but she hit her head pretty hard. I'd like to get her head scanned for internal bleeding. We should check her abdomen as well. How's her neck?"

"I don't know," Drew said, answering his friend while his eyes remained fixed on Alyssa's. "She's moving her hands okay, and she says her leg hurts. Let me check the rest. Allie, let me go for a second, I need to check your feet. Can you feel that?" He touched her left foot.

"Yes. Please don't. It hurts on that side." She bit her lip to keep from crying.

"How about this." His fingers came into contact with her big toe on the right side.

"Yes. Drew?"

"Yes, love?"

"My car?"

"Sorry. It's totaled."

Nauseous with pain and confusion, she gagged and then wailed, "No, I need it. How will I get to work?"

Drew returned to her side, frowning. "It sounds like you're waking up a little. That's good. Allie, you won't be working for a while with this injury."

"I have to." She could hear the panic in her own voice.

"Sorry. You'll need surgery to repair your femur, and you mustn't put any weight on it while it's healing."

Alyssa drew in an unsteady breath. *Oh God, no!* "No surgery. I can't afford it."

"Do you have car insurance?" he asked, his eyes boring into hers.

"Yes." *I'm poor, but I'm not stupid.*

"The other driver's insurance will have to pay for your treatment, and if he doesn't have any, yours will. He was drunk. He's been arrested."

Her circling mind came back to the critical point. "Drew, I have to work."

"Sorry, Allie, there's just no way. Listen, can you move your fingers for me?"

She wiggled one and then another, as directed.

"Good. Looks like you don't have a spinal cord injury." His hand slipped into hers and she squeezed hard. The more she woke up, the worse the pain in her leg became.

"Why are you here?" The question spilled out, seemingly at random.

His expression turned strange. *Or is that me not seeing*

properly? "I'm working. Remember I always wanted to be a doctor? I'm a resident in orthopedic surgery. I'm going to help you with your leg."

Best news I've heard so far. She exhaled, but her sigh shattered into a sob as pain radiated from her leg up and her head down. "Good. Make it better fast, okay?"

"Sure. I'll do what I can. It's pretty bad though, Allie," he told her. *As if I can't tell just from how bad it feels.*

An intern with a pair of scissors began cutting off her jeans. His movements jostled her injury and she moaned. "I know. It hurts like hell."

Drew lifted her face to his, making her look into his eyes. "Okay. I think you're really awake now. We're going to take you for a quick scan of your head and belly and then we'll get you some morphine for the pain."

A sudden wave of fear swamped Alyssa. "Don't go." She clung to his fingers.

He squeezed her hand. "I'm not going anywhere."

A couple of hours later, Alyssa settled in a hospital bed, her leg splinted and in traction, staring at the holes in the ceiling tiles and thinking over her prognosis. *I'm incredibly lucky to have avoided more devastating injuries. I don't have a concussion. I don't have internal bleeding. Apart from the leg, I only have bumps and bruises... and a goose egg on my forehead... ahhh, morphine feels good. It's like I've floated away from the pain. Floating... floating...* Her head fell back on the pillow and she closed her eyes.

A knock on the door shook her out of her stupor and she turned to see Drew coming in. "How are you doing?" he asked.

She looked at him through unfocused eyes. "Not too good."

"This I can see. Poor Allie. Did the morphine help?" He held out his hand. She reached out to take it, and the movement felt odd, dreamlike and surreal.

She answered honestly. "Some, but I feel pretty strange."

"That's normal. It passes." He perched on the edge of the bed, their joined hands resting in his lap.

She nodded. Her head felt like a balloon. "Did anyone call my parents?"

"Do they have a phone these days?" he asked.

"Yes." *Holding still helps. I feel more solid.*

"Give me the number and I'll call them," he suggested. "They should be here with you."

"They can't," she replied promptly.

"Why?"

"Dad's sick again."

"Oh." He frowned and for a moment she feared his lips would fly away from his face. "I always wondered how you guys were getting along."

Under the influence of the narcotic, Alyssa began to babble. "The surgery helped. He was in remission after that for several years, but the cancer came back, and this time there's nothing they can do. He has a couple of weeks at most, probably less."

Drew made an even more unhappy face. *I hope it doesn't break open.* She blinked, and reality stabilized. *Stop thinking stupid things. Listen and talk like a normal person,* she scolded herself as Drew continued. "I'm sorry. It's good that you got eight more years with him."

"Yes," she agreed. "Drew?"

"Yes?"

"Are you my guardian angel?"

He chuckled. "I see the morphine has made you loopy. I'm

no angel, just an old flame who's glad to see you. Sorry it had to be under these circumstances."

She focused on reality, trying to get the words out that were bouncing around aimlessly in her head. "Seriously. Whenever I get beyond my ability to cope, there you are."

～

Drew didn't know what to say to that. Instead, he stroked the back of her hand. "I've missed you, Allie."

"Missed you... so much."

"You sound sleepy. Give me the phone number and go to sleep."

She rattled off a series of increasingly slurred digits and closed her eyes.

Drew scribbled the number down on a piece of paper but didn't reach for the phone right away. Instead, he spent a few minutes regarding Alyssa's sleeping face. *She's so beautiful, even with two black eyes and a bump on her head. I've missed her.* They had never actually broken up, but after high school, they had kind of... drifted apart. He'd been busy with college, and she'd been working so much, and eventually, they just didn't see each other anymore. He'd accepted it as a natural progression. After all, high school relationships weren't meant to last forever, but it didn't mean he'd forgotten, not for a single day.

There had always been a soft spot in his heart for her. Drew had dated a bit, but never very seriously. After Alyssa, all other girls paled by comparison. Seeing her again, he finally understood why. *She's the one. I want her as much as I did at the senior prom.* The feelings, no less intense for all the years that had passed, washed back over him. *She pulled back from me, gently but deliberately, and I allowed it because that's what's*

supposed to happen to high school love. In retrospect, I think I
he hadn't fought hard enough to keep what he'd had.

*Letting her go was stupid. I guess I always hoped one day to
reconnect with her again, and suddenly, here she is, battered and
bruised and in as much distress as ever. And damn it, I'm in any
better position to help her than in high school. I have years of
residency left.* Well, if nothing else, at least he could do what
he'd done in the past. He could be her friend and listen when
she wanted to talk. Lifting the telephone, he dialed the number
she'd given him.

CHAPTER 6

*W*hen Alyssa woke up, Drew still sat beside her, on a chair with wooden arms and pink and green plaid upholstery. *Or maybe he's back. How long have I been asleep?* Must have been a while. My leg's hurting again. She glanced around the sterile white room with the cheap veneer table under the window, and the rolling hospital tray with an unappealing-smelling meal sitting beneath a plastic cover. She grimaced. The medication had made her nauseous and her mouth felt like the Mojave.

"Good morning, Sleeping Beauty."

She turned back toward a pair of concerned green eyes under a shock of reddish brown hair. She tried to smile but knew it didn't look too convincing.

Drew took her hand in his. "Alyssa, we need to talk."

"What is it?" she asked, alarmed at his serious tone.

"It's about your leg. Are you awake enough to listen?"

"Yes." She pushed the button that lifted the head of her bed. "Could you please get me some water?"

SIMONE BEAUDELAIRE

He poured the contents of a pink plastic pitcher into a matching cup. "Here you go."

She grasped it and downed the tepid water in a single gulp. "Thanks. Okay, what's up?" Though she tried to sound calm, her pounding heart threatened to burst through her rib cage.

Drew claimed her fingers, lacing them between his. "I told you this before, but I'm not sure if you took it in. In order for your leg to heal correctly, you're going to need surgery. We're going to have to put some screws into the bone to hold it together. This injury was from a car accident, so auto insurance will pay for it."

That doesn't sound promising. "How long before I can get back to work?"

"Probably about eight weeks, if you don't have to be on your feet too much. The average recovery time from this type of injury is about six months, but it's critical that you don't put any weight on your leg while it's healing."

She shook her head. "There's no way."

His face turned grim. "There's no choice. If you don't keep weight off your leg, it might never heal. You'll be crippled, Allie."

"What am I going to do?" Her voice caught. *Why, God? Why this? Why now?*

"You're going to be strong and get well," he replied. His thumb stroked over the back of her hand.

"Did you call my mother?" she asked.

"Yes. She's very concerned."

"No doubt. Apart from the fact that I'm injured, my income is vital to the family."

His eyes crinkled, showing his strain. "I don't know what to tell you."

∿

Alyssa's lips curved into a sad smile. Even her dimple seemed to be frowning. "You're a doctor. Your job is to fix my leg, not my financial problems."

Damn it, why does that have to be so true? "I never can do enough to help you, can I, Allie?"

She placed her hand on his arm. "It is enough. It's all anyone could ask. You're my saving grace, Drew."

He exhaled. "I wish I could have done more."

She laughed, a bitter laugh that contained in it more than a hint of a sob. Her fingers tightened on his. "The situation was beyond one person's ability to help. It still is. I'll be thankful for what I can get. There is one thing you can do for me though."

"What's that?"

"Hug me." Her voice wavered.

It wasn't professional, but how could Drew say no? He leaned forward and gently took her in his arms.

"When is the surgery?" she asked from close to his ear.

"Tomorrow."

She sagged against him, her head on his shoulder. "Will you do it?"

Finally, a tangible way to help. "Yes. I'll be there."

"Thank you."

He pressed his lips gently to her cheek. "I have some other patients to see today, but I'll come back later." She nodded into the shoulder of his lab coat. He squeezed her, kissed her cheek again, and left the room.

Outside in the hallway, his supervisor didn't look too pleased. "Why were you kissing that girl?" she demanded, nailing him with a gimlet stare.

"She's an old friend," he explained.

Dr. Johannes raised her eyebrow, clearly not fooled.

"Okay," he conceded, "she was once my girlfriend, but that was a long time ago."

"Not long enough, it looks like," she drawled.

Drew's cheeks burned. "I can handle it," he insisted, leaning his shoulder against the white wall of the hallway, trying for nonchalance.

"I don't think so," she replied, casting a pucker-lipped glare at his casual pose. He straightened. "You'd better step aside. You know the rules, Drew."

"Not yet," Drew begged. "She trusts me, and she's scared to death. Let me assist with her surgery tomorrow."

The woman's frown deepened. "It's not good to operate on someone you love."

Leave it to Dr. Johannes to hit the nail squarely on the head. "I have to help her. This is all I can do for her," he wheedled.

She glared at him with narrowed eyes. "I'll let you try, but the minute I feel you're being unprofessional, you're done. After the surgery, switch her with one of Rosie's patients."

"Okay." *Thank you, Lord.*

"Good luck, Dr. Peterson. Don't screw this up."

The next morning, Drew stopped outside the room where Alyssa was being prepared for surgery.

"Is she still awake?" he asked the technician, who was rolling in a portable hook with bags of medicine hanging from it.

"Yes. We're about to start anesthesia," the man replied. He stopped at the sink inside the doorway, scrubbed his hands, and covered them with gloves.

"Let me be here, okay?"

"Okay." The slender Asian man shrugged.

They walked in to see Alyssa lying on a gurney with an IV line running into her hand. She looked terrified.

"Don't be scared, Allie," Drew said as he walked towards her. "I'm here. You're in good hands."

"Thank God." She reached for him, but the movement of the tube running into her hand stopped her.

"Yes. I promised I would be." He sat on the edge of the little bed and took her hand in his. "Look, we're about ready to get started. This is the anesthesiologist, he's going to put you to sleep so you don't feel anything."

"Okay."

He took her trembling, too-thin form gently in his arms for a comforting hug. "It's going to be fine. I'll be right here the whole time."

She nodded. He lowered her back down and took her hand. Then he signaled to the anesthesiologist, who injected a dose of medication into her IV line.

"Go to sleep, Allie. You're going to be okay. I won't let anything bad happen to you." A tear ran down her temple into her hair. He leaned close to her ear. "I'm here for you, sweetheart. Trust me. You're not alone." Her eyes started to close, which was the only reason he dared to whisper, "I love you." Then she passed out.

CHAPTER 7

The surgery went as well as could be expected, and it pleased Alyssa to discover the pain wasn't much worse than the broken leg itself had been. She regarded the cast with a certain numb fascination. Heavily dosed with narcotics, her vision seemed to swim, and her head felt stuffed with cotton.

"You'll need to spend about five days in the hospital," a disembodied voice floated up out of nowhere to tell her. *Maybe if I turn my head, I'll be able to see who it is.* But she didn't. "We'll be monitoring you for infection and rejection of the hardware, okay?" *Voice sounds female. I wonder where Drew went.*

"Okay," she said, her voice slurred. "Drew?"

"He had to see another patient. I'm going to take over your care. My name is Rosa Jimenez."

Still, Alyssa didn't turn. Her head suddenly felt stuffed with rocks instead of cotton, and far too heavy to move. She flopped back onto the bed. "Okay," she said again, her lips fighting against cooperating. "I hope he'll come to see me."

Dr. Jimenez chuckled. "I'm sure he will. You sound pretty out of it, yet. I think I'll save the instructions for later. You have your button if you need anything. Are you with it enough to push it?"

"I'm not sure," Alyssa replied. "I think I might want to sleep."

"Sleep is a good idea. Okay, we'll try this again later," the floating voice informed her. Sneakers shuffled across tile. A door clicked.

Alyssa closed her eyes. *I'll try to understand later.*

Two days later, as she lay in her bed, watching a boring talk show on the television, she thought about Drew. Her bedside table now housed a vase of colorful spring flowers. She could still feel the brief, gentle kisses he'd given her, along with the bouquet. *He's acting like no time has passed since our last date, like he's still my boyfriend. It's kind of nice. I've always liked Drew's version of emotional support, but I'm not sure if it's right to begin depending on him heavily for it.* Once the morphine started to wear off, she realized to her displeasure all the different ways there were to hurt, from the IV, which felt like the worse bruise ever, to the sharp, throbbing pain where she'd been cut, to the deep ache of the broken bone. *And that's not the worst of it. I hate, Hate, HATE being separated from Dad when he's so close to the end. Right or wrong, I need Drew.*

Like the previous night, for instance. He'd sat on the edge of her bed, fingers laced through hers, watching a crime drama on her tiny television.

"You know," he'd said, "this show is boring. You say you always watch this?"

Alyssa had giggled. "Normally it's fun. It figures you'd see the first dud of the season."

"Do you want to watch anymore?" he'd asked, his eyes pleading.

"It's okay if you want to turn it off, Drew."

He'd clicked the remote instantly. "What did you have for dinner? Sorry I wasn't here; there was an emergency and I hate to stay on the clock late."

"You didn't miss much," she'd replied, indicating her half-eaten meatloaf and slimy mashed potatoes. The roll had been too hard to bite and the beans mushy.

He'd made a face at the food.

"What? At least it was hot."

"I'm a bit of... I don't know. A food snob, I guess. Cooking is a hobby of mine. I wish I could make you dinner." He'd thought for a minute. "When you get out, would you care for a date at my apartment?"

"My mouth is watering at the thought. What would you cook?" She'd looked into his eyes and been blown away by the heat she saw there.

"Steak, I think. Twice baked potatoes. Salad. Do you like a glass of wine?"

"I've hardly had any, but I'd be glad to try it. But you should stop." Her stomach had growled. "You're making me hungry. And that..." she waved her hand at her rejected dinner, "isn't going to cut it."

"Poor Alyssa. All alone with an unappetizing meal. I wish I could have been here. Residents are just too busy."

She'd squeezed his hand. "I understand, Drew. I'm thankful for the time you do spend with me. You do more than enough. I'm too needy for anyone to take care of."

"I'm willing to try," he'd said, giving her that burning stare again. Unable to deal with his gaze, her eyes had skated away.

She'd hoped to end the conversation, but he'd lifted her chin back to his and pressed one soft kiss to her unresisting lips. Not another word passed between them, and Alyssa was left confused over how to feel about any of it.

Drew's pager beeped, and the display screen showed the number for Alyssa's room. *Thank goodness I'm between patients.* He ducked in quickly. "What did you need, Alyssa?"

Through trembling lips, she spoke, her voice so soft he could hardly hear it. "My grandma just called. My dad's... dying. I need to get there quickly. What can I do?"

Oh, dear Lord. "Let me work on it." He hugged her and walked out, finding Dr. Jimenez as quickly as he could. "I need to take Alyssa out of the hospital for a while," he told the dark-haired doctor without preamble, the moment he cornered her outside Room 307.

"It's too soon. She can't go," his colleague retorted. "You know that."

"Rosie, her dad is about to die. She has to go, to say goodbye."

Rosie wilted. "Damn. She really needs to stay. What if she exacerbates her injuries?"

"I'll be with her. I'll make sure she doesn't," Drew wheedled.

"Drew, who is this girl to you?" she asked, startled by his vehemence.

"Honestly? She's the only girl I've ever loved." Drew had never admitted anything so personal, especially not at work, and Rosie looked taken aback.

"Oh," she managed to say. Then she steeled herself. "Be very careful. You know what can happen if one of those screws gets knocked loose. She's recovering well, and I don't want her to have any setbacks."

"Neither do I. I'll watch her like a hawk." Rosie gave him a warning glare, but Drew whirled around, ignoring her and retrieving a wheelchair, which he brought straight into Alyssa's room. Setting the brakes, he helped her to sit up and gently wrapped a robe around her hospital gown. She laughed, and it sounded hysterical. "What is it, Allie?" he asked, as he lifted her out of the bed into the chair. It turned out to be far too easy. Years of inadequate nutrition had left Alyssa feather light.

"Most men try to undress women. You're always covering me up more." She rolled her eyes.

Poor Allie. She's about at the end of her rope. "I care about you, Alyssa. You know that."

"Yes, I do."

He wheeled her, with great caution, into the oversized elevator and then down to the parking lot and out to his car. He still drove the same red Trans Am, though he'd had the key marks on the passenger door painted over ages ago. He loaded Alyssa into the passenger seat carefully. "Are you still living in the same place, sweetheart?"

"Yes."

They drove in silence through the familiar streets of the city to the mobile home park. The surroundings had grown seedier than ever, and the Miller home looked shabby and unkempt. *I suppose, in the wake of David's final, hopeless illness, no one wanted to take time to keep the place up.* Old Jax no longer sat in his chair in front of his abandoned and decaying trailer, but other neighbors had taken up his role in various places. *I have to get Alyssa and her mother out of here.*

Now, how am I going to get her up the steps? They were narrow and rickety, and the cumbersome wheelchair seemed unlikely to cooperate. With a sigh, he realized he had no other choice. *I just have to carry her.*

He scooped her, gently and carefully, against his chest. She leaned her head on his shoulder. He kissed the top of her head and supported her injured leg as he crossed the lawn and gingerly climbed the stairs to the door of the house.

An elderly woman let them in and he carried Alyssa back into the bedroom he remembered. On the way in, they passed the priest, Father Aaron, who had just completed giving David Last Rites, and was leaving the family to say goodbye in private.

Inside the room, the shades were drawn, dimming the light down to a single lamp on the table beside the bed. Drew took in the scene as best he could. In the darkness, he could barely see the rose-patterned wallpaper he recalled. The edges of the room faded to thick gray. The meager light illuminated a tableau of grief.

Alyssa's mother sat on a chair by the bedside, her eyes red-rimmed and tears streaming down her face as she held the hand of her lifelong love. It was clearly David's time. He looked terrible, even worse than he had years ago, when Drew had thought death would be a release. His gray skin and sunken, skeletal body resembled those old photos of the concentration camps. The sight disturbed him, and the smell... Drew wanted to gag from it. Even though oncology was not his specialty, he'd been around enough patients in his training to know that vile, necrotic stench.

No rational person would say that continuing to suffer this way would be a good option. Drew crossed to the bed quickly and sat on a chair, cradling Alyssa on his lap.

"Princess?" David croaked.

"Yes, Daddy, I'm here."

"I'm glad. I love you."

"I love you too." Her voice sounded calm to the point of flatness.

David reached across the bed toward her, his hand creeping over the sheets but failing to connect. "Such a beautiful girl. I stole your life. I'm sorry."

"No, you didn't, Daddy. It was fine. I wanted to be here for you." She laid her hand on his arm.

"I want you to go on and live. Don't grieve too long. You too, Beth. Be happy, both of you."

From their matching expressions of disbelief, Drew saw that neither woman could imagine such a thing. They both remained silent.

"Drew?" The word emerged between labored pants.

"Yes, sir?" Drew replied, startled to be drawn into the private moment.

"You're back."

"Yes."

"Don't leave again," David urged. "She needs you. Never was the same without..." he trailed off.

"Sir?"

"I'm giving you my daughter. Take care of her. Never let her go." He released Alyssa's fingers and extended his hand to Drew, who grasped the bony, fragile fingers and shook once.

"Yes, sir. I'll do that. Be at peace."

Silence fell. Beth held one of her husband's hands and Alyssa took the other again. Drew held Alyssa on his lap, petting her hair. David's breathing changed to a strange, harsh rattle, and then stilled, his long struggle over. Beth began to weep, but Alyssa stayed silent. At last, she said, "Goodbye, Daddy."

Alyssa's grandmother Marjorie came into the room and laid her hands on Beth's shoulders, trying to comfort her daughter.

"Ma'am?" Drew addressed Marjorie directly.

"Yes?" She met his eyes. Tears dampened the crow's feet and the grooves around her mouth.

"Do you know if any arrangements have been made with a funeral home?"

She shook her head. "I don't think so. Beth's been too... caught up to attend to the details."

I thought so. "I have a friend who works for one. Should I call him? He could come and get David, get him ready for the funeral."

"I think that would be a good idea," Marjorie replied unsteadily.

"I also have to get Allie back to the hospital. She really shouldn't be out of bed yet, but I don't think it's good for Beth to stay here by herself. Does she have anywhere to go?"

Marjorie wiped her eyes with the back of her hand and nodded. "She can come with me. My condo is small, but I do have a fold out couch."

"Good. I'm glad she won't be alone."

"I'm glad Alyssa won't be alone."

Drew's arms tightened. "She'll never be alone again if I have anything to say about it."

Alyssa's grandmother nodded absently. Drew pulled out his cell phone and made the call. Then he scooped up Alyssa, whose skin had turned gray with fatigue and pain, and carried her back to the car. Setting her carefully in the seat, he fired up the ignition and returned her to the hospital. She never made a sound.

He tucked her into bed and paged Rosie.

By the time his colleague tapped on the door, Alyssa had succumbed to exhaustion, her eyes closed, her breathing deep and even.

"Well, Drew?" Rosie demanded in an undertone.

He didn't answer. He was busy smoothing strawberry-colored strands away from Alyssa's strained face.

"Dr. Peterson!" Rosie hissed in a carrying whisper.

At last, he looked up.

"Did anything happen?" she enunciated.

He raised his eyebrow.

"To her *leg*, Drew."

"Oh." He shook his head. *I'm not thinking clearly.* "No, her leg should be fine. Do you want to check?"

Rosie didn't answer. She simply pulled the blanket back from Alyssa's thigh, checking the incisions by squeezing gently. Alyssa stirred and squinted at the doctor. Her breath hissed between her teeth.

"Sorry," Rosie said. "I'll get you some Codeine."

"No," Alyssa said in a calm voice. "I just want to sleep. I don't need any medicine. Drew, can you please go?"

Her words cut into his heart, but he reasoned that he'd never watched someone he loved die and had no idea what she might need. "Okay, Allie. I'll be back in the morning." He kissed her forehead and followed Rosie into the hallway. Once the door clicked shut behind them, he took the other doctor's arm. "Is she all right?"

"Physically, yes. There was no sign of further injury. I'll watch, but I think she got through it unscathed."

"You understand why she had to go?" he pleaded.

"Yes, Drew," she replied in a tired voice. "I understand. I won't tell Dr. Johannes either. She would surely take a dim view of such proceedings."

"Thank you, Rosie. You're the best." He gave her a brotherly, one-armed hug.

Rosie stepped out of his embrace and gave him an unguarded look. "You know, you might have told me, before we went out, that you were in love with someone else and I never stood a chance."

Not waiting for a reply, Rosie stalked away, reflecting on the several fun but passionless dates they'd shared. *Andrew Peterson is quite a looker, tall and slim, and that dark brown hair shimmering with red – yeowch. Add in piercing green eyes and a face that skimmed the edge of too beautiful to be real.* She shook her head. *I really liked him, but he was never more than friendly to me or anyone else. I never saw passion in his eyes. Not until he looked at Alyssa.* The tender, possessive expression he wore took her breath away. Now Rosie understood why there had never been any hope for any of them. Drew had been in love with this girl for so long. *No one else had ever had a chance.*

She concluded that she needed to let it go. *One thing about Drew... he's a great friend. I want him to want him to be happy. I hope Alyssa's leg heals well, and quickly.* Rosie moved down the hall to her next patient.

A couple of days later, Dr. Jimenez came to see Alyssa.

"You're going to be released soon. I need to go over your instructions," the doctor said, her eyes glued to her clipboard, not looking at her.

"All right," she replied, a little listlessly.

"It's really important that you not put weight on your leg at all until we say it's okay. You don't want to make it worse."

"Of course not."

"So, I'm going to have the physical therapist check you out. You may be able to get by with crutches, but most likely you're going to need a walker. You'll need to come back for regular checkups to be sure the bone is healing correctly. You'll also need extensive physical therapy."

"Is the car insurance really going to pay for all of this?" she queried anxiously.

"Yes." The doctor replied, her voice reassuringly firm. "I've talked to them. We haven't done anything unusual for this kind of injury, and the accident was so clearly the other driver's fault, his insurance company isn't even fighting it. He's lucky you weren't hurt worse."

Alyssa nodded.

"How's your pain?"

"Better. I haven't needed much medication."

"Good. Take it if you need it, Alyssa. You've been through a lot."

She shook her head. "I don't think it's a good idea. I don't like how the narcotics make me feel, and with everything that's happened, I don't trust myself with them."

Dr. Jimenez met her eyes at last. "You won't become an addict. You're too strong for that. Don't make yourself suffer unnecessarily."

"Can I try something less potent?" she pleaded. *I really don't like narcotics.*

"I suppose. Let me see what I can come up with."

"Thank you."

The conversation finished, Dr. Jimenez left, and Alyssa closed her eyes. *What a mess.* She'd talked to her mother on the phone, and they both agreed didn't want to stay any longer in a house with such painful memories, not to mention one in such a disgusting neighborhood. *We need another place to live, a tricky proposition as I won't be able to work for quite a while, and we're still paying Dad's medical bills from his surgery eight years ago. He had life insurance, but a good chunk of it will be going towards his funeral and cremation. Mom could stay with Grandma at the condo indefinitely, but there's no room for me there. I'm homeless. Once I'm released, where will I go?* She pondered her options. *If I still have a job, I might be able to find a room to rent.*

She called the grocery store where she'd worked for the last ten years and asked for Sophie, the owner.

"Alyssa, where on earth have you been?" The woman demanded, her kind voice filled with concern. Alyssa could hear the familiar beeping of the cash registers in the background.

"I'm sorry. I've been in the hospital. I got hit by a drunk driver, and I've been on so much medication that I haven't been able to think straight for days. My mother didn't call you?"

"No," Sophie replied. "We thought you'd just walked off the job. Are you all right?" *Now that's the Sophie I know. Hard words, but the sympathy in her voice reveals her tender heart.*

"Sophie, I would never have done that," Alyssa protested. *I would have hoped, after ten years of loyal service, you would have realized.* "I have a broken femur. It's going to be a long time before I can stand and ring up groceries."

After a long pause, the woman said, "I'm sorry."

"Is there any chance my position can be held until I'm able to come back?"

Silence. Alyssa didn't work for a major grocery chain, but a small family-run store. Though a nice environment, there weren't so many employees that they could easily absorb the loss of a cashier. *It's a lot to ask. I get that but come on. God, if you're listening...*

Her voice, when Sophie spoke, sounded hesitantly apologetic and filled with remorse. "We didn't know you were coming back. We've..."

"You have a replacement already." *Damn.* Tears

threatened, but Alyssa squashed them down. "I understand. Maybe when I'm better there will be an opening?"

"We'll see. There have been a number of applicants." Sophie sounded even glummer to be relaying the discouraging news, but the message remained unchanged by the kindly tone. *Don't get your hopes up.* Alyssa's insides clenched. *Homeless and unemployed. Wonderful.*

"Take care of yourself, Alyssa," Sophie said with the intensity of someone who was almost a friend and the anger of someone who is unable to help a person they care about.

"I'll try. Thanks for... everything."

"You know," at last the store owner's voice had changed to something with a hint of hope in it, "this might be a good time for you to try... something new. I never felt ringing up groceries was the best use of your intelligence."

Now how is that *supposed to work?* Alyssa didn't know, and she didn't feel like talking anymore. "Thank you," she said before hanging up.

She slumped back in the bed. Her thoughts whirled around aimlessly. *There is no solution for this situation. I have no income, no job, and with my injury, no means of working either. It's hopeless. What on earth will become of me? Worst of all, I just feel so terribly numb.* She hadn't cried, though the weight of her misery threatened to crush her. She closed her eyes with a heavy sigh.

"Allie?" Drew's beautiful low voice broke through her misery. "How are you?"

She swallowed hard and opened her eyes. "Not too good."

"What's wrong?"

"We're letting the mobile home go."

He grinned, showing braces-straightened teeth. *I remember teasing him about that tin grin sophomore year,* she thought, dredging up old memories. *How nice he looks now.* She ran her tongue over her own uneven teeth, glad the crowding didn't show too much.

"Good," he said. "I've never liked you living in that neighborhood."

"But I've also lost my job. What will I do now? Where will I go? Dr. Jimenez says I'll be released soon, but released where?" With every word, her hysteria grew.

Drew remained calm. He sat on the edge of the bed and took her hand. "Can you stay with your grandmother?"

"I can," Alyssa said, picturing the option, "but there's not much room. She lives in a one-bedroom condo."

Drew stroked her fingers. Then his eyes lit up. "You can stay with me. I have a spare room and it's going to waste. You can stay for as long as you need to."

Hope flared, followed immediately by doubt. "Drew, do you really think that's a good idea?"

Her lack of enthusiasm seemed to dim his excitement. *Is that really what he wants?* "I don't know, but at least it's an option."

Maybe I could... no. I won't even consider it. I'm not a leech. "Thank you, but no." Her voice held the flat, hopeless tone she was learning to hate in herself.

"When's the funeral?" he asked, changing the subject. *I can see he isn't finished with the discussion of living arrangements.*

"Saturday."

"Would you like me to go with you?"

Now that's an offer I can't refuse. "Yes, please. Having you there would help me a lot."

"Anything for you, Allie." Drew's voice turned dark with intensity.

CHAPTER 8

*T*wo weeks later, Drew took Alyssa on a mysterious drive. She'd been released from the hospital, and he had, as promised, taken her to his apartment, and set her up in the guest bedroom. *He wouldn't take no for an answer,* she thought, leaning her head on the passenger door's window. He'd also escorted her to her father's funeral at the Basilica. *He really was very sweet, holding her hand, waiting to comfort her. But I didn't need it.* Although people who had scarcely known David Miller had wept, Alyssa hadn't. She had sat, still and silent, as the priest spoke over her father, summing up his life in a few kind words. The memory of the funeral and its lingering, unsettling coldness disturbed her. *What's wrong with me that I can't mourn my own father?* She felt dead inside, frozen. As spring bloomed riotously around them, Alyssa's heart felt like a block of unmelting ice.

Not just about Dad either. Drew's trying so hard to be sweet. It almost seems like he wants to resume the relationship we had in high school. I should be delighted. Objectively, he's the solution to all my problems. He would be happy to take care of me, to provide for me. All he wants in return is my heart. Last year, before Dad got really sick again, I would have given it without hesitation. Today, I have nothing to give. No love. No affection. No attraction. Nothing. Sitting in the car beside him, she studied his face. *I want to love him; I just don't know how anymore. One thing's certain, though. No matter how much easier it will make my life, I won't use him that way. Unless I can recover emotionally, I won't ask him to do anything more for me. That would be unfair.*

She turned to look out the window at the spring trees, their leaves small and pale in the weak April sunlight. Closer to the ground, tulips clustered in many gardens and edged the walkways of yards, adding their bursts of color to the soft green of new grass. They passed a row of aging two-story homes, and Alyssa noticed a fragrance. The purple and white lilacs that formed a hedge between two properties, hung heavy with flowers, their branches waving in the cool breeze that carried their perfume through the neighborhood.

The residential street gave way to a row of office buildings Alyssa had never seen before. "Where are we going?" she asked Drew, her eyes still on the scenery.

He considered as he turned left and passed out of the neighborhood. "A few years ago, when I was doing observations at the hospital, I met a woman named Claudia, who was being treated for cancer. Unfortunately, she didn't survive, but while I was working with her, I met her husband, Brandon. He's a career counselor. I thought if you talked to him, he might be able to help you see what's next. You have an opportunity to move your life forward now. I know your dad would want you to use it."

"You mean, like finally go to college?" Drew nodded. "I can't do that."

"Why not?"

Isn't it obvious? "I'm too old," she replied, hearing an unpleasant edge in her voice. "If I start now, I'll be thirty when I graduate."

"Alyssa, how old will you be in four years if you don't go to college?" Drew pointed out. "We all reach thirty if we live long enough, and really, it's not so very old. That's the age I'll be when I finish my residency. Wouldn't you rather face it having accomplished your dreams?"

It figures he'd give sound advice. "Yes, I suppose."

"Good girl. Just see what he has to say," Drew urged as he moved into the left lane and turned into a tree-lined and landscaped parking lot. "There are all kinds of programs to help people get their degrees."

Alyssa nodded.

They parked in the narrow lot of a seven-story brick building, with lilies of the valley planted along the exterior wall. Alyssa hobbled inside on her crutches, Drew at her side, his hand on her back to help steady her. *It's so difficult not to put any weight on my leg.* She made her slow way through double glass doors and let Drew steer her into the elevator at the far side of a brown-tiled lobby.

Moments later they arrived in an attractive office on the fifth floor. Mellow sage-green wallpaper, with a texture like woven grass, soothed the eyes above a serviceable tan carpet. A green sofa with a pattern of leaves, and two black and chrome armchairs provided a waiting area. Above the sofa hung a picture of the half-completed Crazy Horse monument. The office was empty of other clients, so Alyssa hobbled over to the reception desk set up across from the chairs.

A charming secretary with a nimbus of gray hair and smiling blue eyes greeted them, checked Alyssa's name against the appointment book, and placed a call on the black intercom phone on her desk.

"You can go right back," she said. "Mr. Price is waiting for you."

They passed through a door into a second office, decorated much like the first, but with framed photos of the Badlands hung up behind the desk.

Alyssa took one look at the career counselor and her eyes widened with shock. *Oh, my God, he's beautiful!* She thought, unable to tear her eyes away from his copper-skinned features. *I have never seen anyone so attractive in my life. He's so gorgeous he doesn't seem real.* Even Drew, who up to this moment had been the handsomest man she knew, paled by comparison. *Wow.* She shook her head to clear it.

"You must be Alyssa." Brandon smiled warmly, showing straight, white teeth.

Alyssa gulped and shook herself mentally. "Yes. Nice to meet you, sir."

"Brandon Price. Call me Brandon. Please, take a seat."

She hobbled to a chair. Drew sat beside her, pulling her hand into his lap. There was a possessive cast to his expression, as though he hadn't liked the way Alyssa had looked at the counselor.

Ignoring her less than subtle reaction, Brandon turned to the business at hand. "So, you're looking for a career change?" Alyssa nodded. "Okay, so tell me a little about your situation. Do you have any training?"

I wish. "No. I've worked in a grocery store since high school, but when I was injured, I lost that job."

He clicked a key on his computer. "How long were you employed there?"

"Ten years."

He nodded. "Would they provide you good references?"

"I'm sure. I rarely missed work, I was never late, and I always came in if they needed me."

"That's good." He typed briefly and then spoke again. "What about in high school, did you get good grades?"

"Pretty good."

Drew interrupted. "Alyssa was third in our class. She was a straight-A student." He turned to Alyssa. "And how many A.P. tests did you pass?"

"Five," she admitted, biting down on a smirk. *Poor kids aren't stupid, but boy did I shock the hell out of everyone.*

Brandon lowered his eyebrows. "With grades like that, you should have gotten scholarships, gone right to college."

"I couldn't," she explained. "My dad was sick, so I had to work."

"Ah. Is he better now?" Brandon asked idly as he poked away at the computer keys.

"No. He died a couple of weeks ago. He had cancer." The blunt words slapped back against her heart like a hammer blow, leaving her breathless, but still, no tears clouded her vision.

Brandon's jaw tightened. "I'm sorry."

"Thank you."

He took a deep breath, clearly composing himself. "Okay, so this is an opportunity for you. I know it isn't how you would have wanted to do things, but regardless, you have no responsibility to anyone but yourself. I take it being a grocery store cashier wasn't your dream?"

"No," she admitted. *Nor anyone else's for me. But life does what it wants, and you either ride the wave or get run over by it.*

"What did you dream about before all this happened?" he asked, looking over his computer and studying her face. His intense scrutiny made her nervous and obliterated her ability to think.

She shook her head. "I don't know."

"Yes, you do, Allie," Drew interrupted again, "I remember. Brandon, Alyssa was always into music. I can remember her

88

singing all the way back to kindergarten. She was in every choir the school offered. She used to talk about becoming a director."

Brandon's expression turned thoughtful. "Hmm. Our local university has a pretty good music program. So does the Lutheran college. What kind of director would you like to be? Church choir? High school? Elementary school?"

At last a question I can answer. "Elementary. I love little kids. When I thought I was going to college, I used to volunteer at the Boys and Girls club. I was assistant to the music director."

Brandon grinned. "That's very good. I'll contact them and see if they still have information about you on file. So, sounds like going to school to become an elementary music teacher appeals to you."

Hope bloomed in Alyssa's heart, bright as a spring flower. "It does, but how will I pay for it?"

"That's where I come in." He winked at her. "Okay, I need to ask you some pretty personal questions." He turned to regard Drew. Drew looked back, his expression hardening. He crossed his arms over his chest and settled deeper into the chair.

"Go ahead," Alyssa urged Brandon, "I don't have any secrets from Drew. He's known me forever."

Brandon's dark eyes met hers, glanced at Drew, and then returned to her. "Okay, were you ever a ward of the state?"

"No."

He clicked the mouse. "Did you live with a single parent?"

"Nope."

Click. "Were you ever on food stamps or other assistance?"

"Sorry, no."

"They should have been," Drew interjected.

Brandon turned to him with a quizzical expression. "What do you mean?"

"Alyssa nearly starved in high school," Drew stated bluntly.

She blushed at Drew's blunt words. "He's exaggerating."

"I'm not," he insisted. "Did you ever have food outside of school? Why didn't you guys ever apply for assistance? I've always wondered."

Alyssa sighed and admitted the truth. "We were short on food for a number of years, and I'm not sure why we didn't get food stamps. At the time, I wasn't really paying attention, but I think my parents felt they shouldn't need it. They should be able to provide for their family. Pride, I guess."

Brandon jumped back into the conversation. "Do you have financial information from your family? Tax returns?" he asked, his expression considering.

Unless something has gone wrong with the boxes in the closet. "Yes. Why?"

"If you grew up in poverty, it will be easier to get you some grants," Brandon explained. "What about your parents. Did either one go to college?"

"No."

Brandon punched one last key on his computer and looked up, beaming a high-voltage smile. Alyssa forgot to breathe for several seconds, until Drew elbowed her in the ribs. She released her lungful of air in a noisy whoosh. Brandon began talking as though nothing had happened. "Okay, that will help too. I think I can put together a package to cover your tuition and books. Maybe even housing. Lots of money is available for first-generation students who grew up poor. I think you won't have to pay for college at all, except to keep your grades up."

The glimmer of hope solidified into a vision of possibility. *Maybe my life isn't over after all. Maybe this can be a new beginning for me...* And then the darkness descended again. *What kind of thought is that to have? Dad's death provides me an opportunity to live? I really am a selfish monster.*

Brandon kept talking, seeming not to notice her internal

struggle. "All right, give me a few days to work on this for you, and in the meanwhile, go over to the university and apply. They'll need your high school transcripts and your S.A.T. and A.C.T. and A.P. scores."

Drew, always observant, slipped his hand into hers and squeezed her fingers with comforting gentleness.

"Okay, I think I know where those are." *In my closet, aren't they? Or maybe with the family paperwork. I'll have to get into the house and look around anyway. See if there's anything else I need.*

"Alyssa," Drew said sternly, "Don't even think about going back to that house alone. It's not safe. Wait until I can go with you."

"Of course, Drew," she said idly, still mentally searching the rooms. "Can we go right away? I might as well pack up my stuff too."

"Okay," he agreed easily. "I have the whole afternoon off."

"That would be a good idea," Brandon told them. "The sooner you get on it, the better. It would have been ideal if we could have done this in January instead of April, but it's not too late if you hurry. I'll need those documents as well, so bring them to me first and I'll make copies. And your tax returns for as far back as you can go. You can have this, Alyssa. It won't even be that hard."

Head filled with thoughts and plans, Alyssa said, "Thank you, Brandon. I'll get on the paperwork right away." Reaching across the desk, she shook his hand.

Drew passed her the crutches and helped her to her feet. While worked together to get Alyssa situated, the door of the office burst open, and a young woman who looked very much like the counselor ran in, trailed by a small and pretty lady with the lightest blond hair Alyssa had ever seen.

"Hi, Dad," the younger girl said, throwing her arms around Brandon.

"Hi, Maggie. Hi, Selene."

The blond blushed and looked down at the floor, which was a pity because she missed seeing the look of intense longing and desire on Brandon's face. *He has it bad for that one.* Alyssa hobbled out, Drew close behind her.

They headed to Alyssa's mobile home in silence. She seemed deep in thought, her expression far away as she stared out the window at the growing darkness on the horizon. He glanced at her profile. *It's going to be difficult for us to be together while she's in school and I'm still in residency, but I can't imagine doing anything different. I lost this girl once. This time I'm keeping her. Life really hasn't been as good without Alyssa in it, and I still love her as much as ever. I wonder exactly how this should be played out.* Alyssa shifted in her seat and her skirt crept up her thigh, revealing soft, pale skin. Drew swallowed as arousal began to simmer and turned his eyes to the road. *Dad won't like that we've moved in together, particularly if things get... intense, which I suspect they will, but what other choice is there? She has nowhere else to go, and I don't want to let her out of my sight.*

"Do you know something, Drew?" Alyssa asked, her thoughts far away, scarcely paying attention to her companion.

"What's that?" his asked.

"Love's funny."

"How so?" There was a tone in his voice she didn't

understand. She glanced at him but found he was looking at the road.

She explained. "Brandon is completely in love with the little blond who came in as we were leaving," she explained. "I could see she was pretty well enamored of him too. I wonder why they don't just get together."

Drew paused to contemplate his answer. The daylight dimmed as they passed under an arch of huge, ancient oak trees whose branches laced together above the street, blocking out the sky. "Maybe it's not the right time for them yet. Sometimes, even when you really love someone, life pulls you apart. If you can come back together, get a second chance, well it's a rare opportunity that shouldn't be missed."

He spoke with a great deal of intensity. Alyssa, deep in thought, didn't notice.

Drew parked in front of the mobile home. In the time since she'd been away, kids from the neighborhood had made themselves at home on the lawn, throwing soda and beer bottles, cigarette butts and candy wrappers in the once-immaculate garden. Withered, neglected ivy clung like a drowning sailor to the lattice that covered the lower front of the structure. Alyssa fumbled in her purse at the foot of the narrow stairs before realizing it wasn't necessary. The broken front door hung from bent and twisted hinges.

Drew kept his hand on her back as she hobbled up the stairs. The front room lay in disarray. A strong smell of vomited beer hung over the sofa. Someone had taken it upon himself to carve several obscene sayings into the tabletop. Alyssa shuddered and headed to her bedroom. She looked askance at the bed. The evidence of a wild party continued there. The blankets lay, stained and wadded up, in a heap in the lower corner. She rolled her eyes and opened her closet, an awkward move on crutches. The box with her school papers remained blessedly untouched, but the suitcase she had planned to fill with her clothing had disappeared.

"Allie, what are you doing?" Drew demanded as he entered the room carrying a kitchen chair.

"I was going to pack my stuff, but my suitcase is gone." *Why does such a small thing seem like such a big deal?*

"Sorry," he replied. "I know this isn't the best option, but there are some trash bags here." He held up a box of plastic kitchen bags. She gave a curt nod, though the idea of piling her clothes up like trash didn't sit well.

He opened the drawers and his expression went carefully blank. She knew what he was thinking though. *I have so few garments, and many are worn to the point of almost being rags. Clothing has not been my priority in years.* But he made no comment, merely placed the folded items neatly into the bag.

"Is there anything in the bathroom you want?" he asked.

She shook her head. "You have soap and shampoo, and there's no telling what those vandals did to my toothbrush. Leave it all."

"What will the landlord say?" he asked.

What a sweet guy. She shrugged. "I don't care. Neither does Mom. We never did expect to get our security deposit back."

"What about the furniture?" He indicated her ratty cardboard-backed dresser, three-legged particle board table, and single bed.

"Let him have it," she replied. *Drew's guest room is much better appointed.*

"Um, do you think it would be a good idea for me to pack up your folks' stuff? We can bring it to your mom."

She smiled, though it felt thin. *I called you my guardian angel once. You didn't own the title, but it's true nonetheless.* "That's sweet, Drew. Go ahead and pack it. There isn't much.

Oh, and I'm pretty sure the taxes are in an accordion folder in their closet."

He nodded. "I can do that. Don't move from that spot or try to do anything, Alyssa. Protect your leg."

"Yes, Doctor," she replied, but there was no humor to the tease.

As she listened to him moving around her parents' bedroom, she reflected on the ridiculousness of life. *Funny how after only two weeks, his little apartment feels more like home than the mobile home I lived in most of my life.* The closet door in the other room opened with a loud squeal of cheap hinges. *He's packing Mom and Dad's clothes. Getting their tax papers...*her thoughts drifted. *I wonder what exactly he means by keeping me with him. He's such a nice guy, he might just be giving a girl in hard times a place to stay.* The idea made her frown. *On the other hand, he's been acting, since the surgery, like I'm still his girlfriend, although hasn't said anything to the effect. I wish Drew would come right out and say what he wants from me. I need to know, but how in the world does anyone ask such a question?* She slumped in the chair, heat burning her cheeks at the mere thought. *If we're living together,* she realized, *really living together as a couple, I probably should forget about the guest room. It's a small enough thing to ask, to be intimate with someone who's done so much for me.* Even as she framed the thought, she knew she was lying to herself. *It's not a tradeoff. I'm willing, though I don't know what to do.* Even as eagerness tightened down her insides and images of Drew stretched out on top of her, covering her with kisses played inside her eyelids, embarrassment still burned. *It doesn't matter how willing or even eager I might be. I have no idea how to raise the subject.*

A few minutes later Drew returned with the bags in hand. Alyssa bit her lip and forced her unruly thoughts back under control. Drew gave her a questioning look, no doubt wondering why her face had turned so red. She shrugged. He helped her to her feet and escorted her out of the house for the last time, setting the bags on the ground and returning to help her navigate the steps. The drive back to Brandon's office passed in a blink, preoccupied as Alyssa was with unanswerable questions.

"Stay in the car," he told her as they pulled to a stop in front of the same office building they'd just left. "You've stressed yourself enough." She nodded. He took the box from the trunk while Alyssa sat with the windows open and listened to the birds chirping as they flitted through spring-scented breezes. The cool, fragrant air danced through the windows, washing away the staleness of the mobile home and then teasing her senses with the promise of new life. *Everything comes back to life after the winter. Maybe I can too.* But though her body had come alive to the promise of spring and Drew, her heart still felt cold and heavy, not yet warmed by the strengthening sun.

She seemed to lose time again because though the clock on the dashboard said half an hour had gone by, to her it had only seemed like only a few minutes had passed when Drew returned to the car. The slamming of the trunk startled her, and when the driver-side door shut, she jumped.

"Were you asleep?" he asked.

"I'm not sure," she replied, rubbing her eyes.

"Let's get you home. You need a nap."

He held her hand while he drove, and at the apartment complex did more than merely support her. He carried her up to his flat. Feeling wrung out, Alyssa leaned her head against his shoulder and closed her eyes. The bed rushed up to meet her and sleep followed close at its heels.

$\sim$

Drew watched Alyssa crash. *She's worn out, poor thing. Between being stuck in grief over her father and trying to figure out what to do with her life, she seems so lost.* He kissed her forehead. *For now, I'll let her sleep. It's time to make dinner; Alyssa's still much too thin.* He knew that for someone who'd lived so close to the brink her whole life, it felt luxurious to be able to eat as much as she wanted; tasty hot food prepared with good quality ingredients. He'd watched her try not to be greedy, but at first, animal hunger had won out. Now, in less danger of starvation, she was better able to savor and enjoy.

In the kitchen he pulled whole grain dough out of the bread machine and patted it into a rough circle, topping it with marinara and cheese before tossing it in the oven.

The fragrance of pizza awoke Alyssa, but for a moment she didn't know where she was. Lost in a hazy dream, her eyes refused to zero in on anything. She closed them again. The oven door banged, startling her the rest of the way awake. At last, she found herself able to focus on the guest room of Drew's apartment. Though small, it was nicely decorated, the windows framed in honey-colored wood. The antique dresser matched the bed frame; simple, pale Shaker-style furniture.

Alyssa shook her head as her confused thoughts crowded back in on her. *You're such a selfish girl. Out there in the kitchen, making you dinner, is a beautiful man who wants nothing more than to be close to you, and you're taking all he has —food, shelter, affection, help—and offering nothing in return. There's nothing about this that's right. You ought to be passionately in love with him.* Once, she had been. But try though she might, she couldn't feel a thing. She became so frustrated with herself, an angry little noise escaped her.

Drew entered the room in an instant. "What's wrong, Allie?"

She shook her head. *The last thing he needs is to deal with this too.* "Just go, please, Drew. I'm fine."

He perched on the edge of her bed and took her hand in his. "You're not. I know you better than that. Remember what I told you? I can tell."

"Why do you even care?" she asked petulantly, trying to make him angry so he would leave her alone.

He refused to take offense. Instead, he met her sulky gaze with burning intensity. "You know why."

Please stop, Drew. Don't be so nice. Don't be so good to me. She steeled herself and attacked again. "Do I? I did when we were seventeen, but it's been years, Drew. We can't just pick up where we left off, as though nothing had happened."

"Why not?" he demanded, raising an eyebrow at her.

She ground her teeth. "I'm not who I was then."

He shrugged, a half-grin twisting his mouth sideways. "Neither am I. We grew up, Allie. It was bound to happen, but how I feel about you hasn't changed."

She squeezed her eyes shut. Drew reached out and wrapped his arms around her, pulling her close and stroking her back.

"You shouldn't do that." Argumentative hadn't worked, so she went back to flat. She pulled back in the circle of his arms to look him in the face.

Still undeterred, he cupped her face in his hand, his fingers warm on her icy skin. "Why not? You should know, Allie, that I love you as much as I ever did."

Oh God, he actually said it. Now what? The truth, Alyssa. Tell him the truth. "I wish I could say I still love you, Drew. I really do. You're so amazing. But I can't. I'm broken. I have nothing left to give."

He gave her a puzzled lowering of the eyebrows. "What do you mean?"

"You know how it feels when your foot goes to sleep? Well, that's my heart. It's dead, frozen. For God's sake, I haven't even cried for my daddy. I loved him so much, and I can't even mourn him. There's something really wrong with me."

A sad smile spread across his face. The sight made her heart beat a little faster. "No, sweetheart, there's not. Disbelief is one of the stages of grief. You *are* mourning him. This is not the wrong way. You're still in shock because it's so fresh. Don't be angry with yourself for being numb. It's normal." He cupped her cheek in his hand.

She shook her head, not understanding. "How can it be a shock when I've known it was coming for years?"

He sighed, stroking her skin. "Because it's finally over. Don't worry about whether you can feel love right now. It's not time yet. It will come. Just let me take care of you while you work on getting there. You'll mourn when you're ready, and you'll love too. You're not broken, I promise."

"I hate this," she cried. "I want to feel something... anything! Even pain. Isn't there anything I can do to come back to life, to *feel* again?"

Her face heated in the aftermath of her outburst. Drew sat in silence, considering. At last, he said, "Yes, I can think of one thing to try."

His arms around her waist, he moved his face close to his and kissed her. He had kissed her before this, soft little pecks on the lips or cheek, but this was different. She had almost forgotten how wonderful it felt to have Drew open his mouth on hers and dive deep. His tongue slid against hers, tasting her mouth and tempting her to respond. Her arms came up and she slid them around his neck, pulling him close. *This time, there will be no going back.*

He pressed her down on the pillow and leaned over her, kissing her so deeply, and for the first time ever, his hands began to touch her breasts. The gentle stroking turned to a soft squeeze as he shaped the globe with one hand. A gentle, tingling warmth spread through her belly, to the apex of her thighs. He repeated the caress on the other side. These hot, pleasurable touches set Alyssa's heart pounding. Her frozen heart began to thaw in the heat of his desire, and of hers. *I wanted him in high school, but neither of us was ready to act on it. This is different.* Tonight, Drew's hands on her body requested a deeper intimacy, one she desperately craved.

He plucked one nipple between his fingertips. She moaned. "Oh, Drew." She arched her back, offering herself to him. He covered her mouth with his and continued tormenting her nipples. She whimpered.

"I want more," Alyssa whispered when he released her lips.

"Have you done this before?" he asked her, still gently squeezing her breasts.

"No. I never wanted to. No one was good enough, after you."

He pressed his mouth to hers again and began to open the buttons on her shirt, revealing her slender curves. She broke the kiss to pull his shirt over his head, and while she was at it, she unhooked her bra, letting her breasts spill free.

Drew's breathing grew labored. *Get a grip, man. You've seen breasts before.* But this was the first time a woman had revealed herself to him, so he could make love to her. *It's completely different.* He gently touched one little pink nipple, squeezing it softly between his thumb and finger until it strained and grew erect. *She feels even nicer without the clothing.* Then he leaned down and took it in his mouth.

Alyssa made a quiet noise as his tongue softly stroked one breast, and he stimulated the other with his fingertips. While he was moving from one nipple to the other, she deftly opened his belt and unfastened his jeans. Her own skirt had an elastic waistband and would only need to be shimmied down her thighs.

"Drew?" she said, her voice was slurred.

"Yes, love?"

"Let's get out of these."

He wasn't about to argue. He stripped off his pants and boxers before turning to Alyssa. Carefully he eased the skirt around her cast and tossed it aside. Now she wore only her panties... a sexy black thong.

He crooked one eyebrow at her.

"It was on sale."

He grinned. Then he took it off her. *Holy shit. We're naked together,* he realized. *Okay, breathe. Take it slow. Don't get worked up too fast.* To slow himself down, he indulged in a lingering appraisal of Alyssa's body. *She's still too thin.* She had distinctly visible ribs and her hipbones stuck out sharply. *I'll fatten her up soon, but for now, I'm going to feast.* He took an extra pillow from the head of the bed and propped it under her damaged left thigh. "Pretty Allie."

Her cheeks turned a lovely shade of rose, but she harrumphed. "That's better than poor Allie. I don't want you to feel sorry for me anymore."

"Oh no, sweetheart. I'm going to make you so happy everyone will be jealous." *I hope I can figure out how.*

Alyssa smiled, almost a smirk. Her skin felt hot as a furnace. Drew only stoked the heat further. He touched the golden curls between her thighs, massaging gently before sliding one finger between the lips and opening her.

Oh, Lord, is Alyssa wet. Every fold glistened with moisture, so great was her desire, and her clitoris stood swollen and dark. *She truly does want this, thank goodness. It shouldn't take much to bring her to orgasm, and that will make the deflowering much easier on her.* While he understood the mechanics pretty well, experience would have been nice. *Well, there's no help for it now.* He pressed the hood down with his thumb over the eager center of her pleasure and began to circle gently. Alyssa groaned, arching upwards against him. He stroked his index finger down to her opening and slipped inside.

She didn't seem to have much of a hymen, but Drew had studied enough anatomy to know it didn't mean she'd lied to him. *Good. Maybe we can come together without me hurting her.*

Alyssa looked like she was in heaven, tossing her head on the pillow while Drew pleasured her. It wasn't long before ecstasy broke over her in wild waves, tightening her sex around his finger, making her throb under his thumb.

Quickly, Drew positioned himself between her thighs and aligned himself with her entrance. Then he pushed softly against her, a gentle but insistent pressure, and embedded the head of his sex inside her. The tight passage still shuddered at the end of her climax, deliciously warm and wet. He pressed again and again, slowly surging deeper into her. At last, he was buried to the hilt. He stopped for a moment to allow them both to adjust to the sensation.

"Wow," she said softly, "I expected that to hurt."

"I would never hurt you." He kissed her. "I love you, Alyssa."

And then he moved inside her, taking her, gently at first but with growing insistence. She took it all, and the harder he thrust the deeper she moaned with pleasure it until they strained against each other, seeking, and finally finding ultimate satisfaction.

～

A long time later, Alyssa, snuggled half asleep in Drew's arms, started to rouse. She felt wonderful, so relaxed and happy. *I thought giving up my virginity would be scary, but it wasn't. It was sweet. I wish, in that moment of intense pleasure, I had told Drew I love him. I can feel it now.* Her senses had revived. He had fixed whatever was broken in her, and he had done it very well. *I'm so happy it should be wrong... wait, it is wrong. What right do I have to be happy when Daddy's dead? He's never coming back. Even if Drew and I got married, he won't be there to walk me down the aisle. If I have a baby, he won't hold or play with it. If I graduate from college, he won't be there to cheer for me. He's gone.*

At last, the overdue wave of grief crashed over her and she began to sob. Heartbroken, Alyssa pulled the pillow over her face to stifle the sound, so Drew wouldn't hear. She tried to turn over, but her broken leg anchored her in this awkward position, flat on her back like a tipped over turtle, and she couldn't do anything about it but cry.

Of course, Drew woke in a second, tossing the pillow aside and snuggling her close, his body curved around her side. He murmured in her ear. At first, she thought he was trying, pointlessly, to shush her, but at last the soft words broke through. "Let it go, Allie. Let it out. Don't be afraid. I'm here." He stroked her cheek with one hand, kissing her tenderly. After many long minutes, she started to calm. Then another thought occurred to her, starting it all over again.

"I'm a terrible daughter," Alyssa wailed. "How could I do this?"

He regarded her in consternation. "Do what?"

"This!" She waved at the bed. "Make love with you. He's gone, and I just hop into bed with someone like nothing happened."

"No Alyssa, that's not what you did at all," Drew told her gently. His cheek pressed against hers, and the stubble of his russet whiskers scraped against her skin in a surprisingly soothing manner. His scent washed over her. "You were hurting, and you reached for comfort. It's not wrong. It's not surprising. I'm just glad I was here for you. And you're a very good daughter. You worked so hard, so your dad could have the best care."

"What good did it do?" she asked, sucking in a sobbing breath.

He took her wet face in his hands and made her look into his eyes. "What good? Are you kidding? Because of your sacrifice, he had eight more years. Eight, Alyssa. He got to spend nearly a decade with his wife and his child. Without you, none of that would have been possible. I don't think he regretted those years, do you?"

"No."

"And you heard what he told you. He wanted you to live, to be happy. Weren't you happy, just for a few moments there?"

"I'm not sure that's what he had in mind," Alyssa said, wiping her eyes on a corner of the sheet. Mascara smeared on the pale blue surface.

"Likely not," Drew admitted. "But how pleased would he be about you starting college in the fall? Finally working towards becoming a music teacher?"

She smiled. It felt watery but genuine. "He would like that.

He always hated knowing his illness interfered with my dreams."

"Any man would," Drew replied. "I know he was grateful for all you did. Now it's your turn, Allie. Live. Grieve, and mourn, but don't forget to live."

"Hard to forget when you're here, so vital and warm." She hugged him.

"Do you feel any better?" he asked into her hair.

"Yes. I really needed that." She kissed the side of his neck, making him shiver.

"The loving or the tears?" he murmured, heat rising in his voice.

"Both."

He trailed his fingers up her bare back. "Ah. Well, the tears are up to you, but any time you need to be loved, Alyssa, I'm here. I hope you found the experience... enjoyable?"

"Very much. You have such skill."

He pulled back and gave her a funny look she didn't understand. But all he said was, "Are you hungry?"

Her stomach rumbled. "Yes. Always. Did we forget to eat?"

"I guess your heart needed feeding more than your body."

She smiled a little broader. "I'm ravenous."

"I'm not surprised. Let me get you something."

He brought the dinner, cooled but still edible, and they sat together, nude on the guest room bed and shared the meal. Then Drew took the tray back to the kitchen and returned to Alyssa, scooping her up into his arms. She squeaked in surprise as he carried her back to his bedroom and tucked her under the navy cotton sheets.

❀

"This is where you belong," Drew told her, sliding his arms around her waist. He wanted her again, and from the expression on her face, she wasn't too averse to the idea. So, Drew and Alyssa made love, and if the first time had been sweet, the second was even sweeter. Drew kissed Alyssa over every inch of her body, making her burn with desire. He tended particularly to her hard, pink nipples. Then he slid back down along her body, parting her thighs and stroking the tender flesh with his fingers before pressing deep. *She's so wet, so very eager, and now much more relaxed and ready. So am I.* He moved over her, wanting to slide back in, but she protested.

"No, Drew. Let me touch you."

He grinned. "Good idea." He sidled up to where she could reach him, and she took his thick sex in her hands, caressing the shaft. She hooked one arm around his waist and pulled him forward. Alyssa kissed the tip of his penis. He sucked in his breath. *Oh, dear Lord.* Her mouth opened around him and he thrust gently between her lips, letting her taste him. Her tongue teased and circled his sensitive flesh and he moaned. If he hadn't already had one orgasm this evening, he would have come in her mouth in an instant. As it was, he could only take a moment of her caresses. Gently disengaging, he positioned himself between her thighs again. "Are you ready for me, Allie?"

"Yes, Drew. Take me."

He parted her and pressed inside. *This is beautiful. Alyssa's beautiful.* As Drew thrust gently into her delicate passage, he could feel her pleasure rising. Rubbing her clitoris with one finger, driving into her, he brought her, gasping, to a lovely climax, where he quickly joined her.

At last, Drew dropped off to sleep, but Alyssa found rest far more difficult. She had a lot on her mind. *Drew's so passionate and romantic, and the sex felt shockingly good.* It seemed likely he intended this to be a beginning for them, but he still hadn't said so.

And why should he? He asked for sex and you gave it. You know how men are, like Mom always said. They'll take whatever you offer. No reason to suspect he'd mean anything more by it. Especially not from you: the poor, skinny girl from the ugly trailer park. To be someone's cheap lay is all that's expected, after all. Nice boys from good families marry nice girls from good families. Just like Marcie said back in high school, this isn't Cinderella.

You didn't deserve Drew when he was just a nice boy. Now he's a freaking doctor. Yeah, right he wants to be with you. Face it, Alyssa, you're pathetic. He feels sorry for you, so he gave you a place to stay. He asked for sex and you agreed. That's all this is.

Her heart tried to protest, to argue that the feelings between them meant more. "Don't be stupid," it urged. "He told you he loves you, for crying out loud. Back in high school, he told you he wouldn't sleep with a girl unless he loved her. Do you really need more than that?"

Loudly though common sense protested, her self-doubt screamed louder in her head. *I need more reassuring. If I woke him up right now and asked him whether we're a couple, a real couple, with permanent intentions towards each other, he'll tell me, and without a second thought. He's just that kind of man.*

It's a hard question to ask... 'Do you love me enough to keep me'? and I'm not up to it. Nor can I stay in the bed any longer.

She carefully slithered to the floor and crawled, dragging her broken leg, back to the guest room, where she struggled into her clothes and collected her crutches. Hobbling awkwardly, she moved to the kitchen where she wrote Drew a note, explaining what she needed from him. She left it on the table, gathered the bag with her clothes in it, and maneuvered out of the apartment to the elevator, to the bus stop, across town to her grandmother's condo, where her mother and grandmother met her without questions and set her up a pile of blankets on the floor.

She didn't realize Drew had left the kitchen window open. A little gust of spring wind lifted her note and sent it fluttering to the slick wood floor, where it slipped and skidded and finally came to rest under the low bottom of his entertainment center, where it was completely invisible.

All the next day she waited for Drew to call her, but he didn't. He didn't call the next day, or the next. She waited until it became ridiculous. Even after her cast had been removed and her leg, under the care of the physical therapist, began to regain strength, she still waited by the phone many evenings, hoping he would call. When school started in the fall, she took her cell phone with her to class, just in case he might finally decide to contact her.

He never did.

PART III

CHAPTER 9

November 2012
Memorial Hospital

"*D*r. Peterson? I think your phone is ringing."

"You're right, Andrea. Thanks," he told the radiology technician as he fished it out of his pocket and pressed the button, leaning against the wall of the white tiled hallway outside the x-ray room, beside the little light from which pictures of a damaged wrist dangled. "Hello?"

"Hi, Drew," a familiar voice replied.

Dad doesn't call me at work. Hope everything's okay. He didn't sound upset or anything. "What's up?"

"Are you busy this Saturday?"

Curiouser and curiouser. "I have a couple of patients I need to see in the morning, but I should be done by noon. Why?"

"Because I have great news. I just received the most remarkable phone call." James' voice took on the strangest tone.

For some reason it made Drew think he was bouncing up and down on the balls of his feet.

Drew couldn't remember the last time he'd heard his dad sound so excited. "Oh? Who called?"

"Michael. Your brother! He wants to get together this weekend."

Drew's face lit up. He hadn't seen Michael since his mother had left when he was five, taking him, and their other brother Kevin with her. "That's great. What's he been doing all these years?"

"Only good things. He's a doctor too. A Ph.D. in literature, and he's teaching at the university."

Drew's smile stretched until it ached. "Great. I can't wait to see him again. See you Saturday."

Drew hung up the phone and let his mind drift. *Michael. I can't believe it. It'll be so great to see him again. I was just a tiny kid when he left. He seemed too big and dark then, and my friends were all afraid of him, but he was always nice to me, let me tag along. He never got fed up with Kevin either.*

Their middle brother had been born with mental and physical handicaps, and both his older and younger brother had been very protective of him. *Kevin is the reason I became a doctor. I wanted to learn how to help people overcome problems and difficulties. God, I've missed them both.* His bliss faded as he recalled what came next. Amanda and James Peterson had divorced. James had kept Drew and Amanda had taken her sons from previous relationships and left, never to be seen or heard from again.

Or not for a long time, anyway. Sorrow dragged Drew's lips downward. *I'll never forget the sight – or smell – of that halfway house. It was full of the forgotten, throwaway people. The mentally ill, the handicapped, the addicted. People no one was willing to care for. And there was my brother, right in the middle of it, high as a kite. Who sells drugs to a handicapped person? It's disgusting.* Remembering, Drew wanted to retch. *We didn't get back to him in time to save him. We barely found him in time to ensure him a decent place to live for a couple of weeks and a decent burial when his heart finally gave out, just before his thirtieth birthday.* Drew took grim satisfaction in knowing he and Dad had been there. It helped him understand better what Alyssa had gone through with her own father's passing.

Damn it, why can't I stop thinking about Alyssa? I have to let her go. She had made her choice, blatantly, brutally, and I need to respect it. I would never have guessed she'd be the kind of girl to leave a man's bed and disappear without another word. Who does that?

Drew shook his head. *I will never understand women. Now a broken ulna, that I can deal with.* Tugging down the x-rays of the twelve-year-old football player waiting inside the x-ray room, he headed down the hall. *Work is an excellent remedy for women troubles.*

On Saturday, Drew hurried through his visits with his patients. Thankfully, nothing new had been added to his caseload since then, and shortly after noon he handed off his paperwork to the medical assistant for filing and headed to his dad's house to meet his brother. Parking carefully along the slippery curb, he trudged through a new fall of slushy November snow, past the old maple in the front yard, the tire swing hanging forlornly from its naked branches. It had been many years since a child had played here.

He let himself in, hung up his coat, and took off his messy boots, leaving them in the entryway. He could hear voices from the living room; Dad's familiar baritone along with a low, dark, intense male voice and, surprisingly, a woman. Drew approached the room.

His dad perched on the recliner, his back to the doorway. Drew glanced at the sofa. *So, this must be Michael.* He could see hints of the boy he had known in the man seated before him. Same black hair, now shoulder length, pulled back into a shiny, smooth ponytail, revealing a strong jaw; same glittering black eyes above the strong nose and cheekbones. He was dressed casually in a pair of blue jeans and a soft gray sweater that clung to sculpted shoulder and chest muscles. He also had his arm around the waist of a stunning blonde.

Michael's lady friend turned out to be quite the most beautiful woman Drew had ever seen. She had masses of golden curls, pulled into a loose ponytail, friendly laughing hazel eyes, regular features with pale golden skin, and a lush, curvy figure. She smiled, lighting up the room, and he could see his brother's expression change. Drew had been in love before, but he hadn't particularly made a study of the condition in others. However, the look on Michael's face as his eyes took in this lovely woman was one of the most powerful Drew had ever seen. Michael looked at her as though she were his last hope of salvation. She glanced into his eyes and her smile turned possessive. *Good. I'm glad to see she loves him back.*

"Hello, everyone," Drew said. The three all stood and moved in his direction. Drew blinked to see just how tall Michael had become. He and his dad both stood a couple inches over six feet. Michael was taller, maybe even six five or six. His girlfriend though pretty tall for a woman, could easily rest the top of her head on his shoulder.

Michael, his left arm still around the woman's waist, extended his free hand to Drew, and he shook it eagerly. "Michael, I'm so glad to see you. How are you doing?"

"I'm great. I can't get over you, though." His face twisted into lines of discomfort.

He's anxious, Drew realized. *How could I have forgotten his shyness?* Striving to be friendly, Drew said, "Well, it's been a few years. I couldn't help growing up. Sorry." He grinned.

Michael didn't smile, but his expression softened a bit. "Hey, no, you look good. How have *you* been?"

"Pretty good. Can't complain." He turned to the woman and his suave demeanor evaporated. "And this is?" he managed to squeeze out.

"My girlfriend, Sheridan Murphy. Sheridan, this is my brother Andrew." Michael gestured toward Drew with a huge and ink-stained hand.

"Call me Drew." He gave the pretty blond a smile and shook her hand.

"Pleased to meet you, Drew," she replied in a smooth, mellow voice that sent agreeable shivers up his spine. *How is she even real?* "I've heard so much about you. Of course, in all those stories, you were just a baby."

"Yeah, it's hard when families can't stay together," Drew admitted. "But I'm really glad to have found Michael again. He was the best big brother ever."

A hint of color appeared on Michael's tawny cheeks. "It wasn't hard to be nice to you. You were a pretty good kid."

"Then you're lucky, Michael," Sheridan said, her eyes twinkling. "My brothers both used to drive me crazy."

"I'm sure you returned the favor, sweetheart," Michael replied, one corner of his mouth turning upward as he teased his woman.

"I did." She waggled her eyebrows, and everyone laughed.

They all drifted back to the chairs and sat, continuing the conversation long into the afternoon. *After the disaster that had claimed our brother's life, it's a tremendous relief to find Michael well-adjusted, relaxed, healthy, and happy. He pursued a good career and has a beautiful woman at his side. He actually did better than me, as my one attempt at love ended suddenly and unexpectedly after a single night. Now, Sheridan, I can see, has the confidence of a woman who knows she's beautiful, and the humility of one who doesn't take it too seriously. She clearly believes being with Michael is her right, but also a great privilege. They won't have to contend with demons of inadequacy. I'm glad.*

Sheridan also suddenly looked rather ill. Her pretty face had taken on a greenish tint and her throat began working convulsively. "Excuse me," she said, her voice strained. She walked quickly in the direction of the bathroom. Michael jumped up and hurried after her. James trailed along. Drew stayed where he was. He could hear muffled male voices from down the hall and a few minutes later, Michael returned, holding his girlfriend closer than ever. She looked pale, sweaty and none too steady on her feet.

"Sorry to cut this short, but we'd better go," Michael said.

"Are you all right?" Drew asked Sheridan.

"Yes. I'm fine, thank you." She leaned heavily on her boyfriend.

I hate when people said that, and it obviously isn't true.

"Hey, Michael," he said, letting Sheridan's obvious distress go undiscussed. She clearly didn't want to talk about it. "Before you go, can you give me your number? Let's stay in touch this time, okay?"

"Oh, sure." Michael fished a piece of paper out of his pocket and Sheridan dug in her purse for a pen. Michael scribbled down a couple of numbers and gave them to his brother. Drew ripped the paper in half and handed his own number to Michael.

"Will you guys be in town for Christmas?" he asked. "Dad

and I usually get together for Mass and then spend the day together."

"Sorry, no," Michael replied, squeezing his girlfriend's hand gently. "We're going up north to visit Sheridan's family. I haven't met them before."

Committed, are they? Even better. "Sounds daunting. Good luck."

"Thanks." Michael looked nervous at the very thought.

Sheridan gave him a weak little smile and Michael escorted her out the door.

James returned to the room, shaking his head.

"Well, he seems great," Drew commented.

"Yes. I'm relieved," James replied, an unhappy expression on his face. Drew supposed visions of Kevin were flashing before his face.

"Me too," Drew agreed, trying to keep things light. "And what an amazing girlfriend he has."

His father made a face.

What kind of reaction is that, to such an obviously nice woman? "What, don't you like her?"

James responded a little too quickly. "Oh, I do. She's really quite wonderful."

"At least one of us got it right," he commented darkly. *You have to quit saying things like that. Dad doesn't know about what happened, but if you keep hinting, he might ask. You don't want to explain to him, do you, that what you thought was love turned out to be a one-night stand?*

But James, his thoughts clearly far away, didn't seem to notice. All he said was, "Let's hope."

There's something more going on here with Michael and Sheridan, and Dad knows what it is, but it's really not my business, so I have to let it go.

CHAPTER 10

*W*inter deepened. Snow piled up on snow. The streets grew treacherous with slush and ice and the driving wind howled in the bare trees. Two days before Christmas, on a particularly icy and unpleasant morning, Drew sat on the sofa in his apartment, staring out the window at a sky that seemed most reluctant to light up.

I'm not a huge fan of winter, he admitted to himself. *It reminds him too much of Alyssa. I can still see her, wearing the secondhand black coat and the gloves I bought for her, smiling, her dimples showing, as we walked around the high school campus, hand in hand. I still don't understand what had gone wrong. I loved that girl so much. If I haven't begun to get over it by now, I should probably consider relocating once I finish my residency. Going someplace warm and sunny with no snow and no memories. Somewhere I can start again.*

Drew had pretty much given up on dating. No one could compare with what he'd once had so briefly, and it was unfair to those other girls to try. So, he concentrated on work. Winter meant lots of car accidents, some with injuries he could fix.

Also, lots of slipping on the ice and fracturing wrists and pelvises. He certainly kept busy enough.

In between, he spent time with his dad, hung out with friends, and got to know his brother. *Leaving and not seeing Michael again seems sad, as we're becoming quite close. In the time since our meeting, I've found him to be a shy, intense, and introspective man, but a kind one. He genuinely cares about the people in his life, but he also holds them, and himself, to pretty high standards.*

The phone on the end table chimed, and Drew jumped, sloshing tepid coffee onto his clothing. He lifted the device to see Michael's name on the screen. *It's like I summoned him.* Laughing at his own silliness, even as he cursed his clumsy move, he pushed the button.

"Drew, it's Michael. How are you?"

"Cold and grumpy," he replied as the wetness on his sweats slowly grew colder. "How about you?"

"Cold. Less grumpy."

Wow, he sounds really nervous. "What's up?"

"Um, are you doing anything the Friday after New Year's, around five?"

Drew didn't need to check the calendar. "Working."

"Can you get off?"

What? "Maybe. Why?"

"Sheridan and I are getting married," Michael announced.

Drew blinked. "Wow, that was fast."

"Yeah, well. You know how it is. Now that I have her, I want to claim her for life." He rushed through the words, as though he'd rehearsed a script.

This is so weird. "Yes, I can understand that."

"Well, anyway, it's going to be pretty small, but we'd both like it a lot if you could be there."

Naturally. "For this, Michael, I'll make time. Where?"

"The chapel of the Basilica."

Nice choice. Geez, he's even more Catholic than me, I guess. "I'll be there."

"Thanks."

Hmmm. Drew thought, as he hung up the phone, *it's strange for them to be in such a hurry. Something seems a little... off. If I were marrying the glorious Sheridan Murphy, I would plan one of those huge weddings to show off the event. Michael must be a different sort. I hope Sheridan isn't too disappointed.*

On the first Friday in January, Drew put on his suit and tie and drove to the Basilica to sit beside James and witness the marriage of Michael Burke and Sheridan Murphy.

For a small wedding, it's actually quite pretty, Drew realized as he scanned the room. The church had kindly left up the Christmas decorations, so the room looked cheerful in shades of green and gold and smelled of pine. Michael stood nervously in his dark suit, alone at the front. Sheridan and her father, a tall and weathered-looking man, walked in to the music of a violin, a flute and a piano. She wore what could only be a repurposed prom dress, cream colored and with a lot of netting on the skirt. It didn't fit her very well either. *She must have gained some weight since high school. But if she did, it's strangely distributed. In fact, she looks... different than when I met her last month. Her breasts bigger, and she has a little belly I don't recall. Not much, just enough to notice.* Drew's eyes narrowed.

Sheridan set her hand in Michael's, so the ceremony could begin, and he saw her, with her free hand, touch the side of her belly in a gesture he'd seen many times at the hospital.

Suddenly Drew's medical instincts clicked in and he made the diagnosis. *Sheridan's approaching the middle of pregnancy. It explains all the strange things that have bothered me since I met her. She must have had a mild attack of morning sickness* on the day they visited. No wonder they planned such a fast wedding.

So, Michael got his girlfriend pregnant. I'm impressed. Of course, with a woman as glorious as Sheridan, it made sense to claim her as quickly as possible, in ways which couldn't be argued or denied. *I should have done the same with Alyssa.*

The bride didn't seem in the least bit upset with her circumstances either. She gazed up into her husband's face her expression softly adoring. *She isn't sorry to be marrying quickly, and pregnant. She looks delighted, which was good.* Michael's expression as he regarded his wife was intense, passionate and possessive. *They're the perfect couple.*

The musicians began to play a familiar tune; Ave Maria by Franz Schubert. Then a high, delicate voice began to sing. *Oh, good. They didn't get an opera singer.* The pretty voice, soft and tender, seemed to be made for singing to young children. *She sounds familiar, as though I've heard this very woman sing before.* He turned to look and froze with shock.

Of course, it was Alyssa. Off in the far corner of the room, she stood in a black dress next to the instrumentalists, in the curve of the piano. *Damn it, why was it so impossible for me to forget her? Why does she have to turn up, unexpectedly, and shatter my peace?* He regarded her steadily. She looked terrible. She had always been too thin, but now she had grown almost skeletal, her cheekbones in sharp relief, her arms like twigs. *I wonder who she's giving all her food to now. Poverty's such a habit to her, she simply doesn't know how to let it go. She still sounds good though.*

A soft clattering sound pulled Drew's gaze to the seat closest to the musicians. There, a small boy of about three with a shock of reddish brown hair quietly drove a little plastic car over the pew. Drew inhaled sharply. *Don't jump to conclusions,* he urged himself. *There are four musicians there, after all. The* toddler could belong to any of them. *There's no reason to assume he's Alyssa's.* At least, not until the song ended and she returned to her seat. Then the little boy swarmed up into her lap, laid his head on her shoulder, and stuck his thumb in his mouth. She hugged him tight in her arms.

Drew looked at Alyssa and her son for a long moment. *There's little doubt what it means.* A fury the likes of which Drew had never felt before slowly grew inside him. *How dare that bitch not only leave in the middle of the night, but also conceal this child from me for all these years?*

He tried to calm down. *Maybe something happened after we were together,* he reasoned desperately. *Maybe she met someone else. There's no guarantee this boy is my son.*

Oh, but it isn't likely, reason forced him to admit, stomach jumping and threatening to turn itself inside out. *The timing seems right, and the little guy looks like me.*

Drew deliberately clamped down on his rage. *This is Michael and Sheridan's wedding. It has nothing to do with my shattered relationship with their wedding singer. I won't spoil their big day by making a scene. I have to get to the bottom of this, but not now. Today is for Michael and Sheridan, but soon I'll be contacting Alyssa and finding out exactly what she's been up to.*

CHAPTER 11

A couple of days after the wedding, while Michael and Sheridan were off enjoying a passionate honeymoon in the Florida Keys, Drew received a call that was nothing short of life-changing. Unfortunately, it wasn't as pleasant as the one that had reconnected him with his brother or found him attending Michael's wedding. This call came from a nursing home.

After over twenty years of silence, Amanda Burke Peterson wanted her son to come and see her, so he went. He had always wondered exactly why his mother had walked away and never come back. *Maybe I can finally get the answer to the question that haunted my entire life.*

Sadly, he arrived too late.

"Amanda Burke," he told the receptionist.

The woman regarded him from under a bouffant of sandy silver and gold hair. "I don't recall anyone by that name. Do you mean Amanda Peterson?"

Oh, dear Lord. She's using Dad's name still? "Yeah, sure. She asked me to come."

The woman frowned. "Room 217. I... I don't think she's awake."

"Should I come back later?" he asked. "I don't want to disturb her if she's..."

"She's in a coma," the receptionist informed him. "We don't expect her to improve."

"Coma? Listen, ma'am, I don't know what's going on, but..."

She cut in again, her eyes hard and narrow. "She's dying of liver failure. Her son has already told her goodbye and the priest has administered Last Rights. She has a standing DNR. I don't know what you hope to accomplish by visiting at this point."

Drew shook his head. "Dying? No one said that. Look, I'm her son too. I haven't seen her since I was five, I..." words abandoned him.

"Oh." The woman's glare softened. "I'm sorry. Like I said, room 217. She might be able to hear you. I don't know."

Drew nodded and turned, walking unsteadily along the white tile, pointless thoughts crowding his mind. *Why is knowing she's dying so much worse than never seeing her again? Was I holding out hope she might someday actually be a mother?* The toe of his sneaker caught on the tile and he stumbled, placing one hand on the dusty blue wall for support. The door he both did and didn't want to see appeared in front of him. He entered without knocking and approached a figure lying still and quiet on the bed.

She was in a pitiable state. He knew her yellow skin indicated jaundice. Oddly, in addition, scars dotted her yellowed skin in thick profusion his mind refused to interpret. He took a seat in a padded chair and considered whether he should touch her. His hand hovered over hers, but he hesitated, and eventually let it fall away. *There's nothing to do and I have no idea what to say. I guess I sit here so she doesn't die alone.* His breath caught once, and his heart seemed to pound in his chest, but he waited nonetheless, and within only an hour of his arrival, she exhaled for the last time. "Re..." he inhaled and tried again. "Rest in peace, Mom."

A nurse, summoned by the continuous tone of the heart monitor, regarded him sadly. "Are you the next of kin?"

"Yes, I guess so," he replied. "She was my mother."

"Do you have plans for her funeral?" The young man asked, shuffling his feet. "We don't have any information. She..."

"I'll make some," Drew replied, not wanting to know anymore. "Thanks... for taking care of her."

The man dipped his chin, and the conversation ended.

So, Drew planned Amanda's funeral. She deserved at least that much. James refused to attend, but Michael and Sheridan had arrived back from their honeymoon. The three of them sat together at the funeral home and silently bid Amanda goodbye. No one cried.

As Father Aaron spoke a few kind words over the mortal remains of the mother who'd never been there for him, Drew tried to comfort himself with the thought that this priest, due to Michael's intervention, had visited her and given confession and last rights. It provided less comfort than he'd hoped.

It had been such an intense week, attending his brother's wedding, seeing his long-lost love, discovering he might have a child, and saying goodbye to his mother, that as the funeral progressed, Drew began to feel quite overwhelmed. By the end of the brief service, he'd had all he could take and hurried home. But being alone was no help either. *I need to talk to someone*, he realized as he parked the car in the parking garage of his apartment complex. *I need advice. Should I ask Dad? He always knows how to help me think... no. He would be devastated. If... if my guess is right, dealing with Dad will be one thing I need help with. He tried so hard to teach me to be responsible... and I am. This isn't my fault.* Drew sighed. "It doesn't matter whose fault it is," he reminded himself aloud, locking his apartment door behind him and sinking onto the sofa. He stared out the window without seeing the snowflakes drifting past the glass. "A child who could very well be mine is growing up without a father. That is the only important issue. It has to be fixed, but how?"

It wasn't surprising really, how long it took Drew to realize what to do. After all, he hadn't had his big brother in his life very long. But once it dawned on him to ask Michael for advice, he got on the phone right away. The men agreed to meet at a coffee shop near the university during a two-hour break Michael had between classes Monday morning.

Drew arrived in the cozy, gold-plastered café to find Michael already there, seated at a table, holding a steaming cup of coffee. Drew approached the counter and ordered an extra-large with cream from a girl with two rings in her lower lip. Her multicolored dreadlocks swung as she poured from the oversized carafe.

"Um, miss?"

"Yeah?" she asked over her shoulder.

"Can you add a shot of peppermint, please?"

She grabbed the little bottle from the display and poured a generous slug into his cup, before turning to ring up his purchase.

"That will be $5.75," she said.

Drew crooked one eyebrow at her but swiped his card and grabbed the cup. He made his way over to his brother grumbling under his breath. "I should stick to coffee at home."

Then he remembered why he was here and his heart gave a nervous thump. *I don't want to deal with this. I can't deal with this. Maybe I should just pretend I didn't see them.* Then he remembered how skinny she'd looked. *No, I have to get to the bottom of it. I have to be a man.* "Hi, Michael," Drew began, striving for nonchalance as he slid into a chair. "How's married life treating you?"

Michael looked up. A hint of a satisfied smile played across his lips. "Oh hi, Drew. Marriage is great. Everyone should try it. I had no idea it would be so... amazing."

Drew smiled, though he knew the movement of his lips didn't reflect his true feelings. "Glad to hear it. Of course, the wife in question makes a difference."

"You're right." Michael leaned back in his seat, looking even smugger than before. "So, what's up? You sounded a little upset on the phone."

"Yeah. I'm in a... difficult spot, and I was hoping to get some big brother advice."

"Does it involve a woman?"

Damn, Michael sure is perceptive. "Yes."

His brother leaned forward in the high-backed metal chair and sipped his coffee, apparently considering his words. "I'm not sure how much help I can be, unless your situation is very much like mine with Sheridan."

"What do you mean?"

"Sheridan is the only woman I've ever loved, ever been with."

Drew blinked. *How odd for a man who must be thirty-five years old. But then, I haven't been in a rush on that front either.* "Ah, well I'm actually pretty much the same."

"Good. I think it's better that way, don't you?" His eyes took on a faraway look, and Drew imagined a vision of a beautiful blond was dancing in Michael's head.

Drew looked down at the table at a little puddle of spilled sugar. "Maybe if you get to marry the girl and live happily ever after."

"Why don't you?"

"It's a long story." He pushed the sugar around with the tip of one finger.

Michael checked the time on his cell phone. "You have an hour. Get to it."

You wanted advice, Drew. Get to it is right. No dawdling. "Well, I've known this girl forever. We went to elementary school together, but we didn't become a couple until senior year. I really loved her then, but life pulled us apart. She had to stay home and work, and I went to college and became a doctor."

Michael's expression turned knowing. "You never forgot though, did you?"

"Nope. A few years ago, I ran into her again, and it was like no time had passed. I loved her as much as ever, right away. She was in a... difficult situation, and I did everything I could to help her. Things got intense between us. We ended up... spending the night together." Drew looked at Michael, a little embarrassed. *Brother or no, talking about my sex life, such as it was, feels uncomfortable and awkward.*

His brother nodded encouragingly. "I know what that's like." Color stained Michael's cheeks. It seemed he shared Drew's reticence to talk about such private issues.

Drew forged ahead. "But was Sheridan still there in the morning?"

He took in his brother's puzzled look, before Michael answered. "Of course."

"Allie wasn't. I woke up and she was gone." His throat wanted to stick on that confession.

"So, she turned out to be a tramp, then?"

How was it, that four years later, the slight to Allie makes my fists clench? He forced himself to release them, knowing it was a reasonable conclusion. "I don't really think so. She was a virgin too."

Michael's dark eyebrows came together. "It seems very odd."

"I know." He pushed the sugar into a thin line and set the cup on top of it. "Why would anyone do something like that?"

Now the gears began turning. Drew could actually see his brother pondering. *Oh good. He's going to help me think. This I just what I'd hoped for.* "Well, you said she was in a difficult situation. What was it?"

"Her father had just died. He'd been sick for a long time." Drew lifted the cup and sipped. A shower of glistening white fell from the cup's bottom rim back onto the table.

Michael winced. "Ouch. Maybe she felt bad for going to bed with you while she was grieving."

"She did," Drew admitted, "but we talked about it, and I thought she was okay."

"So why didn't you go find her, ask her what it was all about?"

Lost in memories, Drew responded without thought, straight from his bitter, aching heart. "Wasn't it obvious? She got what she wanted from me and she left. Why would I need to hear her say it?"

Michael's heavy black eyebrows drew together, and he pursed his lips. "How do you know that's what she would say? It doesn't make a lot of sense. If someone does something that makes no sense, you should ask for clarification. I think there's more to the story than what you've told me. Why would you assume she was just leaving?"

"Everyone leaves. Especially women," Drew mumbled.

Michael put his hand on his brother's shoulder. "This is

really about Mom, isn't it?"

Was that it? Damn, I didn't want it to be some psychobabble bullshit. Could it really be? But there was something to what Michael was saying. "She left when I was five. She never came back. Most kids with divorced parents spend time with both, but not me. She never visited, she never tried to talk to me. What kind of mother does that?"

Michael took a deep breath and his voice dropped to a near whisper. "A troubled one," he said, turning his coffee cup around and around in his hands, his gaze focused on the Styrofoam. "Mom had... issues. It wouldn't have been good for you to have her around. You were blessed to have your dad. Mom was no great loss."

Drew's jaw dropped. "What a terrible thing to say."

Michael looked up with haunted eyes. "Drew, I lived with her for fourteen years. I know what I'm talking about."

"Well, I don't," he replied stubbornly.

"She didn't leave you. Your dad made her go, made her stay away to protect you from her."

Protect? Huh? "From what?"

Michael took a sip of coffee, exhaled in a loud sigh and spoke words Drew would never have imagined. "From methamphetamine. She was an addict. It was her drug use during pregnancy that caused Kevin's birth defects. She didn't get clean until a few months before she met your dad."

"No." His stomach clenched at the hideous thought. *Meth. One of the deadliest, most addictive drugs on earth.*

Michael nodded grimly. "Did she call you at the end? I asked her to."

Drew's numb lips formed the words clumsily. "She did, but she was already in a coma when I got there. I didn't get to talk to her. What did she want to say?"

"I think just to apologize. That's all she said to me."

Drew shook his head and fell silent. *Methamphetamine. That explains a lot. The scars, the liver failure. Disgusting.* He'd worked with meth addicts before and should have recognized the signs. But who wants to believe their mother is a junkie?

"I'm sorry. I thought you knew." Michael regarded his brother with lowered eyebrows and a sad downward turn of his lips.

"No. I thought she left because she didn't want me." *Wait, don't say that! Shut up, Drew!*

Michael's expression turned sadder. "She did want you. She loved us all. She was just too weak to overcome her demons."

"How did it happen?" Drew asked hesitantly, not sure he wanted the answer. *Why do you need to put yourself through this? How does it help you to know?* And yet, like staring at a car accident, he found himself stuck in horrified fascination, unable to withdraw the painful question.

"She was only fifteen when she had me. I think it was just too much for her." Michael scrubbed his hand over his face.

He blames himself. Another family legacy we share. "I suppose. But still."

"I know." Michael sighed. "So that must have influenced your decision to let your Allie go when you should have been asking her questions. It's not surprising."

Oh, that's right. We were talking about Alyssa, not Mom. Don't get distracted, Drew. "Yeah well, that's not the whole story."

"Okay, go on." Michael circled his hand in an encouraging gesture.

"Let me ask you a question first. Is Sheridan pregnant?"

Michael blushed darkly. "How did you know?" he asked, snapping a sliver off the edge of his cup and smashing it between his fingers.

131

"I'm a doctor, Michael."

He snorted and rolled his eyes. "Right. Yeah."

"How did you... react when you found out?"

Those far away eyes turned sad. "Not well. I wasn't sure I would be able to handle it. It almost broke us."

Broke them? But they love each other so much! "Really?"

"Yeah. We worked it out though, thank God. I don't know what I would do without her." Michael twisted his fingers together, unconsciously revealing how devastating the near-loss had been.

I do know what you would do. I live it every day. "You'd be very sad," Drew told him.

"Right." Michael shuddered, then snapped another bit off his cup and dropped it inside. "So, what's your point, Drew."

Distracted again. Get with it! "Well so anyway, I ran into Allie again recently."

Michael shook his head. Strands came loose from his ponytail and lay, silky smooth and straight, along the sides of his face. He yanked the elastic out of his hair and raked it back. "You did? What did she say?"

"I didn't talk to her. I couldn't. It was the middle of your wedding."

Michael paused, both hands in his hair, and frowned at Drew. "My wedding? There was no one at my wedding, unless you mean Hallie? I thought you said Allie."

"Who's Hallie?" Drew wanted to know.

"A student of mine. She's dating one of my friends," Michael explained.

Drew shook his head and finished his coffee, shuddering at the unincorporated mint syrup at the bottom of the cup. "No, not a guest at your wedding, Michael. You know the musical group you guys hired for the ceremony?"

"Yes?"

"The singer."

"Alyssa Miller?" Michael turned a stunned expression on his brother.

"You know her?"

"Yeah. I had her in class her first semester of college. She's really smart. I don't give out a lot of A's, but she earned one. She must be nearly as smart as Sheridan. She was so sad though, I worried a lot about her."

"Her first semester of college? Okay, I have to ask you something. This is really important." Drew took a deep breath. "Was she pregnant at the time?"

"Yeah."

"Shit." Drew closed his eyes. *Just as I feared.*

Michael continued. "She was due right around the time of finals. It was about even odds whether she would be able to finish the semester. She did, but I heard later that she had her baby about a week after classes ended."

The more Michael told him, the clearer it became that there was only one conclusion. "Did she look all right? Was she... well fed?"

"What a strange question. Yeah, she was thin, but not dangerously so."

Drew explained. "As long as I've known her, Allie has never had enough to eat. Maybe, since she was pregnant, she decided to take care of herself. I hope so." He paused, gathering himself before finally saying aloud the words that had been haunting him. "I'm pretty sure the baby was mine."

Michael gave Drew a sympathetic glance before speaking. "The little boy she brought to the wedding? He did look a lot like you did at that age."

Drew buried his face in his hands. "Now what am I going to do?"

Michael placed a heavy hand on his shoulder. "Well, little

brother, it's time for you to do what you should have done in the first place. You need to find Alyssa and talk to her. Even if she doesn't want to be with you, your son deserves to have a father."

"That's hard. I don't know if I can be civil to her after everything that happened, but the last thing I want is more drama."

"We both know what it's like to grow up without a parent. Do you really want that for your son?"

Michael is going to be a great dad, if asking the hard questions counts for anything. "Of course not."

"You should be sure he's really yours first," Michael suggested.

"I know, but there's not much doubt."

Michael blew out between his lips, blasting his brother with the scent of coffee. "You know something, Drew? Reading people's writing tells me a lot about them. In the early stages of our relationship, that's how Sheridan and I got to know each other. What I read in Alyssa that semester was... interesting. I got a strong sense from her that she doesn't feel good enough."

"Good enough for what?"

"For anything. For college, for friends, to be a mother. She was pretty much in despair."

Drew nodded. "She's always been a little that way. She grew up so poor, and her father's illness and death drained the family dry. I kept trying to tell her she was good enough anyway, that being poor didn't make her of less value, but I'm not sure she ever believed it."

"Maybe that's why she left," Michael suggested. "She didn't think she was good enough to keep you, so she wanted to end things on her terms."

Drew thought about it. "No, that doesn't fit."

"Well, maybe she left hoping you would come after her,

make the big gesture and prove she meant more to you than an easy lay."

Drew wanted to reject the suggestion. *No way. She knew I loved her.* But then he paused and thought more carefully. *Alyssa did have a funny way of interpreting things sometimes.* The more he thought about it, the more sense it made. "That could be it," he admitted, "but still, I did everything I could think of to prepare us to be a couple. She knew I wouldn't sleep with her unless I loved her."

"Did you tell her you loved her?" Michael pressed.

"Yes. More than once," Drew insisted.

"Did you tell her you wanted a relationship?"

Isn't that the same thing? I guess, since Michael is shy, he might understand better what she was up to. "I was working up to it, but it should have been pretty obvious."

"Never underestimate the demon of self-doubt, Drew," Michael advised darkly. "It's a terrible monster."

"How do you know?"

Michael exhaled heavily. "I live with it every day. I loved Sheridan for eight years before I believed we could be together, and even then, she had to ask me. She'd been waiting so long for me to ask her, gave me all the right signals, but I explained them all away because I never believed it would be possible she might be interested in me."

How does that fit with the man in front of me? He has that smoldering darkness that drives women wild. "Wow."

Michael checked his phone again. "Listen, I have to go. My class is starting pretty soon. Let's talk again though, Drew. In the meanwhile, you've got to talk to Alyssa and find out what's going on. Do you want me to get her contact information for you? I still have it."

"No, I don't need it. I have access to her medical records."

And for this, I'll bend confidentiality a bit. If I get in trouble, so be it.

"Okay. Good luck."

"Thanks, Michael."

Drew drove back to the hospital in a state of deep distraction. His conversation with Michael had been enlightening, to say the least. He'd always thought of himself as the strong one, but it turned out he had a deep wound he hadn't even recognized. He'd lost the woman he loved twice, and he had never asked any questions, never fought for her or their relationship. He should have. Perhaps he simply expected to be left, subconsciously believing it was his fate.

Part of me wants her back, he realized. *She did things to my heart...great things as well as terrible ones.* But now, pain and fury clouded the memories. *It will be hard to trust her again after this. I wonder if the damage between us can ever really be healed. Even if it can't, I need to find out whether the little boy is my son and be there for him. That's the most important thing.*

The following Saturday, as Drew pulled on his clothes, so he could get to the hospital to fix up an elderly woman who'd fractured her hip, his cell phone chimed. Shivering and shirtless, he checked the screen and, seeing it was Michael, pushed the button to answer.

"What's up?" *Damn, this floor is cold. I need socks.*

He rummaged in the dresser drawer while Michael spoke. "Just thought of something. Did you have a chance to talk to Alyssa yet?"

"Not yet." He propped the phone on his shoulder and stood on one foot to pull on a thick black sock.

"I hope you don't mind. I asked Sheridan if she

remembered her. She was a T.A. for a while, when she was working on her master's and had Alyssa in her class the semester after she was in mine. Sheridan told me Alyssa had been waiting for someone to call her and I remembered I had trouble with her having her phone in class as well. At any rate, Sheridan is so easy to get along with, Alyssa confided in her a bit. She said she was waiting to see if her baby's father would ever call her. She'd been afraid he was just trying to make her feel better because he was a nice guy and wanted to give him an easy out if he needed it."

By the end of this speech, Drew had both socks on and was trying to figure out how to get into his top without dropping the phone. "Yeah, that sounds like Allie. She has no idea how amazing she is, does she?" He popped the shirt over his head quickly and returned to the conversation.

"She doesn't seem to. Anyway, I think we may have guessed right. She was hoping you would make a big deal out of wanting her, but you didn't. I understand why, but I doubt she did. To Alyssa, she offered you the chance to walk away and you took it."

Drew padded out of the bedroom and into the kitchen portion of his apartment, where his coffee pot waited, filled to the brim with steaming liquid life. "Damn it, that's not what I wanted at all," he said, as he poured himself a revitalizing cup.

"Well, it's going to be hard to convince her this many years later."

Drew gulped his coffee and cursed as he burned his tongue. "I know. I don't know if it's even possible."

"Well, here's my idea. Take it for what it's worth. Sheridan's parents, her brother, and the two of us have all gone in together to buy a cabin in the woods. It's for getaways, family reunions, stuff like that. We're all going for spring break, except her parents. Her dad has to work. If you wanted to spend time with

Alyssa and the little guy, you could invite her. It would give you two a chance to talk, outside of everyday life, and everyone helps with the kids. Sheridan's brother has a son just about the same age. Maybe they could play together. And if she doesn't want to go, you would still be more than welcome. I've checked with everyone, and they're fine with it. Plus, Sheridan has wanted to get in touch with Alyssa for a while. She was worried about her. She really liked Alyssa, saw her as someone she would like to have as a friend, if they could reconnect in a nonprofessional setting."

Socks and coffee made a huge difference, and Michael's idea had definite merit. "You two are great. Thanks for the invitation. I'll see how it works out."

"Okay. Bye."

Drew hung up. Heart pounding, he called the medical assistant at the hospital who looked up Alyssa's records and gave him her address.

As soon as he finished cleaning up after the surgery, Drew got directly into his car and drove over to the apartment building where Alyssa lived with her mother. The sight brought a smile to his face. A handsome red-brick structure gleamed, winter sunlight reflecting off clean windows. The cars parked out front were mostly in good repair. A fenced yard bristled with playground equipment, now half buried in snow. A little row of snowmen waved through the chain-link. *This is, to all appearances, a respectable place for families to live. It looks like with Brandon's help, she got assistance with her living expenses after all.* He checked the apartment number and rode up on the elevator to the seventh floor. Easily locating number 718, at the end of a freshly carpeted hallway, he knocked.

$\mathcal{A}$lyssa sat at the kitchen table studying, or rather frowning in dismay. *I don't like college algebra. Too much time has passed since high school and my math skills are not what they once were.* She pondered the incomprehensible stack of numbers and letter, tilting her head to the left, and then the right, but nothing came clear. *I have to do a good job. If I can get through this class with a good grade, I'll maintain her 4.0. It's not required in order to start student teaching in the fall. They won't mind if I get a B in math, but I'll mind. Still, student teaching. Finally getting some time in the classroom.* The thought of a room full of little children singing filled her with joy.

But first algebra. She squinted hard at the page full of scrawled notes, and then the fifteen practice problems due Monday afternoon, and shook her head. *If they're related, I have no idea how.* A deep sigh emerged from the depths of her being. *I'll probably have to make time to go to tutoring again in the hour-long break between her morning classes. I hate that. It's my one chance to see my son during the day.* Again, she tried to focus on her homework.

A knock at the door shattered her concentration. *I'm not expecting anyone. What on earth?* Whoever it was knocked again, insistently. She sighed and opened the door, only to find herself looking directly into a black sweatshirt. Her eyes traveled up the length of a masculine chest to a face devastating in its familiar beauty. For a moment it seemed her heart had stopped beating. Her lungs drew no air. At last, she managed to croak out, "Drew?"

"Alyssa. We need to talk."

She nodded blankly and stepped aside to let him into the apartment. He looked around and a grim smile spread across his face. She glanced at what he was seeing. The furnishings had come with the place; a functional overstuffed sofa in decent condition, end tables, a fat, old-fashioned television, a plain round table with four chairs. Just an ordinary apartment, but they had splurged on new drapes for the windows with last year's income tax return. The burgundy color complimented the drab taupe that formed the basic palate in the two-bedroom space.

"Why are you here, Drew?" she asked at last.

The grin faded to a glower. "I saw you at my brother's wedding. I realized we had a lot of unfinished business to discuss."

"Your brother?" she asked, unable to process the comment. "I've known you since kindergarten. Since when you have had a brother?"

He shrugged. "Since always. You know my parents are divorced. My mom had two sons from other relationships. When she left, she took them with her."

The pieces fell into place. "Oh Lord, is Doctor Burke your brother? That's the only wedding I've done recently."

Drew lowered his head in a brief nod. "Yeah, he is."

"He's great. He was a fantastic professor, really hard, but I learned so much from him. I'm so glad he and Ms. Murphy got married. They were really sweet together, and I don't even think they were a couple then..."

"Alyssa."

She stopped babbling and her cheeks warmed.

He got straight to the point. "You had a little boy with you at the wedding."

"Yes." *Oh, no, I know where this is headed.* She gulped, feeling a swell of nauseous nervousness in her belly.

"Your son?"

She drew in a wavering breath. "Uh huh."

"What's his name?"

"Ethan. Ethan Andrew. He just turned three."

Drew closed his eyes briefly, then opened them and nailed Alyssa with a burning green glare. "Is he mine?"

Alyssa took a slow deep breath before responding. "Yes."

Drew's jaw clenched. "Are you sure?"

Her cheeks heated from warm to fiery as she admitted the truth. "It's literally impossible that he could be anyone else's."

He nodded. "I suspected as much. So exactly why didn't you tell me you were pregnant?"

Now Alyssa's closed her eyes. "I'd already been enough of a burden on you. I didn't want to make it worse."

He narrowed his eyes. "A burden? Alyssa, when did I ever say or act like you were a burden?"

"I'm not stupid, Drew," she replied.

"At this moment, I'm not too sure."

That hurt, but she pressed on. "How could I not have been a burden? I relied on you for everything... food, a place to live, emotional support. It was more than any person should ask of another."

Something unnamable flared in his eyes. "I wanted to give you those things, and so much more. You didn't have to run away, Alyssa. I didn't want that."

What did he want then? I wish I could understand this man. "Then why didn't you call me?"

"Maybe I'm the stupid one, but I just can't understand why I should have had to! We were in bed together. What more did you need?"

The burn in her cheeks migrated to her eyes. She cried, "To know what you wanted from me! Were you just trying to make me feel better or did you have other intentions? When you didn't call, I assumed we were done!"

Drew threw his hands into the air. "How was I supposed to know what you wanted? You left!"

As if he doesn't know! She turned away from him. "It was all in the note."

His hands closed on her shoulders and he turned her to face him. "Note? What note?"

"The note I wrote you. I put it on the table, where you would be sure to see it."

Drew stared at Alyssa in consternation. *What is going on with this girl?* "Alyssa, there was no note. I looked all over for one."

"I left it. I swear I did." Her voice caught on a sob.

I know it's overwhelming to see each other again, but what on earth is she crying about? Her reaction seemed out of proportion to the situation. Drew closed his hand around her arm. *Such a skinny, fragile arm.* "I believe you. You say you left a note. I'm sure you did, but something happened before morning. It was gone. The only thing I knew was that I'd just had sex with someone for the first time, and she left before morning, never to be seen again."

"The first time?" She blinked watery, ocean-colored eyes and one tear escaped, trailing down her cheek and moistening her dimple.

"Yes, Alyssa. My first time too." He wiped the droplet with the tip of one thumb.

Her lip quivered, before she visibly steeled herself to speak. "I never guessed. Why?"

Okay, Peterson. Lay it on the line. "After we were together in high school, no other woman could live up to your memory. You were the only one I could even consider being with. I was so thankful fate brought us back together."

"And then I screwed it up. God, you're right! I am stupid." Another tear escaped, and she turned away.

Drew refused to be drawn into an emotional scene. Forcing his voice into a sort of chilly neutrality, he continued. "Well, that's in the past. The thing is, I'm not okay with my son growing up without a father. I'm not okay with being separated from him either. Somehow, we have to figure out a way for me to be in his life. A lot."

"Why?" She asked, still facing away from him.

"Because he needs me." Sarcasm trickled unbidden into his tone.

"He has me. I'm a good mother," Alyssa protested.

He turned her gently, one hand on her shoulder. "I'm not saying you aren't, but kids need two parents. I grew up with only one, and it wasn't so great for me."

"Your dad's amazing," she said, meeting his eyes at last.

"He is, but it would have been nice to have a mom too. You're lucky you got both of yours for so long."

Alyssa smiled, and her eyes grew misty at the memory of her father. "Dads are important, aren't they?"

Oh good. She's listening. "They are. I mean, how are you going to teach him how to be a man?"

Her eyelids closed briefly and then opened. "It would be hard. Fine, you're right. Ethan does need you, but how are we going to do it?"

"Well, I don't know. Ideally, a child has two parents who are a couple, but at this point, that would be impossible. I'm not sure I'm able to ... trust you enough to be with you again. I would always be looking for you to leave. And to be honest, I'm pretty angry with you. It's not that promising."

Her eyes swam again, but she answered calmly. "I'm not surprised."

"So, for the time being, we need to work out a schedule where I can see our son, spend time with him."

"Okay. Saturdays are good for me."

He nodded.

Alyssa looked sadly at Drew. "I'm sorry."

He hardened his heart against her sorrow. "You should be. It was a really terrible thing you did, withholding us from each other all these years, Alyssa, and there was no reason for it. You know I'm not a bad man, someone who would be dangerous to a child or who would be a bad father."

"I know." Tears welled in her beautiful turquoise eyes, threatening to spill over.

Time to change the subject. "Tell me one more thing. Do you have enough to eat?"

"Sometimes."

More like rarely, by the look of her. "So, who gets the food now?"

"Ethan."

Of course. "I can't have you making yourself sick. You're way too thin. You have to be well to take care of our son. Let me know what you need."

Her face turned stubborn. "I don't need you to take care of me, Drew."

Is she kidding? "Obviously you do. You've never done a good job of it without me. I'm only giving you two options. Either I'm giving you a debit card for your groceries or I'm shopping with you. What do you prefer?"

If only his voice weren't so cold. Alyssa had died a little every day without Drew. Now, suddenly, he had returned. Too bad the financial aid she got wasn't quite enough. It covered half of this furnished apartment and her car payment and insurance, books and tuition. Her mother paid the other half of the rent, bought groceries, and still, always, made payments on the debts left by her father's illness. There wasn't quite enough food to go around, especially when there weren't many singing gigs to flesh out the checks, but Alyssa made sure her mother and son were well taken care of. *I'm strong and will soon be earning a proper income. Drew found me about a year and a half too soon.* "Maybe we should shop together, the three of us," she suggested in a soft, hesitant voice. "Ethan likes going to the store, and it would be something to do together."

Drew nodded "Where is he?"

"Mom took him to the hill to go sledding. She takes him out sometimes, so I can study."

His gaze moved to the table, seeming to take in the scattered books and paper. "How's school?"

God, does he still care, beneath all the anger and hurt? How can anyone be so kind? "It was really good until this semester."

"What happened?"

"College algebra," she replied.

"Oh, that isn't so bad."

Of course not, you genius. Not everyone's perfect like Dr. Peterson. She squashed down the ugly thought, recognizing it for what it was... overwhelmed emotions. "I've forgotten everything about math. I can't make my brain work at it anymore."

"I suspect malnutrition," he replied in a clinical tone that set her teeth on edge. "It's hard to think when you're starving. Is there anything to eat in here?"

"No. Not much."

Drew opened the fridge. Inside were two apples, a gallon of milk and a package of lunchmeat. He pulled out the plastic tub of ham and found half a loaf of bread on the counter. He quickly assembled the parts into a sandwich and placed them on the table.

"Sit down."

She shook her head. "That's for Ethan."

"We're going to the store as soon as he gets back. Eat."

Alyssa sat. She lifted the sandwich with shaking hands and set it back down. "I don't think I can."

"Do it, Alyssa, or I'm taking you to the hospital. If you're too far gone to eat, you need immediate care."

Undone by his concern, she finally lost control of herself and began to sob.

"Allie?" The old sweet nickname proved to be the last straw. She collapsed into tears. Drew gently gathered her wasted body into his arms. Lifting her, he sat on the chair with her on his lap.

Carefully, he tore off a small piece of the lunchmeat and pressed it to her lips.

"Eat, sweetheart."

"Will you ever stop feeding me, Drew?" she whimpered.

"I will if you ever learn to feed yourself properly." He

tucked the morsel between her lips. She chewed and swallowed.

"Good girl. More." He kept on until the whole sandwich was gone. Then he poured her some milk and made her drink it. "Doesn't that feel better, Alyssa?" he asked, as she set down the empty glass.

"Yes." *But my stomach is cramping. Maybe I did go too far.*

"Listen, we need to work on this."

Distracted by the sensation of being uncomfortably full, she struggled to understand the question. "On what?"

"On how we're going to be parents to our son."

She nodded. Drew set her back on her feet, and not a moment too soon. Beth came through the door, covered in snow, with Ethan's little hand in hers. Drew nodded with approval to see the child so well cared for.

"Mommy!" Ethan ran awkwardly across the room in his outerwear and threw himself into Alyssa's arms.

"Look at you, baby. How cold you are! Here, let's get you out of these wet things. Did you have fun?"

"Yes. I slided down the big hill!"

"Did you? Wow. That's very brave. I would be so scared."

"I hold your hand, Mommy."

"Okay, sweetie, it's a promise." He hugged her tight and kissed her with a loud smack. She tenderly peeled him out of his snowy garments. Drew's throat tightened as he looked at his child and the woman who had given birth to him. He could barely remember being Ethan's age. His mother had also hugged and kissed and talked to him. How had she gone so badly wrong, so quickly? She left two years later.

Alyssa scooped her son up and carried him into the

bathroom, leaving Drew alone with Beth, who gave him an unfriendly look. "So, you're back again, are you?"

Drew leaned his shoulder against the wall. "Yes."

"Why?"

He raised one eyebrow at her. "I found out about Ethan."

"So?" She put her hands on her hips and regarded him with hard eyes.

"I have no intention of letting my son grow up without a father."

Beth raised her head. "He's yours then? Alyssa never would say, but I always thought so."

Drew nodded. "He's mine. I didn't know he existed until a couple of weeks ago, she didn't tell me."

Beth rolled her eyes, dismissing his reasoning as an excuse. "Still, you put her in this position."

"It's not what you think," Drew protested.

Beth scoffed. "It's not? Was it an immaculate conception? Did you or did you not sleep with my daughter and make her pregnant?"

Drew met her gaze steadily. "I did."

"Well then, what part of this isn't your fault?"

Drew straightened, drawing himself up to his full height. "I didn't leave, she did. I still don't understand why. Do you?"

Beth rolled her eyes. "So you would come after her, idiot. Why do you think?"

Take it easy, lady. "I had no idea. For all I knew, she didn't want to see me anymore."

At last, Beth's tone softened ever so slightly. "Drew, Alyssa has loved you since she was seventeen."

I can't think about that. "And she hasn't said so since she was seventeen. That's the last I know about it."

"You know how fragile she is," Beth snarled, hands on her hips.

As if that's an excuse for sneaking out of a man's bed without a word. Seriously. Unwilling to continue this line of conversation, Drew changed the subject. "Yes, more fragile than ever. Would you really have let her starve?"

Beth sighed and broke eye contact, studying the drapes that framed the living room window. "She insists. Until Ethan is fed she won't take a bite. There never has been quite enough for everyone. Alyssa has always been unwilling to let anyone else go hungry. With her son, it's worse."

Drew scowled. "I won't stand for it. She's about made herself sick with malnutrition."

"I know." She made a helpless gesture. "It's been so long since I was able to take care of Alyssa."

"She's grown. Let me take care of her now."

Beth looked at him, considering. "I'll think about it. You have a ways to go to prove you're reliable. You promised my husband on his deathbed you would never let her go. Two weeks passed, and she was back with me, pregnant, and we didn't see you again for years. Only this time was worse. This time you broke her heart."

Drew lost his cool. "*I* broke *her* heart?" he snarled. "My God this family is strange. I did everything for her, and she left me without a word, in the middle of the night, but I've somehow wronged her. I was going to marry her, damn it!"

"It's not too late," Beth pointed out.

He shook his head. "I don't know if I can do this again. Being with Alyssa hurts too much, but one thing I do know. Neither she nor Ethan is going to go hungry if I have anything to say about it."

"That's a good start," Beth admitted.

"I'm taking them to the store. You need more food in this house."

"That's even better." A strange, fierce smile spread across the older woman's face.

Alyssa emerged from the bathroom with the little boy. He ran to Beth. "Gramma, I holded it! I didn't wee my pants."

"Good boy!" She gave him a little squeeze. "You're getting so grown up!"

In spite of himself, Drew smiled. *Ethan's an endearing kid.* Then the little boy noticed Drew and shrank against Beth. Alyssa scooped him up.

"Ethan, this is my friend. His name is Drew. He wants to take us to the store."

Ethan considered the situation with the intense concentration of a child. "Can we get a cookie?" he asked at last.

"I think I can manage that." Drew told Ethan, "but you have to get something healthy too."

Ethan made a face. "Why? I don't want no broccoli."

Drew suppressed a chuckle, striving to maintain a serious tone. "Okay, no broccoli. How about carrots? I'm a doctor. It's important to me that we eat healthy food most of the time."

Ethan thought about that. "Okay."

"Good. Why don't you put on your coat and we'll go?"

"I can do it myself. Look!" Ethan squirmed, and she set him down. He scooped up his dark blue jacket and put it on... upside down. He squinted suspiciously at the zipper, which was now under his chin, as though wondering how it had gotten way up there.

"Looks like you have a naughty coat. It wants to play tricks on you," Drew told him, kneeling in front of the little boy. "It's pretty tough to handle, but I have some experience. Can I give you a hand?"

"Okay."

Drew slid Ethan's coat off and turned it over. "There, try

that. With a coat this naughty, you have to put it in its place sometimes."

Ethan tried again and this time managed to get it on correctly. Drew subtly helped him start the zipper but let him pull it up himself.

Excited with his accomplishment, he ran to Alyssa. "Look, Mommy, I did it!"

"Good job, baby." She picked him up and kissed his forehead. The sight of them made something inside Drew clench in a way he couldn't interpret.

Alyssa returned to the door and slipped on a pair of shoes. Then the two adults walked down to her car and fastened Ethan into his car seat, so they could leave for the store.

CHAPTER 13

The next day, Drew was examining the furniture in his living room when someone knocked on the door.

"It's open," he called, lifting the flap of fabric at the bottom of his couch and peering underneath.

"What are you doing?" Michael's voice startled him, and he jumped, hitting his head.

"Ow. Next time warn a person, would you?" He got to his feet.

"Sorry." Michael chuckled.

Drew turned to face his brother. He'd brought his gorgeous wife with him. *I wonder how I ever missed the signs of Sheridan's pregnancy. It's obvious now. She isn't particularly big, but the curve of her belly is unmistakable.* "Hi, you two. I didn't know you were coming."

"We were in the neighborhood. Is this a bad time?" Sheridan sounded concerned. Perhaps the sight of him scrabbling under the sofa had led her to question his sanity.

"No, it's fine. I've got nothing going on. Why were you in the neighborhood?"

"We've just come from Mass, and we wondered if we could invite you to lunch," Michael suggested.

"Sure. Just a minute though. Sheridan, are you perishing of hunger? If so, I have some granola bars in the pantry cabinet."

"Thanks." She drifted into the kitchen.

"I see you didn't offer me a granola bar," Michael quipped, one eyebrow raised.

"You're not pregnant," Drew retorted, "unless there's something about you I don't know. Of course, your wife is, so that would be a miracle of modern medicine."

"Don't even joke about it." Michael shuddered. "I think I'll leave the gestating to Sheridan. She understands the process better. So seriously, what were you doing?"

"Well, I went to talk to Alyssa yesterday."

"Good. And?" Michael prodded.

"His name is Ethan, and he is my son."

"Oh." Michael made a strange face that resembled a frown, but without the anger. "How are they doing?"

Drew rubbed his forehead with one hand. "Not well. At least she's not. Did you see how skinny she was when she sang at your wedding?"

Michael's eyebrows drew together as he contemplated the question. At last, he shrugged. "Sorry, I don't generally notice other women when Sheridan is around."

For a moment, memories seemed to seize Drew by the throat. "I can understand that. I've felt the same way before." Shaking off the nostalgia, he added, "We're working on an arrangement where I can see him frequently. Then I took them to the store and bought groceries."

Michael leaned back a bit and raised one eyebrow. "What's that got to do with why you were looking under the couch?" he asked, crossing his arms over his chest.

"I asked her why she left." Drew's voice went suddenly

dark, matching the bleak feeling in his heart. "It was like we thought. She wanted me to follow her. She said she left a note, but I never found it."

Understanding dawned on Michael's face. "So, you're looking for it almost four years later?"

"Yeah."

"Why? Does it matter now?"

"It does. I don't know why, but knowing she left a note makes a great deal of difference."

"Are you going to get back together?" Michael wanted to know.

Are we? The question caused a strange mixture of fear and excitement to twist his belly into a knot. "I don't know. I'm thinking about it." *But that's enough thinking for now.* "Okay, she said she left the note on the table. Help me figure this out, Michael."

"What month was this?" the taller man asked.

"April."

Michael scanned the apartment, noting the position of the table. "Were the windows open?"

"I can't remember. Maybe."

"Well, if they were, there might have been a breeze. If it blew a note off your table, it would have gone this way." Michael walked away from the table into the living room area. He looked at the furniture. "I've never seen an entertainment center that sits so low to the ground without actually touching it. Anything that went underneath there would be invisible."

"You're right. It's so low I can't even reach under it. My hand is too big."

"Don't look at me. Mine is bigger than yours."

They both snorted at how wrong the innocuous comment sounded. *Nothing like a brother to snicker at stupid jokes with.*

"Hey, guys, what's happening?" Sheridan asked, walking

over. She had a smudge of chocolate on her lip and Michael gave his brother a look and then kissed it away. She blushed but didn't protest.

"Sweetheart, would you be willing to do your brother-in-law a favor?" Michael asked.

"I guess, since I've stolen his granola bar," she replied with a sunny smile.

"Does your hand fit under the cabinet there?"

"Let me see." Sheridan crouched down and tested the size. "Barely."

"Can you see if you find a piece of paper underneath?"

"How big?" she asked.

Michael looked at Drew.

"I have no idea," he protested. *I only know the note exists, not what it looks like.*

"I'll try." Sheridan reached under and pulled out... a gigantic dust bunny. "Gross, Drew," she said, dropping it in a nearby trashcan. "Don't you ever clean under there?"

"How?" he asked. *There's no broom on earth that'll fit under it.*

"Never mind. Let me try again. I think you may owe me more snacks after this."

"For you, anything." Michael gave him a warning glance, and Drew hastily added, "Because I've never had a sister before."

"Right. Here's something." She withdrew her flattened palm with a paper underneath it. Abandoning it on the floor, she scurried back to the sink to wash her hands. Drew scooped up the page.

"Is it the one?" Michael asked.

"Yeah." He read it.

Dear Drew,

You may think this is ridiculous, and you would be right. I'm sorry. I can't help myself. Since the accident, you've been so good to me, better than I could ever have asked for, better than I deserve. I know you're an amazing person, and that you've always wanted to help me. If that's all this is, then thank you. Your assistance means more than you can imagine. But I have to know whether there might be more. Sometimes I think you care for me as more than just a friend in need, that you're looking for us to be a couple again. I have a hard time believing it, just like I did in high school, but you need to know I'm willing. If you want me to be yours, call me, and I'll be your girl until the day I die. If not, don't say anything, and let me keep the illusion that the best man I've ever known loves me just a little. I leave it in your hands. I love you, Drew.

Alyssa.

Drew closed his eyes. *The answer has been there all along, just out of reach, and I never know. She waited for me all these years but never reached out because it was in my hands. But I didn't know, damn it! She carried and give birth to my child and I never knew.* He swallowed the lump in his throat and looked up at his brother. "Well, there was a note all along. What the hell am I going to do now?"

Michael laid a hand on his shoulder. "Wait and see," he advised. "You're not over her."

"No," Drew admitted, "but sometimes I hate her."

Michael nodded, his face neutral. "One thing I work hard to teach my students is that the opposite of love is not hate. You have to care about someone to be able to hate them. The opposite of love is indifference. If you still care enough to be angry, then there's hope."

Hope? Don't I have to know what I want in order to hope for it? "I don't know if I can dare open up to her again."

"It's hard to be vulnerable to a woman, isn't it? They can really hurt us. The thing is, when they open up to us, they face the same risk. Try to see things from her perspective for a moment."

From her perspective? I don't even understand MY perspective! "I'm not ready."

"Okay, then just let some time go by. Get to know your little boy. Be nice to his mother, because you do owe her that much. See where things go. Nothing has to be decided right now, except where to take my wife for lunch."

Drew glanced at Sheridan, beautiful and curvy, her plump, pregnant belly pressed against the counter while she wiped her hands on a towel. "Be very glad, Michael, that your wife has never gone hungry."

Michael's eyes also caressed her. "I never thought about it before, but I am."

Alyssa stood before her bathroom mirror, getting ready for school and thinking, as usual, about Drew.

Over the last few weeks, he sure has spent time with Ethan and me. He bullied a whole lot of food into me too. Now I don't get a cramp from a sandwich anymore, thank God. He even took me to the doctor, saying he wanted to be sure I didn't have organ damage.

She regarded her reflection in the mirror. Her cheekbones no longer looked quite so prominent and her hips had begun to develop a slight softness. There would be more work needed, but she was starting to look like her old self. *For a while, eating actually felt unpleasant, I was so out of the habit, and my stomach had had to be coaxed with tiny portions. Drew oversaw this process quite a bit. Once he felt sure I was recovering, he left me a bit more to her own devices, for which I'm grateful. Being fed makes me feel like a baby.* Still, now that she was no longer quite so hungry, she found algebra easier than she had thought. *Drew would say it's because I can concentrate.*

Drew. He really is a natural at parenting. Well, he does have a good father to model his behavior after. He shows no signs of losing interest in his son, and the two quickly became pals. It pleased her to see them roughhousing together. *Ethan doesn't get enough of that and is altogether too serious for his age.*

Now she often stood at the playground, despite the biting cold, watching Drew chase Ethan, carefully shortening his steps so he remained just a little behind the squealing boy... for a while. Then he would catch him and tackle him in the snow. She smiled sadly. *If only Drew would warm up to me a little, life would be just about perfect.* He remained guarded, and there was a new hardness to him. He didn't seem like himself at all. *I hope it's temporary. One of Drew's best features was his sweetness. I hope I haven't killed that in him.*

A sudden memory surfaced as she dragged a brush through her golden-red hair. Static crackled and she sighed, reaching for a hair elastic. Yesterday afternoon, before a supper Drew had cooked for their family, the two of them had stood outside. In mid-February, the depths of winter still held Minnesota in its iron grip, and while the thermometer showed a balmy 21 degrees, high humidity sent the chill straight through her jacket and flesh to the bone. She stood in a patch of slanted, late-afternoon sunshine, hoping to catch its rays.

"NO!" Ethan protested, swatting at Drew with snowy mittens. "I do it myself."

Drew chuckled. "Okay, big guy. Let me know if you need me." He walked away from the pile of loose powder her son was attempting to make into a snowman.

"I see you've found the warmest spot in Minnesota," Drew commented, joining her.

"It's not much, but feel free to share my sunbeam," she replied. Then a little gust of wind blew up and she shivered.

"Is that the only coat you have?" he asked, indicating her short, rather thin black jacket.

She replied with a curt nod. *Bad enough I have to rely on him for food. Now he's going to buy me outerwear too.* But the stubborn look on his face said there would be no altering his decision. *And you vowed not to argue with him, remember?*

She glanced at him again. He seemed to be looking away, his expression suddenly nervous. "Alyssa," he said without turning, his eyes on the convenience store across the street, "I have something I need to ask you."

Though he sounded neutral enough, her stomach still clenched with nerves. "What's up, Drew?"

"Um, my brother invited me... invited us to his cabin, the family cabin that is, for spring break. I think we should go."

She looked at him questioningly. *You're still so angry,* she said without speaking, letting her confusion show in her eyes. *I wish I understood what you wanted from me.*

He returned a confused, unguarded look.

Oh, love, no wonder. You don't know either.

But then he spoke. "I'm not sure what the ultimate end of this is going to be, but I think we need to get away from everyday life and all its struggles and just... talk. Focus on being

Ethan's parents, working out a plan we both understand and agree to, okay?

Oh God, a parenting plan? Like a divorced couple? The pain stung her deep and a tear attempted to freeze in the corner of her eye, but all she said was, "I agree. Getting away would be a good idea."

And it still seemed like a good idea today.

CHAPTER 14

*W*ith so much going on, the weeks passed quickly until the time arrived for the family vacation at the cabin. Wednesday morning, Drew picked up Alyssa and Ethan and loaded them into his car. Beth walked them out and gave him a long look. "What are you going to do?" she asked him.

"Try to figure things out," he replied, trying not to take offense at her unfriendly stare. "This is a messy situation."

"Yes." She narrowed her eyes and glared. "Don't get her pregnant again."

Drew's cheeks burned. *Are you going to risk that? Part of you wants to.* But what he said was, "No. That's not really much of a concern."

"I disagree. I see how you look at her."

He closed Alyssa's door, which provided him an excuse to break eye contact without looking guilty. "I can look without touching. I've done it for years."

Beth sagged, releasing a lung full of air in a noisy whoosh. The cold turned her breath misty and visible, and Drew suppressed a smirk and a thought of dragons. Then she shocked him completely with a rapid about-face. "Honestly, Drew, I'm less concerned with you touching her, than with what you do about it."

The burning in his cheeks increased. *Surely that's the wind, right?* "I understand. Give me some more time, Beth. I know what you want. I'm working on it, but..." he hesitated. "She's not the only one who was hurt."

Beth gave no quarter. "I know. But be a man and get past it, would you?"

"I'm trying," Drew replied, more intensely than he intended.

Beth turned and walked back into the apartment building without another word.

Drew climbed into the car and they headed out. *It's bizarre to be going north during spring break. Most everyone else heads south, except the hard-core skiers, and this cabin is on a lake, not in the mountains. In the summer it will be great, but March is pretty unpredictable in this state. It won't be warm, and blizzards are possible. Of course, little kids love playing in the snow. I know Ethan does.* They had spent enough time at it in the last two months, so the little boy should have fun. As for himself, he was long overdue for some serious conversations with the mother of his child, and he wasn't looking forward to any of them.

Alyssa seemed to sense his grim mood and left him to start the conversations.

"Did you have any breakfast?" he began abruptly.

"Yes," she replied softly, seeming confused by his belligerent tone.

"What?" he pushed. *Better not have skimped on it. She's still too skinny...*

Alyssa interrupted his silent and furious tirade with a perfectly reasonable answer. "Oatmeal and toast."

"With raisins," Ethan piped up from the back.

"All right then," he said, but his tense shoulders didn't relax.

"Am I healthy, Drew?" the boy asked.

"Yes, Ethan," he replied in a gentle voice that didn't match his mood. "You're growing up so strong. Keep on eating those good foods, like we talked about, and you'll be tall like me someday."

"Goody." Ethan turned his attention to his toy cars.

Drew glanced at the woman beside him and asked a question he'd been wanting to address for quite some time. "Alyssa, isn't it time to tell him the truth?"

She thought about it. "I don't know. Won't it confuse him?"

Confuse whom? How does concealing the truth make things better? Her answer, which made no sense, irritated him further. "How? Hasn't he ever asked about his father?"

"Sometimes," she admitted.

"Then tell him," he insisted.

She took another moment, looking out the window at the snow-covered fields. "Not yet."

Irritation flared into outright anger. "Damn it, Alyssa," he hissed under his breath, "you're still coming between us."

"I'm just not sure," she answered, voice wavering.

"Sure of what?" he challenged her.

"How long you're going to be around."

That made Drew mad. "Okay, let's not forget who did the leaving here," he said in a cold, soft voice, not wanting to alert Ethan that he was angry. "I've always been there for you. The time we spent apart was your choice, not mine. Don't blame me for that. I'm committed to this boy. He's my son. Nothing will ever change that."

"Soon, Drew, okay?" she wheedled.

Drew didn't answer. He was seething. They drove the rest of the way in tense and uncomfortable silence.

A couple of hours later, they arrived at the cabin. All the passengers in the cherry-red Trans Am stared up at it in astonishment. When they had heard about a cabin in the woods, they'd pictured something small, because all lakefront property was so expensive. This towering, two-story log structure could house an entire extended family.

Despite the remnants of his anger, Drew politely opened the door for Alyssa. A blast of cold hit her, but this time she only shivered a little. *How can I, swathed in the long black puffer coat he bought me?* Once she moved clear of the car, Drew released the seat and reached into the back, holding out his arms to Ethan.

His son unfastened his own seat belt, his latest trick, and scrambled into his father's arms. Unlike his wary relationship with Alyssa, being with Ethan was pure, uncomplicated joy. He snuggled the little boy against his chest, shut the passenger door, and escorted Alyssa up to the front of the cabin.

She knocked, and the door was flung open by a dark-haired boy of about six with a warm grin that revealed several missing teeth. "Hi. Are you guys the Petersons?"

"Yes," Drew said.

"Come on in. Mom's making cocoa."

"Sounds good."

They stepped into the house, quickly closing the door to block the icy March wind. They entered a huge, two-story living room featuring a rough-hewn stone fireplace along the exterior wall, in which a welcoming fire crackled cheerfully.

Behind a comfortable sitting area of red plaid sofa and loveseat, flanked by red armchairs, there was a dining table on one side and a kitchen on the other, along one wall. Opposite the kitchen, a staircase led to a loft. Below the loft was a bedroom and bathroom, and above, a row of five doors, presumably other bedrooms, and a second bathroom.

In the kitchen, a pretty, dark-haired woman about Alyssa's age stirred a pot on the stove. A delicious chocolate aroma wafted through the room. A handsome man in his mid-thirties with brown hair and a friendly face stood close to the woman. As Drew watched, he slid his arm around the woman's waist and pressed his lips to the side of her neck, making her smile.

"Ewwww," A little blond girl seated at the table nearby complained. "Daddy, stop it!" Her legs kicked under the table, sometimes connecting with the wood in a jarring thump.

"Never," he laughed. "You should be glad how much I love your mommy."

"I am, but I don't want to *see* it!" she complained.

Gentle laughter rippled through the room. Drew scanned the surroundings and found Michael and Sheridan seated on the sofa, his arm around her. Michael had a little boy on his lap, a half-read storybook in his hand, and Sheridan held a three-month-old baby against her shoulder.

"Drew, Alyssa," Michael said, "I'm glad you guys made it. Erin, is there enough cocoa for three more?"

"Yeah," the brunette at the stove replied, "I always make too much. Do you guys want some?"

"Oh, that's okay," Alyssa said softly.

"Yes. We would all like a cup." He gave her a hard look. Ethan, sensing the tension, held his arms out to his mother. She scooped him up and unzipped his coat, tucking his hat and mittens into the sleeves and hanging it on a hook behind the door. Then she pulled off his boots and set him down, so she could remove her own outerwear.

They entered the room with hesitant steps, hand in hand.

Erin stepped away from the stove and greeted the new arrivals. "I'm glad you two could make it. I'm Erin Murphy. This is my husband Sean, and all these kiddos you see are ours. The welcoming committee was Jordan, and this is Kayleigh. Over there is William and the baby is Josh." She extended her hand and Alyssa took it.

"Sorry I'm so cold," she said. "I'm Alyssa Miller and this is my son Ethan. And this is Drew."

"I'm Michael's brother, as you may be aware," Drew added, still standing by the door.

"Pleased to meet you guys. Don't worry about the hand. I'm the same way. One foot outside the door and I'm a block of ice for hours." She addressed the child. "Ethan, would you like to sit down at the table? The cocoa is almost ready."

"Do you have any marshmallows?" He looked at her, his eyes hopeful.

"Ethan, we have four children," Sean volunteered. "Of course, we have marshmallows."

"Yay!" Ethan cheered. He let go of his mother and scrambled up to the table.

"And for the grownups, we also have Bailey's. Any takers?"

"I'm out," Sheridan sighed, patting her belly. *Uh oh. Professor Mrs. Burke is quite pregnant. I wondered at the wedding, but now it's obvious. Sheridan must only have a few months to go.* Alyssa couldn't help grinning.

"No worries, Danny. I am too. We'll drink virgin cocoa

together." They looked at each other and laughed. Clearly, they had been friends a long time.

Michael considered. "Just a small splash, okay?"

"Okay," Sean agreed. "No problem. Alyssa?"

"That would be nice, but only a little."

"Sure thing."

"What about you, Drew?" Michael asked his brother.

"Yes, I'll have some. It's so cold, any warming influences would be appreciated."

Soon the kids all sat at the table with cocoa and cookies, and the adults had ensconced themselves near the fire, cradling steaming mugs and inhaling the perfume of chocolate and vanilla. Sheridan set the baby in a portable playpen. Alyssa took a seat next to Drew. *He's still angry. It radiates off him, and it makes me nervous.* She subtly shifted away.

Sheridan took a sip. "Yum, Erin. This tastes like mom's recipe."

Erin beamed at the compliment. "It is." Then she turned to her guest. "So, Alyssa, what do you do?"

"She's a student," Sheridan replied. "I've had her in class."

"So have I," Michael added, "but I forget what your major is."

"Music." Alyssa volunteered shyly.

"Really?" Erin's eyes lit up, "I'm a musician too. What's your instrument?"

"Voice," Alyssa replied, blushing at the attention. "I'm going into elementary education."

"How fun!" Erin exclaimed. "I play the oboe. I have it with me. Maybe we can do a little concert while you're here."

"Maybe," Alyssa said.

"Michael tells us you're a doctor, Drew," Sean said, continuing the introductions.

"Yes," Drew replied. He stretched out his arm along the

back of the sofa but didn't touch Alyssa. "I specialize in orthopedic surgery."

"Wow. That's impressive," Sean said. "I'm glad to know you. With three sons, I doubt we'll get through their childhood without needing your services."

"Well if they do sports, the odds are against you. I think I operate on a teenage athlete every week."

Oh, come on, Drew, Alyssa thought. *No mother wants to hear that.* She glanced at Erin, and sure enough, the young woman's pale face had turned ashen with alarm. Sean quickly changed the subject.

Under the influence of cocoa and liquor, Alyssa started to relax and warm. Sean had, as requested, only put in a small amount, but alcohol was such a luxury, Alyssa almost never had money for it, which left her quite susceptible. She could still feel Drew's displeasure, but underneath it, she could detect a hint of something... else, no less intense, but perhaps a little less angry. Hmmm. *Maybe this trip will be good for us.* Deliberately she let herself drift slightly in his direction, until her left leg – the one he had fixed years earlier – touched his thigh.

He reacted to the touch, looking at her quickly, and then away, but he didn't move. He let her stay pressed against him.

"Daddy," Kayleigh said, sliding into Sean's lap and nearly upsetting his cup, "can we play outside now? You promised."

"Wait until I finish my drink please, princess."

"Okay." She kissed his cheek and scrambled down.

Alyssa remembered her father and her heart clenched. She missed him every day. *I have to work harder on fixing things up with Drew. Ethan isn't going to be deprived of a daddy any longer. Visiting on Saturdays isn't good enough. We need to be a family.*

"Kids are so funny. No sooner do you get them warmed up than they're off getting cold again." Erin sighed.

"Don't worry, baby," Sean said, "I'll take them. I don't feel the cold like you do. Besides, doesn't Josh need a nap soon?"

"Yes," Erin replied, her face brightening.

"I'll go with you, Sean," Michael volunteered.

"Thanks. Jordan has a collection of snowballs with your name on it."

"I saw." He grinned.

"Mommy, can I play outside?" Ethan asked.

Alyssa hesitated. While Sean was clearly a good father, she didn't know him. She didn't want her son to be left out but sending him with a stranger didn't sit right with her. She knew Michael better, but in her mind, he was still Dr. Burke, English professor. She wasn't sure how to see him as someone who would want to play in the snow with her baby.

"I'll go too," Drew said, seeming to sense her internal struggle. "I can bring in the luggage and then keep an eye on Ethan. You stay inside and keep warm."

"Okay then," Alyssa agreed.

All the children cheered. Drew gulped the last of his cocoa and brought in the suitcases, so he could dig out Ethan's snow pants. He took the little boy to the bathroom and then helped him suit up. The other children hurried into their coats and boots as well, swirling and tilting around the room like a collection of tiny tornadoes. After a few moments of furious activity, they all fled, leaving the three women and the baby in the living room.

Josh began to fuss, and Erin scooped him out of the playpen. "I hope this doesn't offend anyone," she said calmly, "but we're all mothers here." She lifted her sweater, opened a flap in her bra and positioned the baby with the skill of an experienced mother. Josh snuggled against her breast, nursing contentedly.

"You know I don't care," Sheridan told her sister-in-law. I've been watching you do this for years, and now I need the demonstration."

"No worries," Alyssa said. "I nursed Ethan for eighteen months, and I was still sad when he was weaned."

"So, have another," Erin replied offhandedly, as though it were the easiest thing in the world. *Maybe for her, it is.*

"I wish I could," she said softly. "It's complicated."

"Oh, come now, Alyssa," Erin scoffed, stroking her baby's fuzzy hair. "Are you going to pretend Ethan isn't Drew's? He looks just like him."

Alyssa nodded. "He is, but we haven't been together in a while."

"You broke up when you had a baby together?" Sheridan demanded, aghast.

"Well, actually, he didn't know I was pregnant. I didn't tell him."

"Why not?" Erin wanted to know.

"It's a long story, and I'm not sure you would find it very interesting."

Erin grinned. "Tell us! There's nothing Sheridan and I like better than helping people fix their relationship problems."

"Me especially," Sheridan added. "After all, I set up Erin and Sean when I was seventeen. And, Alyssa," she continued, "I promise no matter what, no one here is going to judge you. We've both experienced crisis pregnancies. We don't throw stones at anyone."

"Oh, come on, Mrs. Burke," Alyssa laughed. "I don't think being a couple of months pregnant at your wedding is that big of a crisis. It happens all the time."

"Call me Sheridan, please, Alyssa," she replied. "I'm not your teacher anymore, and I would very much like to be your friend. Yes, you're right. This pregnancy isn't a crisis." She laid her hand on her belly. "That's not what I meant. Okay, I don't normally talk about this, but Drew is family, and if we play our cards right, you're going to be as well. I got pregnant when I was in high school."

"So did I," Erin added.

Alyssa gaped at them both.

"Okay, I think we've broken the ice," Sheridan told her sister-in-law, "but she's pretty shy. We'd better tell her the rest."

"Yup. I'll go first. Sean and I started going out when I was a senior." She smirked. "I was a very bad girl and went to bed with him on our first date; the one Danny set us up on."

Sheridan raised her eyebrows and pursed her lips. "It wasn't what I intended them to do. Especially when she got pregnant right away."

"Well, you can see how fertile I am." Josh let go of Erin's nipple and she switched him to the other side, quickly fastening the open flap. The baby looked sleepy now, dazed from nursing.

"Yes, that's true," Alyssa agreed.

"I had a miscarriage." A shadow passed across Erin's pretty face.

Alyssa felt a twinge of sympathy. "I'm sorry."

"Yeah, I was too."

Sheridan interjected. "It was for the best, Erin. You were able to go to college, get your degree. Those are all good things."

"I know, and I'm so busy with my kids now, it doesn't really bother me anymore. Sean and I kind of broke up for a while after that, but I never got over him."

"He never got over you, either," Sheridan reminded her.

"Clearly," Alyssa added. *It's encouraging to see such affection between a couple who had been married so many years.*

Erin smiled. "So, I'm not going to judge you for getting pregnant, or for breaking up with your baby's father. I did both. It worked out anyway."

Alyssa nodded. *I hope someday Drew and I can be happy together, the way Erin and Sean are.* Then she noticed Sheridan sitting with her eyes closed, breathing slowly. "What's wrong?" she asked.

"I hate telling this story," Sheridan replied.

She suddenly seemed less like a teacher and more like any other woman Alyssa might be friends with. "You don't have to," she assured her.

"Thank you, but I need you to understand, to trust me. I wanted to tell you before, when you were hurting so badly. I wanted to be your friend, but our relationship wasn't right for it. I was your teacher. I'm glad we have this chance to spend time together now, but if we're going to be friends, you have to know this about me. It's kind of fundamental to who I am." She opened her eyes and looked at Erin, a silent plea for help.

Erin took up the story, speaking softly, her eyes glued to her son. "Sheridan was a good girl in school. She never fooled around with any boys. She kept her boyfriend on a tight leash. I always thought she would be a virgin on her wedding night. It was what she wanted, and I wanted that for her."

"Sometimes life takes you places you don't want to go." Sheridan's voice caught a little.

"I know about that," Alyssa said. They looked at her. "My dad died of cancer a few years ago," she added by way of explanation. "He'd been sick off and on since I was in high school."

Both women's expressions turned sympathetic.

"Let me do it, Danny, if you really think she needs to know," Erin suggested.

Sheridan nodded.

The dark-haired mother continued. "Danny's boyfriend forced her. He beat her up too. It was really bad. That's how she got pregnant."

Alyssa gasped. "That's terrible!"

Sheridan nodded. "It was. The worst part though was... giving my daughter up for adoption."

Alyssa visualized that. *It's hard being a single mother, but at least I have my son with me every day.* She tried to imagine walking away and couldn't do it. *What strength Sheridan has.* Alyssa jumped up out of her seat in a second and wrapped her arms around her former teacher, giving her a tight hug.

Sheridan hugged back. "It's okay." She took a breath that didn't sound particularly steady. "I stay in touch with her parents. And I'm overjoyed to be pregnant again. It's completely different this time."

"Of course. You're married. I've rarely seen anyone so passionately in love as Dr. Burke is with you."

Sheridan smiled and lit up the whole room. "That's the best part. Everything else that happened was worthwhile, because it all led me to Michael." She ran her hands over her belly, and her smile turned wistful. She took Alyssa's hand and pressed it to her bump. Inside Alyssa could feel the baby pressing and rolling against her. Despite the fear and loneliness, carrying Ethan had been wonderful. She smiled. Pregnancy created a bond among women. *I wish I could have another baby, just as Erin suggested.*

"Excuse me for a moment," Erin said softly. "Josh is asleep." She lifted her tiny son to her shoulder and carried him upstairs, returning a few moments later, yawning and straightening out her clothing. "Good Lord, I'm exhausted," she said as she settled in on the sofa. "I sure hope I don't get pregnant again anytime soon. I've had four babies in less than seven years. It's too much. After Josh is weaned, I'm going to be naughty and get back on the pill."

"What are you doing in the meanwhile? As I recall, the reason Kayleigh and William are so close in age is that breastfeeding wasn't really very good birth control after all," Sheridan commented.

"Well, in an unprecedented move we're trying condoms. I don't like them." Erin made a face.

"Good luck with that," Sheridan said doubtfully. "They certainly didn't work well for me. You might need to try restraint. Alyssa, if you hear noises in the night, don't be alarmed. It's not wild animals in the house. It's just Sean and Erin. They're pretty loud."

Alyssa gaped. *Did Sheridan really say that?* In class, she had always been a perfect lady. Clearly, with family, she was different, more mischievous.

Erin's pale face turned pink. "I told Sean he needed to soundproof the walls. But don't get all superior with me, *Mrs. Burke*. What did I hear last night?"

"Oh, don't say it!" Sheridan begged.

Erin ignored her. "'Oh, Michael,'" she sighed in perfect imitation of her friend, her voice breathy as though with pleasure. "Oh, baby, yes. Do that. Ahhhh."

Sheridan threw a pillow at Erin, who caught it. They both laughed. Alyssa couldn't help grinning. *How silly they are. It must be nice to be able to relax so completely.* The only time she could remember being relaxed in the last decade was right after she and Drew had made love. Everything else had been stress and struggle and hard work. *I'm tired; tired of fighting against the forces that threaten to overwhelm me every day.* She had to keep on, for Ethan's sake, but sometimes she doubted her own strength.

"Okay, Alyssa," Erin said, setting the pillow back where it belonged, "tell us what's going on with you and Drew. Maybe we can help."

Alyssa considered for a moment. *Maybe it will do me some good to spill the whole thing. It will be a relief to get it off my chest anyway.* "Well, I've known Drew forever. We were in the same kindergarten class. We didn't really like each other until our senior year of high school though."

"Wait a second, you two are the same age?" Sheridan gave Alyssa a startled look.

"Yeah. I think he's a couple of months older than me, but not much."

"How old are you then?" Erin wanted to know.

"We're both twenty-nine," Alyssa replied.

"Hmm," Erin said, "you look younger. I'll be turning twenty-nine in September. Sheridan's the baby though. She won't be twenty-eight until this summer."

"You know," Alyssa commented, "it messes with my head a bit that my teacher is younger than me."

"It happens in college all the time," Sheridan assured her. "You're not my oldest student by a long shot."

Alyssa nodded. *It's easier to stop thinking of Sheridan as a professor, knowing she's so young.* She continued her story. "Okay, well anyway when we were seniors, we... got to know each other, and became a couple. He was the sweetest boy. My family didn't always... have enough food, and he made sure I didn't go hungry. He asked me to prom and paid for my dress. I was absolutely crazy about him back then."

"Be honest. Has that really changed?" Erin pressed gently.

Alyssa closed her eyes. "No."

"I didn't think so. I see how you look at him," the young mother said with a smile.

"We were really in love," Alyssa admitted, "as much as two teenagers can be, but we behaved ourselves. Neither of us wanted to go there at such a young age."

"Don't underestimate young love." Erin said, "I fell in love with Sean at eighteen and never looked at anyone else again."

"I know," Alyssa agreed. "That's how it was for me too.

Once Drew kissed me, other boys just lost their appeal. But he's rich and I'm poor, and I didn't want to hold him back. I couldn't go to college because my dad was sick, and I had to help provide for the family, but I knew Drew deserved a girlfriend who was educated, like him. Otherwise, what would we have to talk about or anything? It wasn't fair to keep him, so I slowly let him go. It just about killed me to do it, but I wanted him to have the best possible life."

She regarded her companions. Sheridan looked puzzled. Erin nodded as though this made perfect sense to her.

"Then, about four years ago, I was in a car accident. I was hit by a drunk when I was coming home from work, and in the accident, I broke my thighbone. Drew was in residency by then, and he operated on my leg, and we sort of... reconnected. Then my dad..." She swallowed hard. "He passed away. Drew supported me through it. He even let me stay with him. That's when things got... intimate. We only spent one night together. Then I did something really stupid. I left."

"You did what?" Sheridan gasped, appalled.

Alyssa looked down at her hands, folded in her lap. "I needed to know if he really loved me, or if he just was trying to make me feel better. I left him a note, but he says he never found it."

"Oh Alyssa," Sheridan said sadly, "if there is a worse thing you could have done, I can't imagine it."

"Danny, don't exaggerate," Erin protested. "I understand where she's coming from. Remember, I did more or less the same thing with Sean."

Sheridan rolled her eyes. "Sheridan, remember, Erin? And even he didn't understand it! With Drew, it's worse. You can't imagine how bad this is." She touched her forehead with her fingertips and shook so her mane of curly blond hair swung around her face.

"Why?" Erin demanded.

That's what I want to know too.

"Because Drew is a Burke, like Michael. You have no idea the damage Amanda Burke did to her children," Sheridan stated, as though this should mean something to them.

"Okay, Sheridan," Alyssa said. "Explain. Drew always seemed very strong to me. Are you telling me he's not?"

"No!" Sheridan exclaimed. "He's the luckiest of the lot, because all Amanda did was leave him when he was five and never come back. Didn't you know his parents were divorced?"

Sheridan's intense delivery created a vortex of nerves in Alyssa's belly. "Yes, but I never noticed that it affected him. Did it?"

"Think, Alyssa," she insisted. "His mother left. He was just a tiny little boy, and she left him. He never saw her again until she died a couple of months ago. What did you do?"

A cold sensation washed over Alyssa. "I left." Her lips felt numb.

"And what do you think that did? It confirmed the idea his mother created in him when he was five... that he wasn't good enough to keep a woman in his life."

The words hit like a blow. "Oh my God. No wonder he didn't call me."

"That's right. You were looking to him to heal you of your fears of inadequacy, and all you did was exacerbate his. You must have damn near destroyed him."

Alyssa wanted to cry. "I didn't mean to do that." Her voice quavered. Erin sat down beside her and hugged her, holding her in warm, motherly arms.

"I know you didn't. Sheridan, tell her the rest."

Sheridan took a deep breath. "Even with all that, Drew was the lucky one. James is great, which spared him so much suffering. Michael went with his mother. She used drugs, and he had to live with her addiction until he became a ward of the state at fourteen. He's lucky to be alive. And there was another brother, Kevin, who was born disabled due to his mother's drug use during pregnancy and died in his late twenties. The Burke legacy is one of terrible suffering. It's remarkable Michael and Drew both came out of it as well as they did, but don't assume they're strong. They're both terribly wounded."

"I didn't know. Oh, how could I have been so selfish?" A tear escaped, trailing a burning line down Alyssa's cheek.

Sheridan plunked down on the other side of her and patted her hand. "I did the same thing. Michael seems so strong, and I used him to try to heal my fear of intimacy. I was so happy when I got pregnant, but it wasn't easy on him. Because he's had such poor parenting over the years, the thought of becoming a father really freaked him out. It was hard to come back from it. I thought for a while he would leave me. But he's an honorable man, and he stayed. He learned that from James."

Sounds like we all have our demons, even the beautiful Sheridan. She hastened to reassure her friend. "Maybe James did teach him about responsibility, but he stayed because he loves you, Sheridan."

A hint of a blush stained Sheridan's cheeks, and her lips curved upwards. "Thank you."

Alyssa forced herself to speak. "Okay. So, I've hurt the man I love in the worst possible way. How do I fix this? I want him back the way he was, happy, relaxed..."

"And madly in love with you?" Erin suggested with a broad smile.

Alyssa grinned, though less convincingly. "Yes, that too, Erin."

"Well," the brunette said thoughtfully, "you can expect him to be wary for a while. There's not much help for it. But I think you might be able to work through it as a couple, rather than alone."

Oh please, Erin, give me a way! "How?"

"You'll have to break the ice somehow. After that, talk honestly with him about how you feel and what you want. Don't hint, be shy or anything. Just tell him right out," Erin said.

"That's right," Sheridan confirmed. "Michael and I didn't really make any headway with our issues until we told each other what we wanted, honestly."

"Don't assume anything," Erin continued. "Especially not what he's feeling. You're responsible for Alyssa. Not Drew."

She bit her nail. "That's scary. What if he rejects me?"

"Then he does," Sheridan said bluntly. "You can't prevent it, but you can cause it by being too reticent. Be brave, Alyssa. Isn't having a family worth fighting for? Isn't Drew worth fighting for?"

She closed her eyes and a glowing green gaze floated behind her closed lids. "Yes. But how do I break the ice?"

"You might try seduction," Erin suggested, making Alyssa choke.

"I'm... I... I'm not prepared for intimacy. I really can't afford to get pregnant again, not with things so unsettled between us."

"I can help with that." Erin scurried up the stairs and returned with three condoms, which she pressed into Alyssa's hands.

"Erin, sex doesn't cure everything," Sheridan reminded her sister.

"No, but it does put men much more at ease, and it kind of forces emotional intimacy as well, especially between people who really want it but are holding back. Besides, it's very nice and relaxing. Alyssa looks so stressed, I'm sure she could use it."

Alyssa colored. "I'm not very good at this. I've only done it twice." She looked at the condoms and a strange sensation of nerves and excitement twisted her insides into discomfort.

"Don't worry," Erin reassured her, patting her hand. "You'll be fine."

The conversation ended abruptly as the icy men and children pounded into the house and began shedding garments and scattering snow all over the hardwood floors Sean and his father had lovingly refinished a few months before.

CHAPTER 15

That evening, the oldest children played Old Maid at the table with Erin, while Sean and William wrestled on the floor. Alyssa, sitting next to Drew on the couch, watched their antics. Ethan crept towards the father and son with a rapt expression. It made Alyssa feel a little guilty that he'd missed out on having a dad all these years. Tentatively, he approached the pair and Sean quickly swept him into the fun, growling like a bear and tickling him, making him shriek with laughter. William, jealous at seeing his father playing with another boy, stuck his lip out.

"He's my daddy, not yours," William told Ethan bluntly.

Ethan looked at Sean wistfully. "You're not?"

"No," Sean agreed, "but I guess I'm your uncle."

"Uncle," Ethan said thoughtfully. "I want a daddy." He walked over to Michael, who was sitting on the couch with Sheridan and baby Josh.

"Are you my uncle?" he asked.

"Yes, I'm your uncle," Michael replied.

"Do you have a boy?"

"Yes, I do have a boy," Michael told him gently. He touched Sheridan's belly, "My boy is in here. He's not born yet."

Ethan trailed over to Alyssa and climbed onto her lap.

"Mommy," he said, looking into her face with a wistful expression, "they all have a boy. Do I have a daddy?"

Alyssa's eyes filled with tears. "Yes, baby, you do have a daddy."

"Where is he?" Dylan's lip trembled.

It's time, Alyssa. The only one who wants to conceal this is you, and you're hurting Drew and Dylan for no reason. Let it go. "He's right here," she told her son softly. "Drew is your daddy."

He turned towards Drew. "Are you?"

"Yes, Ethan," Drew said in a scratchy-sounding voice. "I'm your daddy."

Ethan nodded and climbed across his mother into Drew's lap. "Good," he said, leaning his head on Drew's chest.

Drew hugged his son. *Glad no one's talking to me, because I'm pretty sure my voice won't work.*

After a long day of playing, Ethan slowly drifted to sleep.

Finally, Drew spoke. "Thank you, Alyssa."

"You're welcome." She laid her hand gently on his, where it crossed over Ethan's little body, and he laced his fingers through hers. *It's a start.* They sat like that a long time in silence, enjoying being close. Then, Drew lifted the little boy into his arms and carried him upstairs, tucking him into a lower bunk in the room he was sharing with William and Jordan.

Sheridan yawned hugely and kissed her husband, before heading off to brush her teeth. Michael followed her rather more quickly than was subtle, making the other adults smile knowingly. But everyone was tired, and so they all quickly scattered to their rooms, except the Murphys who had to settle their protesting children first.

CHAPTER 16

*A*lyssa lay in bed trying to read a novel, but the events of the day overwhelmed her, and she couldn't concentrate.

In the room to the right of hers, farthest from the children, the bed springs squeaked as Michael and Sheridan settled in for the night. The bed noisily protested Michael's substantial weight. *The interior walls of this cabin are rather thin,* Alyssa decided. The reason the families had been able to afford such a place, Sean had explained over dinner, was because he and his father were both builders. It had been a wreck when they bought it, but the two were fixing it up together as a hobby.

The bed next door squeaked again. *I wonder what they're doing over there.* Her answer came quickly as soft noises began to filter through. First a quiet hum of conversation, the words low and unintelligible, but filled with passion, then a moan, feminine and breathy. Then another. The bed began to squeak rhythmically. *Damn. They're making love.* Alyssa could scarcely imagine anything more awkward than listening to her English professors having sex. She tried to ignore them but found it impossible. *It's also surprisingly hot. They sound like they're having a wonderful time.* Alyssa could remember her brief introduction to intimacy. *It was so perfect. I didn't want to stop. If I hadn't been so stupid, Drew and I could have been practicing all these years, instead of me lying alone in an empty bed, just wishing.*

Through the wall, Alyssa could hear a series of soft gasps as Sheridan reached orgasm, and a low groan as Michael followed her. *Thank goodness it's over.* Or so she thought. On the other side, closer to the children, there was a loud thump, as though a great weight had hit the bed with force. Then, similar sounds, different voices. *Wow, Erin really is loud in bed.*

Alyssa's body burned like fire. *My love, my lover, lies just a short distance away. Everyone else is making love tonight. Why not me?* She gathered up the condoms Erin had given her and went downstairs.

Drew opened the door to an unexpected knock and blinked to find Alyssa there in her pajamas. "What's up, Allie?" he asked.

"Can I come in?"

What's that look on her face? "Okay."

She sat on the edge of the bed.

"Did you need anything?"

She turned burning turquoise eyes on him and answered, "Yes. I've been listening to your brother and his wife get it on for the last half hour. Now Erin and Sean are at it. It's killing me. Can't we please...?"

"Can't we what Alyssa?" *She can't mean what I think she means. There's no way.*

"Make love? Look, I'm prepared." She handed him the condoms.

SIMONE BEAUDELAIRE

Oh Lord, she does mean it. Should I accept? He looked at the handful of prophylactics, and then he set them on the nightstand. "I'm sorry. I can't do it."

She gaped at him. "Why not? We've made love before."

"It was different then," he said, trying to verbalize what he only half understood.

"In what way?" she demanded.

Okay, think, Drew. How do you explain this? "In every way." He sat beside her and took her hand, wanting to be sure she got his point. "Alyssa, why do you think I made love to you?"

"Because I was hurting, and I needed it."

Is that really what she thought? Doesn't she know the difference between love and pity? "No, that's wrong. If you were hurting, I would have held you, but I would never have slept with you. I did what I did because I believed we were in love, that we were starting a relationship that would be for life. I had it all planned out. In the morning, I was going to take you over to my dad's house and reintroduce you to each other. We would pick out a ring and plan a pretty summer wedding. That's why we had sex, Alyssa. I always told you I wouldn't sleep with anyone unless I loved her. Did you really think that had changed?"

Alyssa closed her eyes. "And then I left. God, what a stupid mistake. I'm so terribly sorry, Drew. I didn't mean to hurt you. I was selfish."

He gave her a little one-armed hug. "Yes, and foolish too. If you needed reassuring, couldn't you have done it in a less dramatic way? If you had just woken me up and said you needed to hear where this was headed, I wouldn't have minded a bit."

"I know. I was afraid. I just always felt you were so high above me." Alyssa looked down at the red comforter on the soft double bed, stroking the fuzzy fabric.

Drew grasped her chin and lifted her face. "That's a lie you tell yourself, Alyssa. Stop. I told you in high school and I'll tell you now. Your value has nothing to do with how much money you have. Your income never mattered to me."

The tender words shattered the wall around Alyssa's heart and her deepest longing spilled free. "Drew, can't we please... try again? I swear I won't do anything so stupid. I'll be brave and ask for what I want right out."

He withdrew slightly, his gaze shuttering. "I still don't know. Sometimes I want to, but it's hard."

"It would be best for Ethan if we could be together," she reminded him.

"I know. I'm keeping that in mind."

"So, couldn't we please just...?"

Drew stood and extended his hand. She took it and he helped her to her feet, walking her slowly towards the door. "No, I can't do it. I won't. If we really can be together, committed, then yes, we'll make love again, but I'm not ready, Alyssa. I'm sorry. Please go back to bed, they should be done by now."

Alyssa slowly trailed out, her expression both disappointed and a little embarrassed. Drew returned to his bed, thinking back playing with the children outside.

Jordan had taken Ethan under his wing, tugging the little boy behind an intricate snow fort that must have taken days to construct. The boy had cleverly built it with a shaggy pine at the back, so no one could attack him from the rear. Behind it, truly daunting pile of snowballs waited for his younger brother and sister, who huddled behind a much more rudimentary fort, furiously balling up the snow to create ammunition for Jordan and their new acquaintance. As the men watched, all four children wound up and let fly, wild throws zooming off in random directions.

"You know something, Drew?" Michael said.

"What?"

"This way you're going about wooing Alyssa, by glowering at her, I don't think it's going to be very effective." He raised an eyebrow.

"I know," Drew replied. "She made me mad."

"I can understand that," Michael agreed. "She's made a lot of silly decisions, but they're in the past. You should let it go."

"Maybe so," Drew conceded, "but damned if I know how."

"You might consider just forgiving her," Michael suggested.

"How?"

"It's a choice, Drew, not a feeling. You just decide not to hold on to the anger anymore, and every time you feel it creeping back up, you remind yourself to let go. Prayer helps."

Good, wise advice. Exactly what a big brother should provide. "How do you know so much about it?"

"I forgave Mom. Did you?"

"No."

"Maybe that's why you can't forgive Alyssa," Michael said. He leaned his shoulder against a tree. In the background, Jordan took a face full of snow and went down, laughing and spluttering. Ethan tried to clean him up with ice-encrusted mittens. "You're punishing Alyssa for Mom leaving. She couldn't help it, you know."

"Alyssa left me too," Drew reminded him.

"Yes, but you chose an insecure girl," Michael pointed out. "You had to expect to deal with her issues."

"I didn't think they would play out quite like this."

"That's the risk. Being with Sheridan scared the hell out of me at first. I had to learn to trust her. The good part is, she's never betrayed my trust."

"Lucky you," Drew replied dryly.

"Oh, believe me, I know it. But we have our own issues to work out, too."

"Like what?"

"Well, I told you about my... childhood. It's had a big impact. Sheridan has her own problems."

"The glorious Sheridan? She seems so... perfect. What problems could she possibly have?"

Michael regarded his brother, considering. "Well, this is in confidence, but she had a... bad experience with a man, before we got together. Sometimes it still affects her."

"She was abused?" Horror dawned. *Who would dare harm such a sweet woman?*

"No. Assaulted," Michael replied, his tone bleak. Just before he shuttered his gaze, a flicker of rage flared.

"Oh God." *Sickening.* Drew tried hard not to visualize the circumstances.

"Yeah, it was horrible. Do you know she actually forgave the rapist, right to his face? She was really smart about it too. She told him she wasn't forgiving him because he deserved it, but because she wanted to be free from him. Drew, as long as you stay mad at Alyssa, you'll never be free. Even if you don't get back together, do you really want to carry that with you forever?"

"Of course not."

"Then why not just let it go? Forgiveness doesn't mean what the other person did was right. It means you value yourself – and your relationship – more. Being angry will never make you happy."

"That's good advice, Michael. I'll think about it."

The two of them had gone back to watching the snowball fight, but throughout, Drew kept on pondering his brother's words, and he continued thinking about them throughout the evening. *Alyssa came to me, apologized sincerely, and asked for another chance. Now I have to choose. I can stay angry, punish her for her mistake, or I can let it go and try to be with her again.* It wasn't as easy a decision as he would have imagined.

He thought about her. She had never lost her appeal, even when thin to the point of emaciation, but now she regained her beauty with every passing day, becoming soft and feminine, losing the angular sharpness. She seemed happier too. That dimple he had always loved appeared in her cheek more and more each day. *She wants to make love with me again, too.* If they got back together, he could have her over and over, day after day. *She needs it. So do I.* Having once tasted her, it had been impossible to move on. No one could ever suit him like Alyssa did. But he would have to trust her. He couldn't lock her in a room. He had to trust she would choose to come home to him every day, choose to sleep beside him at night and still be there in the morning. *How can I trust in her, when my own mother left and never come back?*

Oh, God. Michael was right. I'm holding on to my anger at my mother and punishing Alyssa for it. It's wrong. We have to deal with our own situation, without the specter of Amanda Burke hanging over us. He couldn't forget, so he had to forgive.

"Mom," Drew said aloud, "Michael says you're in heaven now, and if so, I know you can hear me. I'm sorry I missed out on talking to you at the end, because there were things I needed to say. It killed me that you left me. I didn't know you had so many problems, but really, couldn't you have tried harder? Couldn't you have loved your sons more, loved us enough to stay clean? Did you have to run back to the drugs that killed you, that killed Kevin? That wasn't right. I know you could have done better, because I met someone who had it just as hard as you. Her name is Alyssa. She was desperately poor, and she had a baby to care for, but she did a great job. She never used drugs. She's such a good mother, she almost starved herself trying to keep her son fed. It can be done, Mom. Why couldn't you have just tried harder?" Drew's composure cracked. His voice wavered.

"Michael says I need to forgive you, so Alyssa and I can make peace and finally be together, be a family. It's important, because that little boy she loves so much is my son. He needs me, so I have to find a way.

"It wasn't right, Mom, for you to leave your husband and baby. It wasn't right for you to do what you did to Michael, putting him through all that suffering and fear. It really wasn't right for you to use drugs when you were pregnant and make Kevin all messed up. It's hard to let go of these things. They hurt a lot, Mom.

"I forgive you. There. It's a choice. God, help me to live it. I don't want to keep being angry. It's not getting me anywhere. It's just hurting me, and I don't want to hurt anymore."

Drew fell silent. His grief cut too deep for tears. He let himself feel it, really feel it, the way Alyssa felt hers that night in his apartment. It hurt like nothing he could have imagined, like fire, burning him up. But with the pain came truth. The truth was, as long as he blamed himself for his mother's abandonment, he could never grieve it properly. He had to try to keep earning the right to be loved by a woman. That was why he had felt so drawn to Alyssa. She had needed so many things he could give, and by giving them, he had hoped to earn her love. But it wasn't possible, not because there was something wrong with him, but because there was something wrong with her, a deep fear of not being good enough, which made her hold back her heart from him. Neither Alyssa nor Amanda had left Drew because there was anything wrong with him.

A thread of peace began to weave through his misery. It felt supernatural. *You're a good man,* it seemed to say. *You're deeply loved. You have a lot to offer. You need to try again with Alyssa, because you love her, and because Ethan deserves a proper family, but if she can't handle it, it still won't mean you're inadequate.*

That was a lie I told himself, he realized, and *I'm not going to lie to myself anymore.*

"Okay, Mom. I really do forgive you. Be at peace." Somehow, he knew she was.

Exhausted, he lay down on the pillows and fell into a deep and healing sleep.

CHAPTER 17

*I*n the morning, Drew woke up feeling like a scrub brush had been taken to his insides. He'd been cleaned out of a lot of unpleasant gunk, but also felt kind of raw and uncomfortable. He joined the families in the great room, where chilly adults in pajamas sipped coffee and nibbled toast while the children ate cereal at the table. Alyssa wasn't up yet, but Ethan was stuffing Cheerios into his mouth with a gigantic soup spoon. Drew scooped the little boy up and received a tight hug around the neck. He pressed lips softly on his son's head and plunked him back down in front of his bowl before heading into the kitchen to pour himself a steaming hot mug to take to the sofa. Erin sat on the loveseat with a blanket draped over her. Josh's tiny feet stuck out from underneath.

Good for Erin. He offered her a supportive smile. She returned it, her cheeks pink but her gaze steady. She had been a mother for a while.

Sean sat down next to his wife and laid his arm around her shoulders. He looked very relaxed. *Well, he should. Alyssa wasn't the only one who heard a bit more of the Murphys'*

SIMONE BEAUDELAIRE

evening activities than was comfortable. Erin leaned her head on her husband's shoulder. *Those two should go into the business of promoting marriage. They make it look awfully appealing.*

Adjacent to the loveseat, Michael sat in an armchair with Sheridan on his lap. The two of them snuggled, his hand and hers on her belly, feeling their child move.

Suddenly, Drew fiercely wanted what they all had. He wanted to be with Alyssa through pregnancy. He wanted to touch her belly and feel his baby inside, and know their love had created a new person. He wanted to be at her side while she delivered and hold her while she nursed their child. *I missed it all, and now Ethan's three, still little, but no longer a baby. That's so sad.*

Of course, there is a solution. I can give Alyssa another baby. Not right away. Not when all is in crisis and disarray between us. But if I can coax her back into my life, to stay this time, if I can marry her, then we can try again, the right way this time. The appealing thought seemed much less daunting than it had the night before.

He remembered the note Sheridan had found under the entertainment center. Alyssa hadn't abandoned him. She'd made a foolish mistake, but her intention hadn't been to hurt or to leave him. *It does make a difference.*

A door opened upstairs, and Drew looked up. There she stood, lovely in her faded gray pajamas, her strawberry blond hair pulled into a casual ponytail, her eyes soft with sleep. He wanted to go to her, to gather her into his arms and hold her close, the way he always used to do. He also needed to tell her he forgave her, that he wouldn't hold her mistake against her anymore. *It's over. The point is to move forward.*

At about the third step from the bottom, she suddenly collapsed, tumbling to the floor. Drew shot to his feet. He found himself at her side before he even realized he was moving. She lay still, her eyes closed.

"Allie? Are you all right?" *I shouldn't move her until I know what her injuries are*, he thought, even as his instincts urged him to pick her up.

She opened her aquamarine eyes, beautiful, deep and unfathomable, like the Mediterranean. "I'm fine, Drew. I'm not hurt."

"Are you sure? What happened?" His heart was still pounding.

"Nothing. Sometimes my leg just... gives out for a moment. I must have stepped wrong."

"You had your eyes closed. I thought you hit your head." He ran his fingers over her hair, feeling for bumps.

"No, I didn't hit anything." She arrested his nervous probing with a gentle touch. "I was embarrassed about being so clumsy. I'm sorry if I alarmed you."

"You're sure you're okay?" he demanded.

"Yes. Nothing hurt but my pride." She smiled ruefully.

"Thank God." He wrapped his arms around her, pulling her into his lap.

"Goodness, Drew," she started to say, but he interrupted by bringing his mouth down hard on hers.

Alyssa tasted delicious. He had forgotten. She tasted like toothpaste, but also like warm, succulent woman. He opened her mouth with his tongue, so he could taste her better. Far from resisting, she wrapped her arms around his neck and pulled him closer.

What are those sounds in the room behind me? People are there. He didn't want anyone to look at him while he kissed Alyssa, so he stood, lifting her close to his chest, and carried her into the bedroom, slamming the door shut with his foot.

~

"Mommy?" Ethan said, startled by the unexpected turn of events. Sheridan recovered first and went to him.

"Don't worry, Ethan. Your mommy and daddy just need to talk for a few minutes. She'll be right back. Would you like some more cereal?"

~

Inside the bedroom, Drew deposited Alyssa on the bed, lying down beside her.

"I have to have you, Alyssa, right now. Will you let me?"

"Yes. Oh, yes. Right now."

She pulled her pajama top over her head and tossed it aside. His sweatshirt flew, and they pressed together, naked flesh to naked flesh, loving the sensation of each other's bodies. Alyssa pulled Drew back down, so she could kiss him thoroughly. She stroked his back. Her fingers were chilly, but he was beyond caring. The kiss stretched on, long and wet and luscious.

Finally, endless moments later, he pulled back enough to finish undressing them both. Alyssa parted her thighs, so he could kneel between them, and he lifted her breasts in his hands, kissing and licking first one hard pink nipple and then the other. Alyssa moaned, all sense forgotten, as Drew pleasured her. Her back bowed, turning her hips into a cradle for his loving. She reached down with one hand to caress the thick sex she wanted inside her.

He touched her intimately, wanting to be sure she was ready. "Oh, Allie, you're so wet."

"For you. I need you, Drew."

Passion had Drew in a stranglehold, but he had enough

196

awareness left to remember his promise to her mother and grab a condom from the bedside table where he'd left them last night. Rolling it over himself, he lifted Alyssa's hips into just the right position and slid home in a single sure thrust. *Home. That's what this is, deep inside her body, holding her in my arms, listening to her make soft, passionate noises as I push in and pull back.*

Alyssa was so ready, so aroused, that when Drew plunged himself into her, she just about came immediately. *He's nicely thick, filling me right up, filling all the empty places in my heart too. With Drew, I never have to hunger. He satisfies me.* His sweet loving satisfied her again. He felt so great that, despite her desire to hold back and enjoy being taken, she reached her orgasm quickly.

Drew looked on in satisfaction as Alyssa went wild under him. He loved how her spasming sex caressed him. He thrust harder, taking his own pleasure inside her. He drove into her again and again, prolonging her peak and reaching his own, growling with his release.

Then he rolled over, taking her with him, spreading her over his chest like a blanket and hugging her tight with one arm.

Alyssa kissed Drew on the lips, neck and chin. He grasped her thigh, carefully feeling through the soft flesh to the bone beneath.

She giggled and squirmed. "What are you doing?"

"Checking out my work." He squeezed her, feeling the scars where he had cut into her skin to try and save her leg function, the thick calcification where her broken femur had healed, the lumps of metal screws inside her flesh. *Sometimes surgery still amazes me.* Drew switched on orthopedic surgeon mode. "It gives out?"

"Every now and again," she replied.

"Do you have any pain?"

"When the weather changes. It's better than I expected."

"Good. I'm glad."

"Drew?"

"Yes, love?"

"I need to get up. I have to go to the bathroom, and I need to check on Ethan."

Drew's insides clenched.

It must have showed on his face because she quickly added, "I'm not leaving. I'll be right out in the other room. Drew, I... I don't know exactly what this means, but I'm not going anywhere. When the time is right, we'll talk about it, okay? And I'll be here."

"Right."

She pulled her pajamas back on and walked out of the room, quickly closing the door behind her. Deep in thought, Drew removed and discarded the condom and got dressed for the day. As he emerged, he saw Alyssa had done exactly what she said. He found her on the couch, Ethan on her lap.

"Mommy," the little boy said, "why were you crying?"

"I wasn't crying," she replied.

"I heared you," he insisted in a childish lisp.

She blushed. Looking around the room at all the knowing glances didn't do much for her composure, he could see, as a deep blush suffused her cheeks.

"Is my face wet, baby?" she asked.

Ethan touched her cheeks. "No."

"See I wasn't crying."

"Okay. Were you and Daddy talking?"

"Yes."

Remember what she said all those years ago? Talking like teenagers do? He smiled, poking out his cheek with the tip of his tongue.

"What did you say?"

Alyssa gulped and suppressed a guilty grin. "We said we were very lucky to have such a wonderful little boy, and we were thinking of ways where both of us can be with you all the time."

"Oh. Good."

Drew poured Alyssa a cup of coffee and brought it to her, scooping Ethan into his own arms.

He gave her time to process everything that had just happened. *I want her ready when I take the next step.* Eventually, Ethan squirmed, and Drew set him down. He ran off to play with the other children, who were building with Lincoln Logs in front of the fireplace.

Alyssa finished her coffee and carried the cup into the kitchen. Drew followed her. In the partial privacy beside the refrigerator, she turned to him. "What does it all mean, Drew?"

That she would even ask such a question, after everything that had happened, bothered him. "You know the answer. Tell me."

"I think I do, but..."

"No, Alyssa. No 'I think so' no 'but'. I don't want to talk to your demons anymore. Okay, we're going to do this the simple way. I'm going to ask you a question, and I want you to answer with just one word. No explanations. No backpedaling. Got it?"

"But, Drew I..." He put his finger on her lips; shushing her.

~

Across the room, Sheridan didn't like what she was seeing. It looked forceful, and that made her nervous for her friend. She started to get up, intending to intervene, but Michael wrapped his arms around her tightly. "Don't go, sweetheart. Let them work it out."

"But..." She squirmed in his grasp.

He released her, placing a hand on her arm to get her attention. "He's not hurting her. He's not going to hurt her. He loves her."

Sheridan looked her husband in the eyes. "I don't trust him."

"Do you trust me?"

"Of course."

He hugged her. "He's my brother. He loves Alyssa. He has to be with her. Let him do this his way." Sheridan subsided and cuddled against her husband's chest.

Back in the kitchen, Alyssa stopped trying to argue. She nodded, agreeing with Drew's request.

"Okay, Alyssa," he began in a calm, neutral voice, "did you love me four years ago, when Ethan was conceived?"

"Yes." *Of course, I did. If only I'd said so.*

"Did you mean to leave and never come back?"

She bit her lip at the pain in his eyes. "No."

"Are you sorry I found you?"

"No." *How could I be?*

"Do you want to be with me?" A hint of passion flared in his tone.

"Yes," she stated emphatically. *If only I could be sure it's what he really wants as well.*

"Do you love me?"

Oh, that's hard. He's making me say what he needs to hear and not offering anything in return. Okay, time to be brave. Alyssa took a deep breath and finally told him the truth. "Yes, Drew. I love you."

"Will you commit to me then?" His expression turned pleading in a way that was, in itself, a sort of answer. His hand closed around her upper arm.

Alyssa dipped her chin. "Yes."

"Will you marry me?"

What? Really? "Oh, Drew…" her lips parted.

"Will you, Allie?"

"Yes." She closed her eyes.

He pulled her to him, hugging her tight. "I love you, Alyssa."

She wrapped her arms around his neck.

He kissed her softly. "Okay, now listen, Allie. I don't want you out of my sight again. You're going to sleep beside me tonight, all night. I want you in my arms when I wake up tomorrow morning, and every day for the rest of our lives. It's nothing other than the deepest commitment two people can share. Do you understand?" His expression pleaded with her to stop fighting, to accept what had always been inevitable between them.

Alyssa wanted nothing more than to assure him. "Yes, I understand, Drew. I'm going to be your wife. We love each other. That's why we made love."

He beamed. "Right. That's right. Now you've got it."

She returned his smile with a wry grin. "It only took me eleven years to figure it out."

He tugged on the end of her ponytail. "Well, I loved you then, too."

"I know. You've always loved me, haven't you, Drew?"

"Yes."

"Good. I've always loved you too."

"Good. That's the way it should be."

"Yes."

"You see," Michael told Sheridan as they watched the couple lean in close for another long kiss, "I told you he wouldn't hurt her. Burke men never hurt their women."

"Well, that's certainly true," she replied.

After several minutes, Alyssa and Drew emerged from the kitchen, hand in hand. Alyssa felt a little embarrassed to be on display, after they had made such a scene earlier, losing control and heading off to make love so blatantly and apparently so loudly. Now, she looked like what she was... a well-bedded woman. In the bathroom, moments ago, she'd seen the pink marks on her cheeks where Drew's whiskers had rasped her. She also had a visible love bite on her throat. The only saving grace was that these people around her were no less passionate with their partners and would be unlikely to take offense. She wanted to slink around quietly for several hours, until the intensity died away. All eyes in the room fixed on them.

Drew it seemed, would have none of it. "Everyone," he said, "I have an announcement. Allie has done me the very great honor of agreeing to marry me."

Erin and Sheridan immediately pounced, pulling Alyssa into a loud squealing hug. Judging by their reactions, she would have thought they'd been friends their whole lives. The overwhelming support quickly had Alyssa in tears.

"Allie?" Drew stepped forward, not certain what to make of it all.

"It's all right, Drew," Sheridan told him over Alyssa's shoulder. "She's just happy."

Erin nodded in agreement. "Nothing to worry about."

"Ahem," Drew turned. Sean was standing beside him. "Yeah?"

"Um, look. It's been great to meet you and all. Really it has, but you're a doctor, right?"

"Yes," Drew replied, "why?"

"Because that means you can afford to buy your own damned condoms. I have a beautiful wife. I need mine."

Drew chuckled. "You do. They're on the table in the bedroom. I'll pick up some more when we go into town this afternoon."

Sean punched him playfully on the shoulder and they both laughed.

CHAPTER 18

*O*n Monday, after spending a perfectly wonderful weekend with his beloved, Drew called his dad during his lunch break. "Dad?"

"Hello, Drew. How are you?"

Drew's stomach churned. "Um, I'm great. Listen, I need to talk to you."

"Sure, what's up?"

"Do you remember my high school girlfriend?"

"Which one, Marcie?" James sounded suspicious.

"No, Alyssa."

His dad sighed. "I had so hoped you would forget about her."

Drew was dumbfounded. "Why?"

"Because she wasn't good for you. She reminded me of your mother."

This statement confused him even further. "How? She's nothing like that."

Dad sucked in an audible breath. "Drew, you might not know this, but your mother was..."

"I know. An addict," Drew interrupted. "Michael told me. Dad, why did you marry her anyway?"

James let out a heavy sigh. "When we met, she said she'd been clean for over a year. I didn't find out until later that it had only been a few months. I also knew very little about addiction, particularly to such a powerful drug. All I knew was how attracted I was to Mandy. She was beautiful then and she seemed so fragile, so tragic, with her tiny sons and her sad story. I wanted to help her. Instead, well, I made her pregnant again."

"Oh, I see." Drew hoped his face wasn't burning. *I really didn't want to know this.*

"I wasn't sorry though," James added fiercely. "Not until later. Alyssa always reminded me of Mandy. She had those same hungry eyes."

"It's not the same, Dad," Drew protested. "She's a good woman, a strong one. She's almost finished with college too. She's made something of herself, despite her rough start."

Another deep breath crackled the speaker. "All this sounds very present tense, son. Are you back together?"

"Yes. And there's more."

"What's that?" James didn't sound like he wanted to hear anything else.

"Well, we got together once before, a few years ago. We have..." Drew took a deep breath. "This is really hard. Okay. We have a three-year-old son."

Silence.

"His name is Ethan. I'd like to bring them over soon to see you."

"Tonight, Drew. Bring them tonight." James' voice sounded tight and brittle.

"Okay, Dad. I will."

~

That night, with pounding hearts, Drew and Alyssa drove to the red brick house with the tire swing in the front yard. Alyssa carried Ethan through the lingering slush on the sidewalk with Drew's arm around her waist. She prayed like mad with every step, for a way to explain the mess she'd made of everything to Drew's wonderful father; a way that would eventually lead to him giving his blessing on their relationship.

Drew knocked on the door and James opened it, silently ushering them into the warmth of the living room.

"Dad," Drew said, stepping away from Alyssa and hugging his father. He held out his arms and Alyssa handed him their little boy.

"Dad, this is Ethan, our son. Ethan, this is your grandpa." Ethan looked at James skeptically. He had certainly gained a lot of new family members in the last few days.

"Hello, Ethan. I'm very glad to meet you," James said. "Listen, I have some cookies in the kitchen. Would you like one?"

"Yes, please," Ethan said, demonstrating the manners Alyssa had worked so hard to teach him.

"What about you two?" he asked, turning to Drew and Alyssa.

"Sure, Dad, thanks," his son agreed, eyes alight.

Looks like my boyfriend has a sweet tooth.

"Drew, why don't you and Ethan go get them," James suggested. "You can... show him around. I need to talk to Alyssa."

Drew gave her a questioning look and she nodded. *This is necessary.* He hugged her and carried Ethan into the kitchen.

"So, Alyssa." James regarded her with a look she couldn't read.

She tried for courtesy. "Hello, Mr. Peterson. It's good to see you again."

"How's your father?" he asked.

"He passed away about four years ago." She bit her lip against a burn of tears. *No matter how many years go by, it never gets easier to say.*

"I'm sorry." Alyssa studied James' face. *He seems sincere.*

Alyssa smiled sadly. "Me too. Not just about Dad though. I'm sorry for so many things. Did Drew tell you anything?"

"Not really." He proceeded straight to the heart of the conversation. "Why did the two of you keep Ethan a secret from me?"

Oh, dear. What to say? "He didn't. I didn't tell him I was... expecting. He only found out about Ethan at Michael's wedding. I was singing. I didn't see him, though. I had no idea at the time that they were related. When I sing, it's hard to pay attention to anything else, and I had Ethan with me so..."

He cut off her long-winded explanation. "Why didn't you tell him at the time?"

Alyssa responded with brutal, self-deprecating honesty. "I made a terrible mistake. I always thought Drew was so far out of my league. I didn't want to be a burden on him. I... I was stupid."

"I never wanted you two to be together," James told her in a flat, emotionless voice.

Alyssa closed her eyes in pain at those blunt words. "Why?" she choked. "We love each other."

"You remind me of his mother. I didn't want him to go through what I did."

"Oh, please, Mr. Peterson, not that. Don't say that." Tears sprang to her eyes and she struggled not to break down. If there was a more painful comparison, Alyssa couldn't imagine what it would be.

He continued. "She wanted to be rescued, but no one could rescue her from herself. Are you saying, after everything that's happened, that you don't see Drew as your ticket out of poverty, your white knight?"

Alyssa shook her head, steeling herself to continue the conversation. "I don't want to be rescued. If I can't take care of myself, of my child, what good am I? Besides, I don't need the help. I'm almost done with school. Soon I'll be able to support us both. I'm grateful for Drew's help, but I would have managed without it."

Suddenly fierce, James took both of Alyssa's slender arms in his hands, holding her tight, but not hurting her. "Swear to me, Alyssa; swear you've never used drugs, that you never will."

"Oh, no, never. I would never do that!" she exclaimed. *Oh, God. Is that what he thinks?* "I've never tried them, never even wanted to. Mr. Peterson, I grew up in a poor family, but a respectable one. I did have good parents. They taught me better."

Relieved, James released her. They looked at each other in silence for an endless moment. "Sorry. I had to know. No one should have to live through that."

"I'm very sorry you did," she replied.

He shook his head. "I made my own choices. I won't see Drew suffer for them anymore."

"He won't. Not from me. I'm not his mother, I swear I'll do better than that."

James scanned her face again, and she watched the fierceness drain away from him until he looked wary but much more like the James Peterson she remembered. "You know, you do need to be rescued, Alyssa, and you also need to do the rescuing. From what you're saying, it sounds like you've gone too far in the opposite direction. You try to do everything yourself, take all the burdens on yourself, so you never let anyone down. Life doesn't work that way. It has to be give and take. You've never wanted others to take care of you, have you?"

She thought about his words. "You might be right. I didn't know before how to count on anyone else, but I'm starting to understand now."

"Ask for help if you need it," he said. "Don't suffer in silence until you break under it."

"No, right," she replied. "I'm learning how to ask." Unconsciously she fingered the ring on her left hand.

James noticed. "So, you're engaged then?"

"Yes," she admitted. *No point in lying now.* "We need to be a family. All three of us need to."

He nodded. "You do. Drew loves you?"

"Yes." *I know he does.* Even the thought illuminated her heart with a flare of hope. *With Drew to love me, I can survive anything.*

"I think he always did," James commented. His frown held a hint of... something in it.

"That's what he tells me. It's amazing and wonderful."

"Okay," James said, half turning away. *Seems the third degree is done. Thank goodness.* Let's go get some cookies."

"That would be great, thank you. Oh, and Mr. Peterson..."

"Please, call me James."

"James." Alyssa dimpled prettily. Then her expression grew serious. "I'm very sorry I hurt your son, and you."

"I'll forgive you this time," he replied.

It's enough. There will never be a next time. We're a family now.

EPILOGUE

*a*nd so, the weeks and months passed. The couple lived frugally. Drew still had another year of residency, and while his income was adequate, it was not extravagant. Besides, they had a bit of saving up to do. For Alyssa, having as much food as she wanted was luxury enough. She had a hard time imagining what life would be like once he began to earn his full doctor's salary. Drew still fed her from time to time, but not because she needed him to anymore, just because he enjoyed doing it. She did too, and it often led to more passionate activities.

Then one Saturday in July, just around Alyssa's thirtieth birthday and two months after Drew's, she put on a pretty white dress. Then she made the long walk, arm in arm with her mother, up the aisle at the Basilica. She glanced at Beth as they went. *My wonderful mother. I'm so blessed to have her.* After Alyssa moved out, Beth had left the apartment and moved in with her own mother, who was having a hard time managing alone in her condo. Beth saved a fortune in rent, and the two widows were happy to be close. A few months later, at the grocery store, Beth had run into an old acquaintance, the oncologist who had tried so hard to save her husband's life. The two had started talking, and even though he was about three years younger than Beth, he took her out to dinner sometimes. He sat in the front row on the bride's side, waiting for Beth. Alyssa smiled. *I'm not sorry Mom's dating.*

As they walked on, they passed the Murphy clan. Erin, looking slim and lovely, and thankfully not pregnant, sat with little Josh on her lap and her two older sons, like stair steps, between her and Sean. *All the boys are being fairly quiet... so far,* Alyssa noted with a grin. Since the time they'd spent together, Erin and Alyssa had become close friends, despite the three-hour distance between them, and spoke frequently on the phone. Another family reunion was being planned at the end of the month, and the Petersons would be invited.

As they neared the altar, Alyssa's eyes fell on James, sitting near the front, holding a tiny new baby with a wisp of black hair. This was Sheridan and Michael's child, his grandson, christened Kevin James Burke.

In the last few months, Alyssa had had several intense conversations with Drew's father. It had not been easy, but he'd finally accepted her as his son's future wife and embraced her as part of the Peterson family. *I'm so glad.*

Beside him sat Kayleigh, dressed in white and holding a basket that had at one time been filled with golden sunflower petals, and Ethan, dashing in his new suit, with a pillow that had a ring on it.

And then, she met eyes with Drew. His gaze intense, he stood beside Michael, waiting for her. Beth kissed Alyssa on the cheek and handed her to him. He took her arm in his and led her toward the priest. Sheridan, still looking a little pale after the delivery of her son a couple of weeks before, had dressed carefully in a gown cut to conceal the pregnancy curves that had not yet quite subsided. She arranged Alyssa's skirt and took the bouquet from her, so the bride's hands would be free. *I adore having Sheridan for a sister.* The two of them spent a tremendous amount of time together. *Being with her through the last few months of her pregnancy and seeing the new baby gave me the urge to try again myself, soon.*

But now, it's time for me to get married. Alyssa tried to focus her attention on the priest, with Drew standing beside her, she struggled. *Sometimes I still struggle to believe that after everything that had happened, we're really together, but I strive to accept it. I have never been so well loved and cared for in my life. My only regret was Daddy isn't here to see Drew fulfill the promise he'd made.*

Just for a moment, Alyssa thought she could feel him there with her. *Perhaps, those we love who have gone on to Heaven aren't completely cut off, after all,* she thought. *Perhaps they are allowed, in spirit, to visit from time to time. I hope so. I know he would approve of what I'm doing. He wanted this for me all along.*

"Do you, Alyssa Jeanette, take Andrew Caleb to be your wedded husband..." the priest began, startling Alyssa back to the present. *I need to pay attention now. I'm about to make my vows.* For her, it was a particularly important one to make. *Never again will I disappear from this man's life, no matter how I needed reassurance. I'm promising to let go of my shyness and neediness and dedicate myself to meeting the needs of my husband, leaving his to me.* So, she vowed, in front of the priest, her friends and family, and God, "I do."

"Do you, Andrew Caleb, take Alyssa Jeanette to be your wedded wife...?"

Drew's beautiful green eyes grew even more intense and took on a teary shine as he vowed to love and care for his wife, for better or worse, in sickness and in health, until death did them part.

Drew brushed his lips against Alyssa's tenderly and they turned to face the room and be introduced. Alyssa smiled, the dimple showing deeply in her right cheek. *It's done. After all the years, after all the suffering, the mistakes, the hurt and disappointment, we're finally married. And it's wonderful.*

ONE OCTOBER MORNING

PROLOGUE

"What did you say?" Mindy looked up from her coffee and stared, stunned, at her husband.

"You heard me," Max replied, rubbing his hand over the smooth baldness above his bushy black eyebrows.

Mindy blinked. "Are you serious?"

Max flung himself to his feet from the leather sofa they'd picked together for their anniversary and began pacing the room. "Totally serious, Mindy. I mean, be honest. How long has it been since we've had anything like a real relationship? Five years? Ten? We've been going through the motions for at least a decade. We need to stop pretending."

"So, stop," Mindy replied. "I never said you should pretend with me, did I? I never asked you to lie. Be real. But if we're going through the motions, don't you think, before we throw away eighteen years of marriage, we ought to at least try to reconnect?" Though her words sounded calm, a stunned little girl inside Mindy cried "Nooo!"

Max shook his head. "I've stayed this long for Andie's sake, but she's off in college now, on her own, and I don't need to pretend anymore. It's over, Mindy. I want a divorce."

He stalked out of the room and returned with a manila envelope, which he thrust at her. "Here," he said. "I've been fair with you. I haven't tried to cheat or manipulate you at all, I promise. But if you want to hire an attorney to look it over, that's probably a good idea."

Mindy opened the envelope and drew out a sheaf of papers written in dense legalese. Her breath seemed to catch in her throat. "Max, you know how impulsive you can be..." she started.

"Be quiet, Mindy," he retorted. "I know what I want and you're not going to be able to change it. I've contacted a realtor. He's going to be by to take pictures of the house this afternoon. Can you... just make sure the place is cleaned up before then?"

He walked out of the room leaving Mindy alone. She stared at the papers, too sad to rage, too stunned to cry. While a whirlwind of confusing emotions tore her insides apart, a single, bitter thought coalesced. As she considered it, a tear escaped unnoticed to slide down her cheek. The irony made her want to choke.

I have to call Cindy and Joan and let them know... and cancel the party. Today was her fortieth birthday. She'd planned a small get-together with her best friends from work and their families. Looked like instead of barbecue, cake and a few gifts, the only present she was going to receive to mark the event was divorce papers.

CHAPTER 1

Four years later.

*M*elinda glanced at the thermometer hanging outside her front window and shivered. Only October and it was already freezing. *Well, fifty degrees anyway. That sure feels cold. I'd rather go back to bed.* "Come on, Mindy, move your butt," she said aloud. "If you don't get any exercise, you're going to look like a beluga again in no time. Besides, the pretty leaves are almost gone."

Pulling on her sneakers, lined hoodie, and gloves, she stepped out onto the porch and locked the door, hanging her key around her neck on a purple lanyard. Before heading out for her habitual hour-long stroll around the neighborhood, she took a moment to regard at her home. One story with red brick up to a black roof. White shutters on the windows. Lilac bushes, now long since dormant, crowded under the bay window of her living room. A set of cream curtains obscured the view into the house. In the small front yard, a single enormous evergreen thrust upwards towards the sky. She took a moment to bury her face in the fragrant branches. Then, sighing, she took to the sidewalk, walking briskly.

You're not doing too badly, she thought to herself. *All in all, life is manageable. You have plenty of income, a job you love, and good friends. What more can you ask for really?* She didn't answer the internal question. Instead, Melinda focused on the beauty of the leaves; oaks in rich red and brown. Maples in brilliant scarlet. Willows in shades of gold. Acorns scattered across the sidewalk, to the peril of the unwary... and the delight of the squirrels. As she made her way to the end of the street, she took a moment to enjoy the antics of the bushy-tailed rodents as they chased and squabbled over the coveted nuts, preparing their winter hoard.

She smiled. Squirrels reminded her of kindergarteners. Busy, frantic, and completely sincere. She arrived at the corner and turned.

A loud *WOOF* broke through her concentration and a large shape flew in her direction. Squirrels squawked and scattered, running for their trees. On pure instinct, Melinda snagged a length of red leash. The galloping beast reached the end of his slack and nearly jerked her off her feet. She set her heels and pulled back, bringing the dog to a sudden stop. He turned and gave her a comically dirty look.

"Rufus!" a low-pitched voice yelled. Melinda stopped staring at the dog and turned to his owner. He appeared to be about fifty years of age; rugged and handsome, his blond hair streaked with silver. She tucked a strand of her own gray-dappled brown hair behind her ear.

"Oh," he said, coming to a sudden stop in front of her. "You caught him. Thank you."

"You're welcome." Melinda smiled and received a smile in

return. It only served to make her own grin wider. Though attractive when his face was in a neutral posture, the turning up of his lips and the sparkling of his eyes transformed him into something that froze her grin and turned her casual conversation into a lame stutter. She handed him the leash.

Get it together, Mindy, she ordered herself fiercely. "Your friend here was headed for Lyndale Avenue," she informed him. "I didn't like the thought of him tangling with all that traffic. It's bad enough when the squirrels get run over."

"Thank you," he replied, tugging the lead. Melinda could have sworn the mutt on the other end was pouting. Without thought, she sank to her knees, holding out her hand to the pug-faced white canine. He gave her a soggy lick to her gloved fingers before taking the initiative to jump up on her and bathe her face in saliva.

"Hey, watch it, buddy," she said, laughing and wiping at her slobbery cheek. A hand appeared, and she grasped it, letting the man help her to her feet.

"I'm James," he said, turning the hand up into a handshake. "And I believe Rufus already introduced himself. My son calls him Doofus. I think you can see why."

Melinda couldn't help laughing. "Just a bit," she said. "I'm Melinda, by the way. Melinda Summers."

"Pleased to meet you." He was still holding her gloved hand in his. "I think we're sort of neighbors. Don't you live at the end of the street, next to the park?"

"I sure do," she replied. "Tiniest lot in the neighborhood."

"I have the second tiniest," he boasted, waving his free hand. "Across from you and two down."

"I know," she replied. "I've seen you a time or two in the mornings. Heading off to work, is it?"

James nodded. "I'm the speech pathologist for the Richfield School District. I travel campuses."

"Oh!" she exclaimed as the pieces fell into place. "No wonder you seem familiar. I teach kindergarten. One of my babies met with you last year."

"Jordan Paulk. I still have him. He's making great progress."

They beamed at each other, and then Melinda laughed again. "What a couple of nerds," she said.

"Absolutely," James replied, laughing along with her. She enjoyed the way the corners of his eyes crinkled.

"So, James," she asked, teasing, "do you have a last name, or are you a single moniker star like Prince, or Madonna?"

"Please, it's 'The Artist' now," he said, reminding her of the odd local celebrity's penchant for changing his stage name.

"You?" she asked, widening her eyes and pretending to be gullible.

"Sadly, no. I'm one of the ubiquitous Petersons." His face fell into an ostentatious pout.

That made her chuckle again. "Well, Mr. Ubiquitous, you've now held my hand for over a minute, so it's going to have to be nicknames for us."

Is it embarrassment or wind that made his cheeks so pink? He glanced at her glove and then back at her eyes. He didn't let go. "Nicknames sound good, except... I don't have one. Do you?"

"Mindy," she replied.

The smile disappeared from his face in a heartbeat. His mouth dipped downward, and deep, bracketing grooves appeared.

"I take it you don't like that?" she asked mildly, slipping her hand from his.

"Sorry," he replied, clearly struggling for calm. "My ex was named Mandy. I don't think I could handle something so close."

"Must have been one hell of a divorce," she commented, not shying away from stating the obvious. "Recent?"

He shook his head. "Over twenty years ago."

Melinda quirked one eyebrow. "Okay, that must have been horrible. If Mindy won't work, what will?" *Please don't let this be the end of the conversation. I haven't had so much fun in ages.*

He considered her for a long moment. "Okay, Mel," he said at last, but his smile didn't return. He seemed to be gauging her reaction.

"Okay, Jim," she replied.

He squinted at her. "No one calls me Jim."

"No one calls me Mel," she replied. "But that's okay. I like it. *My* ex calls me Mindy, so letting it drop seems good for closure."

He nodded.

"Well, Jim, what do you say we continue this walk together? Walking alone is a drag," she suggested, pleased by her own boldness.

"Sometimes literally," he replied, nodding at Rufus, who had stretched out with his head on Melinda's foot. Ribbons of drool festooned her shoe. "And to answer your question, yes. That would be very nice."

"Up, Rufus." She nudged the slobbery dog gently with the toe of her sneaker and the three of them set off at an energetic pace.

That night, Melinda called her daughter. Excited about making a new friend, and missing the girl, she couldn't wait to have a long Saturday night conversation. Except Andrea never picked up her phone.

CHAPTER 2

Six weeks later.

*M*el knocked on the door of Jim's house. He answered, still in his socks, his gaze on the cell phone clutched in his hand. Rufus nudged his leg and whined. He patted the dog absently.

Beyond him, Mel could see into his living room. The TV was on, and from the sound, playing a football game. Warmth wafted from the room, along with the aroma of homemade beef stew. *Curling up in there sounds like much more fun than walking in this,* she thought glaring at the icy drizzle spitting down from the steel-gray sky.

"Jim, what's up? Are you not walking today?" she asked.

He blinked, shaking his head, and his eyes focused on hers. "Oh, hi, Mel. Yes, I'm walking. Just let me get my shoes on. Um, here, come in," he urged. "Don't stand outside in the cold until we're ready to go."

She stepped through the door into the cozy space. Plaid and leather furniture surrounded the TV. Taking a chance, she removed the phone from his hand and set it on the coffee table. Next to the device was the remote, and she switched off the game.

"Uh, Jim," she said, giving her friend a look.

"Hmmm?"

"Are you planning to walk in *those*?" she waved at the polished dress shoes he was tying.

"Crap." He quickly pulled off the shiny black lace-ups and slipped his feet into his Nikes. Muttering under his breath, he dragged on a coat and gloves. Rufus brought Mel his leash, and she clipped it to his collar. His squashed, slobbery face seemed to be smiling.

"Don't get too excited, big boy," she told the dog. "It's one step away from miserable outside."

Rufus whined and lifted one big white paw to scratch at the door.

"Jim, I'm taking him out," she said. "I think he needs to wee."

Her companion nodded. She led the dog into the cold outdoors. While the spitting sleet had stopped, the clouds had thickened, and the cold had ratcheted down to a bone-chilling blast. Mel winced.

"Hey," Jim said, making his way down the steps and joining her near his oak tree. Rufus lifted his leg. Mel looked away from the dog.

"Hey yourself," she replied. "What has you so distracted, Jim?"

"I'm... stunned," he replied, and he looked it. His eyes remained unfocused.

"So, I see," she replied dryly. "Okay, spill. What happened?"

"My son just called me." He said this as though it were momentous.

She looked at him askance. "Doesn't Drew call you every week?" she asked.

"Huh? Oh, yeah. He does. Sure, but I don't mean Drew."

Now Mel felt even more confused. "Jim, how many kids do you have? Drew's the only one you talk about." *And you talk about him all the time.*

Rufus lowered his leg and lumbered over to them, licking his chops and urging them to move.

"Good idea, buddy," Mel said, taking the dog's suggestion and stepping out onto the sidewalk. Jim trailed along after them.

"I actually have... had... three," Jim explained.

"Hon, you're not helping me out much," Mel complained. "Last I heard, you had one son, Drew, who's a resident in orthopedic surgery. Who the hell are the other two?"

"The thing is," he said, slipping his gloved hand into hers and squeezing gently, "um, remember when I told you about my ex?"

As if I could forget anything you tell me. "Mandy, was it?" She glanced at him. He winced at the sound of the name but nodded.

"Yeah, she came to me with two little boys. They had no father, but while we were together, they felt like mine. I always thought of them that way."

Mel nodded. *Jim's sweet like that.*

"After we split, I asked for joint custody, but since I wasn't their biological dad, the judge said no." Jim looked sadder than ever. Without the sparkle of good humor, the lines on his face looked harsh and unwelcoming. She squeezed his hand. "So just like that, I went from three kids to one."

"Ouch," Mel said gently. "Sorry."

"Yeah, it was horrible," he replied. "Michael... well, he was only five when Mandy and I got together, and Kevin was even smaller. Great boys. I never saw Michael again."

"And Kevin?"

"He passed away a couple of years ago." Jim's voice wavered.

Mel stopped walking, completely frozen in her tracks. "Oh God," she said. "Jim, oh no!" He ceased moving forward. She turned and hugged him. "I'm so, so sorry," she said. *And no words will ever come close to expressing how sorry I really am!*

He accepted the hug and then pulled back to look into her face. "Thank you, Mel," he replied. "I miss him."

"I bet," she said.

He blinked hard and changed the subject. "I just got a phone call from Michael, though. Can you beat that? Almost twenty years since the last time I saw him, and he's coming to lunch on Saturday!"

"Jim, that's great," she said, tightening her arms around him again. He squeezed back. For one electrifying moment, his blue eyes lit with joy and other, more complicated emotions. She licked her lips. He seemed to be moving forward, and then, up ahead of them, a car honked, breaking the spell.

"Come on, Mel," he suggested. "Let's walk."

She trailed along after him, happy he'd had such a positive surprise, but disappointed the threatened kiss hadn't materialized. *He's so nice,* she thought to herself. *If only...*

That night, Mel called Andrea. For some reason, every time she dialed the number, Andie either didn't answer or ended the call quickly.

"Sorry, Mom. Can't talk. I'm on my way out to study group. Later."

The phone went dead in her hand.

Saturday night, Mel and her girlfriends sat around a table at their favorite restaurant, regaling each other with tales of kindergarten madness and giggling over drinks and breadsticks.

"You're putting us on," Mel laughed. "There's no way!"

"Yep," Cindy replied, chortling. "He asked for ice cream. I couldn't believe it. Only in kindergarten can a kid throw up all over the floor, his classmates and himself and then ask for dessert."

Julie, the youngest teacher present by many years, looked slightly ill, but the other three had seen enough vomit not to be worried about it anymore.

"What do you do if they barf like that?" the first-year teacher demanded.

"Call the janitor," Mel replied, "and then take the kids to the gym. Otherwise, they'll all stare."

"If the kid's messy," Cindy added, "send him to the nurse. She has extra clothes."

Julie looked from Cindy to Mel to Lucille, a teaching veteran of many years, on the brink of retirement. Julie sighed.

"Don't worry, honey," Lucille said, "you'll get used to it."

Mel took a sip of her merlot. "That's enough talk about work. How's everyone doing otherwise?"

Julie's disgusted face turned to a grin as she held up her left hand. "Greg proposed," she announced.

"Oh, that's great!" Mel exclaimed. Cindy oohed and ahhhed over the generous diamond adorning the young teacher's slender finger. Lucille smiled and toyed with the large rock on her own finger. She and her husband had just celebrated their fortieth anniversary.

Max and I didn't even make it to twenty, Mel thought sadly, but then she suppressed it, hoping the idealistic young woman didn't notice her momentary lapse in happiness.

"Are you planning a summer wedding?" Cindy asked.

Julie nodded. "Yes, outside by the river. It's going to be so pretty. I can't wait!"

"Sounds great," Mel said. "Will we get invitations?"

"Of course!" Julie exclaimed. "You ladies are like mothers to me. I wouldn't dream of leaving you out."

Mel smiled, but a bit more sadly this time. *I miss my daughter. I wish Andie would call more often.*

"But enough about me," Julie continued. "What about you guys? Cindy, how's your husband?"

"He's well enough," Cindy replied. "He had his last round of chemo, and the results are promising. No new growth in the tumor. I think they'll have to operate to remove it, but the doctor says they might be able to go through the nose, rather than open his skull."

A clatter of china diverted their attention. Apparently, the waiter who was bringing them their pasta had heard more than he wanted to. He gulped and quickly set the plates in front of the ladies.

"Enjoy," he said and hurried away.

"Hmmm," Mel hummed at his retreating backside. "Cute."

"A bit skinny, don't you think?" Cindy retorted. "You can't fool me, Mel. Quit playing 'Stella'. There are better ways to get your groove back."

Julie giggled into her napkin and Lucille guffawed.

"Oh yeah?" Mel retorted. "Like how, smarty?"

"Well, if you like the young ones, there's always Lance."

"Ugh," Mel replied. "The gym teacher isn't any older than

Julie. I don't want to date someone young enough to be my son. I still haven't decided if I want to date at all."

"Who said anything about dating him?" Lucille asked, waggling her eyebrows. "He would be a fun boy toy."

Mel choked on her wine. When she managed to get the merlot out of her windpipe, she hissed, "I don't like younger men."

The other three ladies laughed. Then Cindy gave her a searching look and said, "So who is he?"

"Who is who?" Mel asked before taking a hearty bite of spaghetti noodles with shrimp and cream sauce.

"The older man who has your cheeks glowing," her friend replied.

"That's windburn," Mel replied, patting her mouth with a napkin.

"Bull," Cindy retorted. "Name, please, and you might as well not try to hold out on me, Melinda Summers. I can pester you day and night if I have to."

Mel sighed, knowing she was beaten. "Jim," she said.

The other woman blinked. At last Lucille spoke. "Okay, out with it. Who is Jim, how do you know him, and why have we never heard of him before."

"Jim is my neighbor," Mel replied. "I know him because we go for walks together... just about every day. And you haven't heard about him because we're *friends*. Not a couple."

"Hmmm," Cindy hummed. "Sounds promising."

Mel started to shake her head.

"Don't pretend with me," Cindy insisted, waving her hand in the air, "I can see plain as day you'd like to be. A couple, that is."

Mel gulped. "I don't know if I want to be a couple with *anyone* again. Tell me honestly, Cindy. After so many years of marriage, how easy would it be to start over with someone else? I'm not even sure I care to try."

"I can see your point," Cindy replied. "That would be hard. But you're the one who tells us – every time the state comes out with new requirements, mind you – that just because something is hard doesn't mean we don't have to do it. You're a great professional, Melinda, a great teacher. You do so many things well, but when it comes to relationships, you chicken out. Do you want to spend the rest of your life alone? I mean, if you did, I wouldn't worry about it, but I can see how lonely you are."

Mel looked down at the table, eyes stinging.

"You know what, I have an idea." All eyes at the table turned to Cindy.

"We're so good at setting professional goals and helping each other achieve them. But when do we ever set personal ones?" Heads nodded. "Here's what I propose. Let's each set a personal goal and try to keep each other on track. I'll start. I need to spend some time on myself. Between work and my husband's... condition, I haven't even taken the time to get my hair colored or my nails done in almost a year. My goal is to spend time and money each month doing something entirely for myself."

Mel nodded. "That's a great goal. You'll really enjoy it too. When I decided to go for a walk every day, just because I needed to lose twenty pounds before Type II diabetes set in, my outlook really improved. What started out as a weight loss technique became the highlight of my day."

"Not least of all because you have a compelling companion to keep you on track," Lucille pointed out.

Mel blushed and shut her mouth.

Cindy continued. "Julie, your goals are clear. You need to spend time preparing for your wedding."

Julie nodded.

"Lucille?" Three sets of eyes turned to the older woman.

"I intend to have more sex," she said, and then cackled while the other three blushed and stammered. "What? You think there's no sex after sixty? Dream on."

"Okay," Mel said, still choking a bit. "Good one, Lucille."

"You need the same goal," the older woman insisted. "There's sex after forty too, dear."

"I suppose," Mel said, her face burning hot enough to warrant a call to the fire department. "But unlike you, I don't have a partner handy."

"Sure, you do," Cindy jumped in. "Jim. He's already your friend and you already like him. Maybe he's your happily ever after."

"Or maybe he's my walking buddy," Mel replied, scowling, "and if I proposition him, he will be so embarrassed he won't do that anymore."

"Bah." Lucille dismissed Mel's words with an irritable cut of her hand. "Are you sixteen years old, to be embarrassed of your own sexuality? If you ask him to make love to you and he turns you down, you can still be friends. And if you try it and the heavens don't move, you can decide not to do it again, but at least you tried."

"What do you say, Melinda?" Cindy urged. "I think you should set a goal to get laid by your next birthday. That's not until July, so you have plenty of time to work on it slowly."

Mel took a large gulp of her wine to cover her embarrassment.

"That's a pretty big goal," Julie piped up. "I think we should help her break it into manageable steps. Step one, after your walk, invite him into your house for a cup of coffee. Easy."

Hmmm. That is easy. And how nice too, to have Jim, not hurrying down the street, but just sitting on the sofa.

"Ooooh, she likes that idea," Cindy drawled, shaking Mel from her reverie and setting her to blushing again. "Be sure you follow our esteemed colleague's sage advice. By next month's ladies' night, I want to hear you've had coffee with Jim at least twice."

"More than twice," Lucille suggested.

Cindy shook her head. "She'll never do that. Twice would work better."

"I'm not promising anything," Mel insisted. "We'll see."

Then she applied herself to eating her dinner in silence. But all the while, the thought of inviting Jim in for coffee, and that never-delivered kiss, kept her eyes twinkling and her mind spinning. Her friends noticed of course, but they didn't say anything.

CHAPTER 3

*B*y Christmas, the Saturday and Sunday morning walks had morphed into something completely different. Unlike the weekday strolls, which time restricted to exercise only, the weekend ones had stretched to include, not only coffee, but brunch, with Mel and Jim taking turns cooking for each other, eating together, and sharing conversation of an increasingly personal nature.

Mel was falling hard for her new friend, but hesitated to voice her feelings, fearing he wouldn't reciprocate. The almost-kiss had proven to be an aberration, never repeated, but every now and again, Mel could swear she saw heat rise in Jim's eyes when he looked at her, only to be quickly repressed.

The Saturday after Christmas, having concluded a cold and snowy stroll, the two sat in Mel's kitchen, sipping coffee with cream and waiting for the cinnamon rolls to come out of the oven, when Jim spoke. "Guess what?"

"What's that?" Mel asked. The oven beeped, and she jumped up to retrieve the pan of golden, fragrant rolls, setting them on the stove and drizzling icing over the top.

"Remember my long-lost son, Michael?"

How can I forget? You talk about him as much as you do Drew. "I do remember. What's up?"

"He's getting married," Jim replied. He smiled, but there seemed to be a hint of strain around his eyes.

"Is that a good thing?" Mel asked. "You don't seem too sure."

"It is," he replied. "It's just... well... they're expecting."

Mel giggled. "Oops."

"Yeah," Jim replied. "I'd say something about doing the right thing, but that's not why they're marrying. They just want to. The baby only changes the timing."

"Well, good for them," she said. "Is the girl nice?"

Jim thought about this for a long moment. "I've only met her the one time, but she seems sweet. Gorgeous and brilliant. Almost too good to be real. Poor Michael looks like he's been clubbed over the head." He chuckled.

"I'm so glad you found him... or rather, he found you," Mel said, using a spatula to lift two fragrant rolls onto a plate and bringing them to Jim.

"Me too," he replied. Then his eyes focused away from the food onto her face. "What's wrong?"

"Oh, it's nothing," she replied.

"Mel." He took her hand. "Tell me."

"It's just... My daughter, you know, Andrea?"

He nodded.

"I tried to call her again yesterday. She's so busy she never has time to talk. I mean never. I haven't had a conversation with my little girl in ages. I know she's a grown up now, a senior in college, but does that mean she has to give up talking to me altogether?"

James gave her hand a little tug, bringing her around the chair to face him. He rose to his full height, a perfect 6'2, and slipped his arms around her waist. The scent of his cologne teased her, heating her libido while the warmth of his hug melted her heart.

"Keep trying," he urged. "It's no good to lose touch with a child, even a difficult one."

Mel nodded. She slid her arms around his neck and looked up into his face. *Funny, the features I thought handsome when we first met are now even more powerfully moving.* Again, awareness sparked between them. Mel let her eyes go soft, pleading with him not to back off this time. But apparently, even a silent appeal was more than Jim could take. He dropped his arms to his sides.

"These smell delicious," he said, slipping from her embrace and plunking down in his seat. Mel sat down, her thoughts rueful. *His divorce is so much older than mine. Why does he still seem so wounded?*

With neither answers nor kisses forthcoming, Mel applied herself to cinnamon rolls and conversation.

CHAPTER 4

When Mel knocked on Jim's door that day in March, she knew immediately something was up with her friend. He still wore in his sweats, and grizzled silver and gold stubble crowded his cheeks.

"What's wrong?" she asked bluntly, stepping through the door and closing it behind her. She could see there would be no walk today.

"Nothing," he replied, but something about his manner pleaded with her not to drop it.

"Bullshit," she replied. "Don't give me that, Jim. I can see you're hurting. I'm your friend. Out with it."

"I can't," he said. "I've burdened you with too much of my drama. Would you believe my life was... almost boring up until this last year? I mean, a single man in his fifties with an empty nest and a well-established career doesn't generate much."

"Your drama doesn't scare me, Jim," Mel replied, taking his hand. He allowed the touch. "You're my friend and friends help each other. Not to mention that I'm overjoyed to talk about adult problems from time to time. Think about it. My day is bathed in kindergarten drama; boo-boos and hair pulling, vomiting and people calling each other 'poopy-heads'. And the odd round of head lice or a potty accident. Besides, as many times as you've listened to me vent about my daughter... so what's up?"

"Let's get some coffee," he suggested, tugging her hand and ushering her into the kitchen. She helped herself to a mug. Jim, she noticed, already had one for himself. He sipped thoughtfully, apparently considering his words. "Drew came by for a visit," he said at last.

Mel took a swallow of coffee and gave him a questioning look.

"He's engaged."

"Congratulations?" Mel posed the response as a question. Jim's glum demeanor seemed at odds with his news. "Is that a bad thing?"

He took a deep breath through his nose. "I don't like the girl. Not at all. I never have. They were together in high school. I've never been so happy as the day he stopped talking about Alyssa."

The harsh response seemed so contrary to everything she'd known about Jim up to this point that Mel could only stare. "What's wrong with her?" she asked at last.

Jim shrugged. "I can't exactly put my finger on it," he replied. "Ever since the first time I met her, I felt... uncomfortable. She reminds me of... of Mandy. I don't want my son ending up suffering like I did. And he's already lost his mother. Did I tell you? Mandy contacted Drew. She asked him to come visit. But then she passed away. He was sort of devastated."

"And what about you, Jim? Were you devastated?" *Oh, Lord. If he's still hung up on his ex, it would explain so much.*

He shook his head. "I don't think so," he replied. "Not

really. I mean, it's been twenty years. I've been divorced from her three times longer than I was with her."

And you've counted every year. Oh, Jim. What happened to you? Her eyes filled with sympathetic concern, and she hung on his every word.

"And then to find out Drew is back with Alyssa, and – here's the real kicker – they have a three-year-old son they never told me about. Here I was, all excited about my first grandchild; Michael and Sheridan's, coming this summer. Now I find out I've been a grandfather for three years and never knew it? That hurts way more than Mandy passing away. I think... it's probably a mercy she's gone. Michael made sure she got last rights and everything."

A lot of what he was saying didn't make sense to Mel, but she didn't interrupt. The words poured out of Jim like pus from a lanced infection and she didn't dare stem the flow. She set her coffee cup down on the table and arranged her chair, so she was seated directly at his knee. Wanting to offer a comforting touch, she laid her hand on his leg and then gave a surprised little "Oof," as he grabbed her hand and hauled her into his lap. His words had halted, but his arms tightened around her.

"Jim," she said softly, "why do you dislike this Alyssa so much? A superficial resemblance to your late ex-wife is no reason to dismiss her. That's unfair, and I've never known you to be unfair."

"I don't want Drew to suffer the way I did. I don't want him to love an unworthy woman," he insisted, returning to the same reasoning.

Mel slipped her arms around his neck and tugged him down until they were forehead to forehead. From this angle, he looked like a Cyclops. "How do you know she's unworthy? Is she a bitchy girl? A mean girl? Lazy? What? What real reason do you have? Because if your son loves her, and wants to marry her, and has a *baby* with her, separating them will be damn near impossible. And if your reasons are weak, you won't have a leg to stand on. Tell me about Alyssa."

"She's not bitchy," he said at last, as though with great reluctance. "She's... fairly timid. But sweet. She used to be mean to Drew, back when they were in school, but he was mean to her too. They fought like cats and dogs until they fell in love. *God,* I wish she'd stayed gone."

Mel ignored the comment. "So, what is it you object to?"

"She's so... I don't know. She's trailer trash, Mel."

Mel's teeth clenched. From between them, she hissed, "How dare you say that? As if she could help growing up poor. You know how many of my babies live in trailers? Does that make them trash, Jim? Does it?" She grabbed his shoulders and gave him a little shake. "I thought the point of education was to help people better themselves. Is she still in that trailer?"

He shook his head. "I think she lives with Drew now," he replied. And then, with the air of someone having several teeth pulled, he added. "She's about a year from finishing up a music education degree."

For shame, Jim Peterson, she thought, but then a flare of understanding dawned. She pulled back, so she could meet his eyes properly. "So, my friend, what girl would have been good enough for your son?" she asked. "Having suffered through such a terrible experience, a divorce so painful you're still hung up over it twenty years later – and don't think I didn't notice your references to denying your ex contact with Drew – I imagine you've become very comfortable trying to keep dangerous people away from him, isn't that right? But is there anything actually wrong with Alyssa?"

Jim sulked. His mouth turned down and his lower lip showed signs of poking out. "No."

"And Drew is, what, in his late twenties?"

"He just turned thirty."

"And has a little boy with this girl?" Melinda pressed.

Jim closed his eyes.

"Before you say anything to him, one word, before you risk damaging the most important connection in your life, stop and think. Is your disapproval about Alyssa, or is it about you?"

He opened his mouth. She placed her hand over it.

"You don't have to answer me. This isn't about me. This is about you and your relationship with Drew. Be sure you think of the long-term consequences of your actions before you speak."

Over her fingertips, Jim's bright blue eyes met hers. She watched as a whirlwind of emotions raged behind his eyes. Then, something happened she had never expected. Jim kissed her palm. Startled, she dropped it away from his lips.

"Jim?"

"What would I do without you, Mel?" he asked, his voice intense. He tightened his arms around her waist. She lowered her cheek to his shoulder.

"I'm glad you're not throwing me out. It was a risk. I didn't want to piss you off."

"Hey, no way!" he replied. "It takes a true friend to tell someone he's screwing up his life."

"You didn't..."

"I almost did," he replied. "I could have. I suppose I'll need to make peace with Alyssa."

"I think that would be a good idea," Mel said softly.

"It's been too long since I've had a woman in my life to explain all this emotional stuff to me," he said. And then his voice grew wistful. "So long alone."

"I know," she said, returning to empathy. "I know how much it hurts to be alone."

"Sometimes I can't stand it."

SIMONE BEAUDELAIRE

"Me either," she said.

"Mel, I..."

Whatever he was going to say disappeared. She reached for him and without hesitation, laid her lips on his.

Jim inhaled sharply through his nose at her surprising movement. But then, after a moment, he relaxed and leaned into the kiss.

For endless moments, they lingered mouth on mouth, and then tongue to tongue, natural as breathing.

At last, when the need for oxygen grew overwhelming, she pulled back, panting.

"Oh, Lord," Jim breathed. "That was..." He looked just as stunned as she felt.

"I know," she replied.

"Mel, why?"

"Why did I kiss you? I don't know. I guess I had to. I've been waiting for you to kiss me forever, but you never did, so..."

"What... what does this mean? God, I feel like a dunce." He slapped his hand to his forehead. "I've been single so long, I can't remember how all this stuff works anymore."

"It means, Jim, that we're friends, close friends, who are attracted to each other. Maybe, someday, it could grow to be more. I don't need to rush that part. But it would be nice to acknowledge the possibility, don't you think?" *Oh please, oh please let him think so.*

"More... like... a relationship?"

So damned neutral. He's not telling me anything. "Yes."

Instead of answering, he took her face in his hands and captured her lips again.

While Mel didn't exactly understand what he meant by this embrace, she remembered her friends telling her to try, even if it didn't work out in the long run. Jim seemed willing to experiment, and she was glad.

242

She released his lips with a pop and then rose to her feet. He joined her, but only to haul her back into his arms for another deep, thorough kiss.

Mel's insides turned liquid in the heat of Jim's passion. Whether he wanted her or just wanted not to be alone made no difference whatsoever. She would ride this wave wherever it took her. *Hopefully to the shores of paradise.*

"Ahhh," she sighed against his mouth as a frantic hand closed around her breast, shaping the generous globe with tender roughness.

"Mel, I... I want... can you...?"

"Oh Jim, yes! A thousand times, yes!"

"Come on then." He tugged her down the hallway to a room she'd never entered before; a masculine bedroom with wood floors and window trim, a green and blue bedspread and a huge flat screen television mounted on the wall. *Such a man's room,* she managed to think before he lifted her sweater over her head and then his own. At last, bare chest to almost bare, they returned to the passionate embrace they'd been sharing in the kitchen. Jim unhooked Mel's bra and slid it to the floor. Layering kiss after devastating kiss on her lips, he slowly brought his hands up to cradle her naked flesh. Pure, sizzling pleasure shot through her belly and straight to her sex, moistening her for his eventual entry. He released her and pulled back a bit, taking in her body.

It occurred to Mel, for the first time in her life, that sex was not about perfect figures and porn star shimmies. Though she'd lost the twenty pounds she'd gained after the divorce, and felt proud of her form overall, age and gravity had made changes to her C-cup breasts. Her belly, beneath the jeans he was sliding down her hips, retained a distinct outward curve. Her stretched-marked hips flared a little fuller than fashionable, but the heat in Jim's eyes, as he beheld her standing before him clad only in a pair of satin and lace panties, burned with desire. Clearly, the imperfections of her shape did not dissuade him in the least. Nor was he a hard-bodied sex god himself. He had love handles, not huge, but visible, and more than a hint of a paunch. Overall, he appeared fit, but not perfectly so. Undaunted, Mel reached forward and boldly unbuckled his belt, sending his own jeans to pool around his ankles. Then she stepped close and pulled his head down, so she could claim his mouth again.

His hands skimmed her hips, sending her panties to the floor. *Naked at last,* she thought with a sigh. He led her to the bed and pulled back the covers, revealing serviceable cotton sheets. He lowered her to them. She reached for him, urging him to join her. He didn't require a great deal of convincing.

"Jim," she said, "I want you to make love to me."

"Oh yes, Mel," he replied. "That's what I aim to do." He wriggled out of his underwear and let her feel the firmness of his erection against her hip. She reached for him, wanting another kiss, but he grasped her hand, staying her movement.

"Wait. I want to taste you," he urged.

A fluttering sizzle shot through her belly. She rolled to her side and arched her back, offering herself to him. He cupped a breast in each hand and lifted them, kissing one erect nipple and then the other, teasing the sensitive peaks with his lips and tongue, and the gentlest edge of his teeth. It had been so long since Mel had enjoyed a man in her bed. Even before the divorce, Max hadn't been the most urgent lover. But having Jim devour her nipples went a long way towards making her feel alive, like a real woman again. He sucked hard, drawing a breathless whimper from her.

"Do you like that, sexy lady?" he asked.

"Oh yes, Jim," she panted. "Again."

He repeated his tug on the other straining nub. She sighed as her back arched. "That's soooo good," she said.

As Jim made free with her breasts, her hands roved feverishly over his body, enjoying the interplay of skin, hair and muscle. He stroked her too, caressing her arms, her sides, her belly and finally delving between her thighs. Mel bent one knee, allowing him greater access. He cupped her, stroking the coarse hairs there before spreading her lips and feeling her wetness.

"Hmmm, nice," he murmured against her breast. He easily located her clitoris, engorged with blood and slick with fluid. He stroked the button gently, knowing just how much pressure to use to bring her to orgasm. His talented fingers stoked her fire easily. She flopped to her back. He followed, seeming to enjoy watching her response unfold before him. Her hips shifted, lifting, trying to reach that perfect moment, that utter ecstasy.

Slowly it began to dawn on her that she needed more. While he might bring her to orgasm this way, it wouldn't be enough.

"Jim?"

His blue eyes met hers with burning intensity.

"I need you now. Please?" She reached out to him.

"Are you sure?" he asked.

She nodded. "I'm about to explode. I want to share that with you."

He grinned and shifted, kneeling between her legs. She opened widely, reaching low to grasp his penis, which she caressed from head to root several times, until it jumped in her hand and a drop of semen beaded at the tip. Then she aligned him with her opening. He pushed inside.

Mel's neck arched, and he kissed her throat. Her breathing

grew shaky and harsh as Jim began to drive into her, pull back, and return. This was sex at its most primal, obliterating the senses, driving need to a fever pitch. She wrapped her arms around his chest, enjoying the softness of him, his weight and heft as he drove her into the mattress with eager thrusts. Her body yielded to his penetration with slick, passion-moistened acceptance. That orgasm teetered again on the brink, but this time she was ready. Jim filled her to her limit and she came apart, crying out with pleasure and squeezing him tight. Her ecstasy triggered his, and his release began before hers concluded. They froze, joined together, locked at the height of pleasure, bathed in sweat that defied the icy weather. Mel clung to Jim, wishing she could prolong this moment, make it last forever.

But as passion gave way to relaxation, she found the peace of his sated body in her arms just as compelling as the coupling had been.

Later, when the pleasurable drowsing had passed, Mel, her head resting on Jim's bare chest, spoke in a soft, hesitant voice. "Jim, what does this mean for us?"

He ran his fingers through her hair and then down her back until he was cupping her bottom. "What do you want it to mean, Mel?"

"I don't know exactly," she replied honestly. "I think it's obvious that I'm really attracted to you. and if what just happened is any indication, you feel the same way, right?"

He leaned up and kissed the top of her head. "Yes, Mel. Of course, I am. I... I'm not ready for this to be a... romance yet."

She swallowed hard, but thinking about it, she actually agreed to a certain extent. "Can we say it has the potential to grow into one?"

He smiled, a huge, perfect smile that crinkled the corners of his eyes and made the bright blue color look even brighter. "Yes. That sounds just right. In the meanwhile, I hope you will consider the occasional... repeat performance?" Now his gaze had turned hesitant.

She gave him a reassuring smile. "Of course. That was soooo nice. I wouldn't mind doing it again." She leaned up and kissed his lips once more.

"Sorry, Mel," he said, his voice a rueful chuckle. "I'm done for today."

She laughed. "Excellent," she reassured him. "I feel wonderful... and quite satisfied. Although it is Saturday, so there's always tomorrow too."

"Hmmm. I think 'tomorrow' is my new favorite word."

"It feels so naughty," she commented, "to have a friend with privileges."

"Naughty good or naughty bad?" He waggled his eyebrows.

"Naughty good. Like a delicious secret. Well, Mr. Peterson, shall we go for that walk after all? It's probably warmer now, and I bet Rufus is about beside himself. Um, where is the boy anyway?"

"Out back," Jim replied. "You should have seen him sulk when I sent him out the door."

"Get him," Mel urged, "and let's walk. Our Saturday brunch will become lunch if we don't get moving."

Jim stretched, rose and pulled his clothing back on. "Part of me feels about seventeen years old," he said.

"Good," she replied, glowing with pleasure and knowing exactly what he meant.

~

All that week, Melinda had the hardest time concentrating, which is deadly when one teaches kindergarten. While the children pulled each other's hair and called names, she tried to force herself to maintain her grip on reality, her mind wanting to go back to the weekend she'd spent in bed with Jim... even to the point of sleeping over Saturday night. While they both had said it wasn't a romance, it sure felt like one. And she, for one, intended to enjoy every second.

Well, every second that didn't involve six five-year-olds digging in the mud far too close to the swing set and one taking a flying knee to the head in the process.

She felt powerfully relieved to lock up the classroom door Friday afternoon and meet her friends for adult conversation at last.

They, of course, showed her no mercy. Cindy took one look at her face and crowed loudly enough that the other tables could hear, "Someone got laid!"

Melinda blushed and ordered a strawberry daiquiri but didn't comment.

"Out with it," Lucille ordered. "Is this one full of hot air, or did you finally find a partner?"

Melinda gulped and grabbed a piece of bread from the basket. Then she inhaled deeply. "Yes," she said in a soft voice. Then she held up her hand to prevent a prolonged round of squealing. "Yes, I let my friend make love to me. It was enjoyable. We're not a couple at this point, but we're entertaining the possibility. And as a lady, I can't give you any more details than that." And she didn't. She nibbled her dinner while her friends pestered her with questions to which she did not respond. *It feels so nice to have a few mysteries for a change.*

Melinda felt pretty good when she arrived home. So good, she decided to make one more attempt to contact Andie. She dialed her daughter's number, delighted when someone picked up. *This time, I'm not going to take no for an answer.* But the voice on the phone was not her daughter's.

"The number you have dialed is no longer in service," a mechanical-sounding recording informed her.

Shaken, Melinda hung up the phone.

CHAPTER 5

*W*inter passed into spring. The snow slowly melted, revealing tender shoots of new, pale green grass. Bulbs burst into flowers. Slowly and with many false starts, winter loosened its grip and life began to take hold. And with the spring blossomed new feelings of hope in two hearts for whom winter's grip had been too long embedded. Slowly, the Saturday and Sunday brunches evolved into weekend-long sleepovers. While Mel and Jim never spoke of a long-term relationship, in Mel's heart it felt like one. Lying with Jim's arms around her waist, she could just imagine how it would go; *slow and easy. No heavy drama, no intense conversation. Just the gradual admission that we've been a couple for a while. Eventually, I'll move into his house. When people ask, of course, we'll say we live together to save money.* She smiled in the darkness. *Of course, we will. And maybe, far off down the road, we'll stand side by side in Jim's backyard in front of a justice of the peace and say simple vows in front of friends and family. I'll wear a yellow sundress, or maybe a blue one. It doesn't much matter. It's the best future I can imagine,*

and it seems wonderfully plausible. Now if only I could get ahold of Andie, I think life would be about perfect.

And then thought failed as sleep washed over Mel. Cradled safe in her lover's arms, she felt happy and at peace.

~

"So, you ready for the long weekend, ladies?" Lucille asked.

"I am," Julie replied. "I have so much to do before my wedding, and I only have a month left. I need every second of that day off!"

"Don't panic, honey," Cindy urged. "Everything will be fine and beautiful, and you'll be much better off if you let go of the idea that it needs to be perfect. There's no such thing as perfection. Try to have a little fun this weekend. Melinda, what do you have planned?"

Mel smiled, a bit dreamily. "Jim is having me over for barbecue."

"That's all?" Lucille demanded. "Don't you two spend all your weekends together?"

"We do, pretty much," Mel replied, "but this time his kids will be joining us. Isn't that great? I get to meet his sons, Michael's wife, Drew's fiancée and the grandson." She beamed at her own excellent news.

The other ladies beamed. "That's great!" Julie exclaimed. "Are you officially a couple yet?"

The question took a bit of the wind out of Mel's sails. "No, not really."

"You might need to give him a bit of a nudge," Lucille suggested.

Mel shook her head. "If he's not ready, he's not ready. Why would I push him?"

"Because he's playing games with you," Cindy said, as

gently as she could. "Not intending to be mean or cruel, he is playing a game. Are you going to let him toy with your affection?"

"And if he breaks things off because I was too pushy?" Mel demanded.

"Then you'll know he isn't serious," Cindy replied, patting her friend's hand to soften the blow.

Drinks arrived, along with a dish of cheese dip and toast squares, sparing Mel from further conversation. *Thank you, Lord, for appetizers. I didn't want to have that conversation anymore.*

That night, Mel called her ex-husband.

"Max," she said without preamble, "I need Andie's new phone number. I know you have it, now give it to me."

"Who is this?" a breathy, female voice asked.

Though the woman couldn't see her, Mel raised one eyebrow in a disapproving gesture. "This is your partner's ex-wife. The mother of his child. Can you please put Max on the phone? I'll be quick."

"Max," the woman's muffled voice still carried over the phone. "She says she's your ex-wife. She wants your daughter's phone number."

"Mindy?" Mel noted with detachment that the sound of her ex-husband's voice no longer stirred her.

"Hello, Max. I need Andie's new phone number. She never gave it to me."

"I can't believe it took you this long to ask," he commented. Then he rattled off a series of digits so quickly Mel had to ask a second time. "So why did you wait?" he asked.

"Because it's awkward to call you," she replied dryly.

"Especially as I have no idea whom you might be... entertaining when I call. Not that I care," she added quickly. "I just don't want to interrupt. Do you know why Andie won't talk to me? Is this some kind of convoluted plot to get us back together?"

"Nope," Max replied. "She's crazy about Ingrid. They get along great."

Mel wasn't sure why she found the information so deflating, but she felt like a damaged soufflé. "Thanks for the number. Good night." She pressed the button and dropped the phone on the bedside table. *I'll call Andie soon and make her talk to me.*

Mel used her elbow to ring the bell on Jim's door. Normally, she would have come right in, but her hands, full of stacks of serving dishes, couldn't operate the mechanism. Not without dropping the hot casserole dish of beans currently burning her hands right through her potholders, the dish of potato salad perched precariously on top, and the bottle of soda tucked under her arm.

Instead of Jim, a young woman opened the door. "Hello, are you joining us?"

"You bet," Mel replied. "I come bearing side dishes, as you can see."

"Well, come in," the girl urged. Mel grinned and stepped through the door. She wondered which one this was. Jim had described his sons' ladies' personalities but not their looks, so the strawberry blond hair and aquamarine eyes provided no clue. "I'm Mel," she said, as she began to hot-foot it to the kitchen, eager to set down her burden before she did any damage to her fingers. "I'm guessing you're either Sheridan or Alyssa. Am I right?"

"Alyssa," the young woman replied from behind her. "Let me get that soda before it falls." She retrieved the bottle and Mel set her burden on the kitchen table, quickly removing the potato salad from atop the beans before it could get any warmer. She popped it in the refrigerator.

"Nice to meet you, Alyssa. I've heard a lot about you." Mel shook the young woman's hand and gave her a longer look. Alyssa seemed a bit scrawny, and her eyes seemed to swallow up her whole face, giving her a haunted, fragile appearance.

"Mommy!" A tiny boy with russet hair ran into the room and hurtled himself at Mel's companion. She scooped him onto her hip.

"I haven't heard about you, I'm afraid," Alyssa said. "Are you a friend of James'?"

"I'm his neighbor down the street. We walk together. You know, for exercise," Mel explained. *This is the woman Jim hates for his son to be with?*

"Ah, well it's a pleasure to meet you," Alyssa replied. "Come on out back. It's a beautiful day and the meat is almost finished."

So, Jim hasn't told his family anything about me, eh? Interesting. And yet I'm here meeting them. Having no idea what it all meant, Mel walked through the house to the backyard. Sure enough, Jim presided over his showy, stainless steel grill. *If I didn't know better, I'd say he was compensating for something... but Jim's nicely endowed. Must just like grilling.*

She regarded the other guests. Two younger men, both appearing to be thirty-something, sipped beer from sweaty brown bottles and chatted. The younger one looked a bit like Jim, though his hair was auburn like that of the young boy. *This must be Drew, the biological son and doctor, though he looks nothing like a medical professional, in loose brown shorts, a short-sleeved button-up shirt, and sandals.* Alyssa and her son crossed quickly to him. He planted a kiss on her forehead and scooped the little boy into his own arms. Her face lit up. *Just a sweet, ordinary girl. Nothing at all to worry about.*

She turned to the other man and noted he looked quite different. Ridiculously tall with black hair tied into a shoulder-length ponytail, Michael was clearly not of Jim's bloodline. He looked non-European. He wore slim-fitting jeans and a fitted tee that revealed bulging biceps and chest muscles. Her guess as to the man's identity was confirmed when a lovely woman in a loose-fitting pink dress emerged from the house. Her belly bulged heavily, indicating late pregnancy. *That's right. James mentioned Michael and Sheridan were expecting* Michael's gaze, filled with pure, possessive heat, resembled a panther eyeing its mate... or its prey. The young woman seemed unintimidated by her husband's ferocious smolder. She walked right into his arms and tugged him down, kissing his lips. A laugh like a chime spilled from her. She laced her fingers through his.

"Mel!" Jim called, drawing her attention back to him.

"Hello, Jim," she replied. She spared a quick glance at the two couples before approaching her host, plucking the tongs from his hand and hugging him. She brushed her lips across his cheek. *There. Let them all make of that what they will.*

"Everyone," Jim announced, "this is Mel. My..." his eyes skated over her, then over his family. "My friend."

"We walk together," she elaborated. "The two of us and Rufus."

Drew laughed. "Who walks whom?" he demanded. "Do you two walk the Doofus, or does he walk you?"

As though realizing he was the subject of conversation, Jim's slobbery dog sauntered over to Mel and laid his head on her foot, groaning. Ribbons of saliva dripped through Mel's sandal and soaked her big toe. She grimaced at the slimy sensation but knelt anyway, taking the dog's wrinkly, snub-nosed face in her hands. "He's a perfect angel," she said, ruffling Rufus' ears. "Aren't you, baby?" The dog moaned in response.

Gentle laughter sounded from the assembled guests.

"The food's ready," Jim announced.

"Let me wash my hands," Mel replied, "and I'll bring out the side dishes."

"You going to wash your foot too?" Drew asked.

"I might," she replied, lifting it. Laughing, she hobbled into the house.

By the time she emerged from the bathroom, Jim had entered the kitchen, where he appeared to be gathering up paper plates and cups.

"Hey, you," she said. "Come here, big boy." Feeling amorous and aggressive, she grabbed Jim and planted a wet kiss on his lips. For a moment, Jim seemed startled, but then he relaxed, leaning into the kiss, giving her a quick plunge of the tongue.

After all too brief a moment, he pulled back, meeting her eyes. "More of this later, my dear," he said.

She winked and then, as though nothing had happened, she gathered up the potato salad and a handful of napkins, stalking out of the house with a sexy swivel of the hips.

"Watch out, little lady," Jim drawled, imitating a southern accent, "or you might get more than you bargained for."

"That a promise?" she replied cheekily, scooting out the door before he could pop her on the butt with a rolled-up towel.

Mel passed an enjoyable afternoon and evening with her friend and his family. She found all the young people delightful.

Drew, though possessed of a smart mouth and a sharp wit, was never scathing or sarcastic. Alyssa said little, but the way her eyes followed Drew around spoke of a deep and abiding love for him... and also a hint of disbelief. *Their relationship is far from settled.* Drew doled out constant reassurance in the form of little squeezes to the hand, kisses to the temple, and other tender gestures.

Michael, for his part, slowly transformed in Mel's mind over the course of the visit. What had at first seemed smolderingly dangerous, as she observed, became shyness. And once he relaxed, the tall professor revealed himself to be a brilliant and well-spoken man. Much of his relaxation could clearly be attributed his wife, who softened his glower. *As if anyone could withstand such cheer.* Sheridan, all smiles and smart, well-informed conversation, presided over the table like a friendly and benevolent queen. When the fullness of her belly began to shift visibly under her dress, she invited both Alyssa and Mel to feel her baby moving. *It never gets old,* Mel thought as the little one – whom Sheridan had informed them was a boy – pressed hard against her hand.

"We're going to name him Kevin," she announced, drawing all eyes to her, "unless anyone has an objection."

Mel watched the reactions of the group. Alyssa smiled shyly, but both Drew and Jim grew a bit misty-eyed at the information.

"I think that's a fine idea," Jim said at last in a gravelly voice.

"A fitting testament," the young doctor concurred with a sharp nod.

And then, finishing the meal with a scrumptious rhubarb and strawberry crumble Sheridan had made, the young couples departed, leaving Jim and Mel alone.

"You have a marvelous family," she said softly as she stood in the doorway, watching the taillights of Michael's Firebird disappear around the corner. Jim's arm came to rest around her waist and he led her back into the house.

"Now then," he scolded as they walked inside, "you were doing some powerful flirting back there, little lady. I want to know what you meant by it."

She giggled. "I don't know," she replied. "I guess I just got excited seeing you. You know you're going to have to field quite a few questions after this."

"How so?" Jim came to a stop in front of his kitchen table and turned to face her.

"You brought me to a family gathering. Does that mean..." she trailed off, too nervous to continue.

"Mean what, Mel?" Suddenly serious, his blue eyes bored into hers.

She remembered her friends telling her to give him a nudge. "They'll think we're a couple. Are we, Jim? Because it sure feels like it."

"You know, it does," he replied, reaching up one big hand, calloused from years of yard work and washing dishes. "What do you say, Melinda? Want to be my girl?"

"I'm forty-four, Jim. I'm hardly a girl." She ruined her faux-serious demeanor by giggling again, as much with nerves as with excitement.

Jim shrugged. "Semantics. Do you?"

She nodded. "To be honest, I think I have been for a while."

He dipped his chin in agreement and boosted her up onto the table, stepping forward to kiss her. "Hmmmm, nice," he mumbled against her lips.

"Very nice," she agreed, teasing his lips with her tongue. *Turns out there's no wrong age for a romance.* He tipped her onto her back and tugged her skirt up to her waist, revealing her panties. As always, she wore pretty lingerie. *No reason to risk being caught in granny panties.* He slipped the black satin briefs down her thighs and lifted her knees, settling them on his shoulders.

"Feel okay?" he asked her.

"Yeeeees." Her answer turned to a squeal as he leaned forward and lowered his mouth to her sex.

Her swollen clitoris reacted instantly to the gentle touch of his tongue, wringing a soft cry from her lips.

"Oh, Jim, oh God," she panted as he made love to her with his mouth. Within moments she was drenched and throbbing, aching with need for her man... for their lovemaking to be consummated. "Please, Jim. I need you. Please."

"All right, sweetheart. God, I love it when you beg." He opened his belt, letting his pants fall to his ankles, and dragged her to the edge of the table. A hand under each of her thighs to support her legs, he moved into position. She grasped his penis and aligned him. No slow merging, he joined their bodies with a hard thrust.

They both groaned as he sank home inside her. Mel loved every moment. *Doing it on the table like horny teens is dirty fun. Half-dressed is even better.* If her forty-something body could turn her man on this much, she must look just fine.

Jim hammered into Mel with the vigor of a man half his age, until both were sighing in sweet release. Then he helped her down, gathered their scattered clothing, and led her to the shower.

In a two-bedroom apartment across town, a young couple also reclined in bed in each other's arms. Drew kissed Alyssa on the forehead and snuggled down onto the pillows. She cuddled close to him.

"Drew?" she said.

"Hmmmm?" he replied sleepily.

"What did you think of your dad's friend?"

He opened his eyes. "She's nice. Why? You don't think they have something going on, do you?"

She grinned. "I'm sure they do," she replied.

Now Drew really seemed awake. "How so? Women's intuition?"

"Nope." Alyssa's smile began to look more like a smirk. "I saw them kissing."

Drew rolled his eyes. "That peck on the cheek? Friends do stuff like that sometimes, Allie."

"No, honey. This was in the kitchen. And unless friends tongue-kiss, it was a bit more than a casual gesture."

Drew's jaw dropped. "The hell you say?"

"I'm serious," she replied. "They were making out like kids."

"Wow," Drew said at last. "I'm speechless."

Alyssa suddenly grew worried. "You're not upset about it, are you?"

He shook his head. "Dad's been alone too long, so it's about time he met someone. I'm okay with it."

"Good," she said. "I love you, Drew."

CHAPTER 6

$\mathcal{B}$y the time of Drew and Alyssa's wedding, Mel was starting to think she'd found her one true love, her soul mate. Something about Jim that spoke to her heart in a way she'd never experienced before. Even growing old seemed less daunting if he would go there with her.

They sat in the same pew for the event, Jim on one end, holding Michael and Sheridan's newborn son while the new parents acted as attendants for the bride and groom. Between her and Jim, little Dylan sat with a pillow on his lap, watching solemnly while his parents married. A little girl named Kayleigh, Sheridan's niece, held an empty basket on hers. Mel's years of experience teaching tiny kids prepared her to corral the children, and she doled out coloring pages and crayons, small, non-messy snacks, and finally toy cars and a miniature doll from a restaurant kids' meal to keep them occupied during the hour-plus long Mass.

Jim drew in more than a couple of unsteady breaths as he watched his son marry the girl he'd never liked, though after several more meetings, Mel felt more confused than ever about

Jim's objection to Alyssa. Though shyer than Sheridan, the young woman had a quiet and understated friendliness Mel found charming.

After the ceremony, Mel and Jim sat together at the bridal table at the dance hall, surrounded by bouquets of irises in a rainbow of colors. Bright cloths decorated the small round tables along the periphery of a parquet dance floor.

"Congratulations, Drew," Mel said, leaning behind Jim to address the groom. "I'm so happy for you both."

"Thanks," the young man replied. "I didn't get a chance to say this before, but I'm glad you and Dad got together. I think you're a nice couple."

Mel beamed. "I think so too. Thanks, Drew. That means a lot to me."

"Any time." Then, like the besotted lover he was, Drew's gaze returned to his bride. He leaned over and kissed her cheek as the guests whistled and cheered. She blushed. Michael tapped his knife on his wine glass and all eyes turned toward the tall, long-haired groomsman.

"Welcome, guests. Maybe you're not familiar with our family story, and I don't intend to belabor the point now. Drew was born when I was in elementary, and a boy could never have asked for a better little brother. Even when he did trail after my friends in his annoying little brother way, I couldn't stay mad for long."

The guests chuckled, and Drew glared at his brother. Then he laughed too.

"Life dragged us apart for way too many years, but I never forgot my little brother. And I'm overjoyed we've had a chance to reconnect. And now he's marrying his high school sweetheart, a girl I never got to meet until now. But I can see she's an angel. Drew, you're a lucky man. Don't try your annoying little brother tricks on her, okay?"

Alyssa blushed and giggled.

"To Drew and Alyssa!" Michael raised his glass and the rest of the room followed suit. Then Drew kissed his bride and the party continued.

Midnight had long since passed before Mel and Jim stumbled, yawning, into his bedroom. They collapsed on the bed.

"Sorry, Mel." Jim yawned. "I don't think I'll be able to..."

"No worries." Weariness made it difficult for her lips to form words. She settled against Jim's back, draping her arm around his waist. She kissed his shoulder. He lifted her fingers to his lips.

"Mel?"

"Hmmm?" she hummed, struggling to focus against the crushing urge to sleep.

"Was I completely wrong about Alyssa?"

Mel wanted to groan. Fatigue was about to bowl her under and Jim wanted to ask deep questions? "Yes, honey," she replied in the kindest voice she could manage. "Alyssa is a nice, sweet girl and she and Drew will be fine together."

Jim grunted, but she thought it had a hint of an affirmation to it... before she slipped into the darkness and slept.

The next day, Mel sat in her kitchen, watching the wallpaper, where a real ladybug climbed up a printed vine. A half- empty glass of red wine sat in front of her. A new disposable cell phone rested next to it. Third was the number Max had given her. After repeatedly attempting to call Andie from her own cell and receiving no response, Mel had resorted to desperate measures. *I feel like a stalker, but I'm her mother. Surely she can at least explain why she's avoiding me.* She raked her fingers through her hair, making it stand on end, bit her lip and swallowed a big gulp of the wine, then another, as she built up her courage. *I'd better take it easy or I'm going to get dizzy and forget what I'm trying to say.*

"All right, Melinda, you've been dawdling for an hour. Get to it!" At last, she dialed the number.

"Hello?"

Mel closed her eyes at the sound of her daughter's voice. Years of memories rolled over her. The scent of Andie's shampoo. The softness of her baby skin. Tears stung Mel's eyes.

"Hello, is anyone there?"

"Mel, it's me. Don't hang up."

"Mom?" The voice sounded disbelieving... and unhappy. "What do *you* want?"

Stung, Mel demanded, "Hey, what's up with that? I want to talk to you, honey. You're my daughter, and I love you. Besides, you must be graduating soon. I want to know when and where so I can be there."

"I graduated last week," she replied, "I didn't think you'd want to know, since you only ever cared about yourself." And then the connection went dead.

Mel stared at the phone as though it had bitten her. The tears that had stung at the thought of talking to Andrea had been replaced by stunned disbelief. *She didn't even call to tell me about her graduation? Didn't send me a note? What the hell is going on? I always thought we were close.*

Her eyes returned to the wallpaper, but the ladybug had disappeared. Her hand closed around the stem of the wineglass and she lifted it, downing the contents in three big gulps. She choked, swallowed hard and set the glass on the table, waiting for something to happen.

Come on, Mel. Feel something. Cry. Something... Don't just sit here like a zombie. But to her surprise, the first emotion she felt was rage. Sweeping the glass off the table, she shouted, "What the hell, Andrea? Why are you doing this to me? I've always been there for you. Always. How can you say I didn't care? What on earth is happening?"

At last the bitter tears burned in Mel's eyes and spilled over. "Andie," she whispered.

"Mel, is everything all right?"

Her head shot up and her breath caught at the sight of Jim standing in the kitchen doorway.

"Watch out," she said, her voice unsteady. "There's glass. I broke a glass..."

"I see." In fact, it seemed he saw a great deal. The half-empty bottle of merlot on the counter. The shattered fragments of glass on the floor. The splatters of dark red. Mel's tear-streaked face. The corners of Jim's mouth tightened. "I have to go," he said, turning on his heel and stalking out of the house.

"Jim, wait!" Mel called. *Don't go. I need you.*

The living room door slammed shut.

Mel jumped from the table, trying to skirt the jagged mess, but the alcohol had muddied up her brain and she miscalculated, driving a shard deep into her toe. Cursing, she hopped on one foot as she yanked out the offending glass, and then, limping and wincing, she hobbled into the street.

"Jim! Jim, please come back. I need to talk to you."

On the front step of his house, he turned and glared at Melinda.

Her weight came down hard on her injured toe and she wobbled, catching the railing for support. She staggered up the steps. "Please, Jim. Tell me you have a moment. I really need you."

He looked her up and down and she flushed to realize what a mess she must look, hair messy from earlier housework, clothes filthy, staggering with a bloody toe, her eyes bloodshot and her face tearstained.

Jim slowly shook his head. "I don't think we should see each other anymore." He stepped inside his house and shut the door.

CHAPTER 7

"*A*nd then he just closed the door in my face," Mel sobbed. "What's going on, Cindy? Why did my daughter and then Jim turn on me? What did I do?"

"I don't know," Cindy replied, hugging her friend from her seat on Mel's couch, where she'd camped out after her friend's incoherent phone call the previous night. "It doesn't make a bit of sense, any of it."

"What do I do? I can't lose either of them. I can't stand it."

"Hush now, honey." Her friend rubbed her back. "Let me think... do you have Andrea's phone number?"

Mel waved in the general direction of the kitchen. Cindy gave her an extra squeeze and rose, walking into the other room. She returned, dialing from her own cell phone. Mel watched in teary curiosity, wondering what Cindy was up to.

"Andrea? Yes, this is Cindy Jones. I know you must remember me." There was a pause and then, "Don't take that tone of voice with me, young lady. I know your mother taught you better manners than that." Another moment passed, and Cindy snapped, "Bullshit. That's crap and you know it,

Andrea, unless you've completely lost your mind. You've broken your mother's heart with your behavior and there's no reason for it. The least you can do is explain to her what the hell is going on."

Cindy held out the phone to Mel, who placed it tentatively to her ear. "Hello? Andie?"

"Mom." The chilly neutrality of the voice brought fresh tears to Mel's eyes.

She looked up at Cindy, who mouthed, "Don't take any shit."

"What's going on, Andie? Why won't you talk to me, and don't say you thought I wouldn't be interested. I've been trying to get ahold of you for most of the last year. You've been avoiding me. Don't deny it."

"I'm not denying anything, Mom," that icy voice replied. "But I'm not avoiding you exactly. It's more like... I know you don't want to talk to me and I'm trying to let you know you don't need to perform your duty towards me anymore. I'm a big girl. I don't need you."

The words cut into Mel's heart like blows from a cleaver.

"I know you don't need me, honey," Mel said quietly. "You're doing great on your own. But does that really mean you have to cut me off completely? I tried to give you a little space, but that doesn't mean I wanted to lose touch."

"Cut the crap, Mom," Andie sneered. "We both know you never saw me as anything but a burden."

Mel's jaw dropped. She stared at her friend for a silent moment before anger welled up. "Are you insane?" she shouted. "Where are you getting this garbage from? I never, not once, saw you as a burden, Andrea Summers. I never said it, implied it or thought it."

"Mom..."

"No!" Mel interrupted her. "I won't listen to this. I didn't do anything to deserve it and I'm not taking it. Not from you or anyone else. It's nonsense. Now you'd better explain where exactly you got these ideas from, because it certainly wasn't from me."

"Wasn't it?" Andrea burst out, angry now instead of sarcastic. "Didn't you work by the hour when you should have been taking care of me? Didn't you join committees and spend long hours on the job while I was growing up? You loved everyone else's kids, Mom, but what about your own?"

Nonplussed, Mel simply blinked for several moments. "What?" she demanded at last. "What do you mean? Yes, I worked. Lots of mothers work. But that doesn't mean I didn't love you. Don't you remember how you'd come to me? I signed on for bus duty, so I could meet your bus every day, and then you'd sit in a desk near me and work on your homework, and I'd help you if you got stuck?"

"Yeah, I remember," Andrea replied, sounding sulky.

Mel looked out the window at two robins pulling worms from her front yard and took deep breaths while she pondered her next words. "Didn't I always come home and cook a good dinner, and we would sit together, the two of us, or the three, if your dad was around, and enjoy a family meal with conversation?"

"Yeah."

"And in the summer, when I wasn't working, didn't I take you camping? We'd sit on the porch of the cabin, just the two of us, and talk girl talk for hours, Andie, drinking hot cocoa and laughing. Or fishing from the dock. Tell me you remember all this."

"I remember, I remember!" the girl exclaimed, exasperated.

"Then where did 'burden' come from? I wanted to do those things. I enjoyed them. I enjoyed sharing my time with you and watching you grow, Andie. How did you get that so turned around in your mind?"

"It's just you... you're so... I don't know. So passive when it comes to relationships. You don't fight for your family or your friends. You just float along, keeping things superficial, and when someone wants to go, you just let them walk away, like you did with Dad."

"Wait just a minute, did your dad tell you all this?" Mel demanded. "Did he paint your whole childhood with his perceptions of me? Honey, think! If there's blame to be laid for our breakup, it's on both sides. Listen, maybe I did let our marriage slide a little. It's hard, working full time and taking care of a kid, cooking and cleaning and holding life together. But if you think back, your dad wasn't around much to help out, so a huge part of the burden fell on me. Something had to give. If the consequence was my marriage ending, so be it. That can't be changed now. But, Andie, that doesn't mean I didn't care for you!"

"Sure, Mom. Blame Dad like you always do. He didn't want your marriage to fall apart. He tried..."

"He served me with divorce papers, honey," Mel pointed out. "I don't think he wanted very badly for it to work. But that's between him and me and shouldn't mean you have to choose one over the other. The first three years we were okay. What happened?"

"Wait," Cindy interjected loudly enough to be heard over the phone. "Did Max get into a serious relationship in the last year?"

"Yeah," Andie replied, and Mel nodded, so Cindy would know the answer.

"Did he talk to you and his girlfriend about his marriage, try to explain what went wrong?"

"Uh huh."

Mel dipped her chin again.

"Then I'm sure he tried to paint the breakup as Melinda's fault, with himself as an innocent victim, so his girlfriend would keep faith in him. That was for her, not for you, Andie, and I'm surprised you fell for it."

"Hmmm," Andie replied, clearly considering.

"You see, honey?" Mel took over. "Look, I'm not blaming your dad for anything, but I need you to know that while I may not have been a perfect mom, or apparently a very good wife, I always loved you. Do you know why you're an only child, Andrea?"

"I always thought it was because you realized having more kids would destroy your career."

Mel shook her head sadly. "Not a chance, honey. I wanted a houseful and would have given up teaching if my job interfered with my babies. No, your dad and I had some kind of fertility problem. We tried for two years to have you, but nothing happened. The doctor gave us some kind of drug to help. It worked, and you were born nine months later, but then it never worked again. I figured, if you were the only one I was getting, I'd better maximize the time I had with you. That's when I chose teaching, mainly so I could have regular hours and plenty of time off with my little one. I love my job, Andie. I love those babies. But they don't substitute for you, my own child."

A long moment of silence ensued. Mel sat breathing slowly, trying to convince her heart to stop pounding. *Andie's listening to me. She's thinking. Maybe all is not lost after all.*

"Do you really think," the girl eventually said, "that Dad made that stuff up to impress Ingrid and it's not true at all?"

Somehow, Cindy had managed to hear the question and shouted "Yes!" in the direction of the phone.

Mel waved a hand, urging her friend to hush. "It might

have been somewhat of an exaggeration. If he actually said I didn't have time for you, think back and you'll know that's not true. But if he said I was a bit passive with our marriage and let it slide... I don't know. Honesty compels me to admit there might be some truth in that. But not with you, Andie. Never with you."

"I guess, if you're being honest, I should be as well. What you're saying fits better with what I remember than what Dad said."

"Thank you for that, Andrea." Mel bit her lip to keep it still.

"Mom?" The girl suddenly sounded so wistful.

"Yes?" Mel replied.

"You really aren't trying to push me away?"

"Goodness, no, Andie!" Mel exclaimed. "Not in the least. That's the last thing I wanted. I was only giving you the space you seemed to be asking for, so you wouldn't feel like I was encroaching on your adult life. I wanted to let you set the pace is all."

"Oh." Andie heaved a huge sigh. "Mom..." This time when she spoke her voice sounded hesitant, not angry or sarcastic the way it had. "That was a bit passive too, you know. I was kind of waiting for you to make a big deal, get all over me about not being around. When you didn't..."

Mel gulped. "Okay, sorry. I didn't realize what you wanted. But that's not what I meant at all."

"I know," Andie admitted. "But sometimes you do give up on things kind of easily. Remember the year it was predicted to rain all week, so you canceled our camping trip?"

"Yeah. I remember you were thirteen and complained for two weeks that you'd rather stay home and hang out with your friends than 'sit in the woods and watch the trees drip'."

"I was actually kind of looking forward to it," Andie said.

"All my friends had been telling me how much it sucks to hang out with your parents, and I felt like I had to act that way around them. I didn't mean for you to cancel it."

Mel's eyebrows came together. "I wish you'd told me so privately, hon. I'm not a mind reader."

Andie sighed again. "Mom, I really do have to go. I'm interviewing for a job in half an hour, and I need to get ready. But I'm glad you called."

"Me too, or rather, I'm glad Cindy called and made us talk." Cindy smirked. "Good luck at the interview. From your tone, it sounds like a job you really, really want."

"My dream job." Andie inhaled loudly. "I'm underqualified and in no way likely to be chosen, but I have to try."

"I understand that feeling, but it might go better than you expect. Act like you have every right to be there. Do you remember what I always told you about confidence?"

"Yeah," Andie chuckled. "Fake it. No one will know the difference. They're all too busy faking their own confidence."

"You got that right, honey. Good luck. I love you."

"Love you too, Mom. Bye."

This time when Andie hung up, Mel smiled. She handed Cindy's phone back to her. Her friend was seething. "That jackass. How could you put up with him all those years?"

"Who, Max?" At Cindy's nod, Mel explained. "Andie isn't wrong. I did let my marriage slide. I didn't have enough strength to do everything. And what I didn't tell her is that I did do everything. Worked, paid the bills, cared for her, did all the chores. Everything, everything."

"Max didn't work?"

"Oh, he did," Mel assured her friend, "but he didn't actually want kids. We agreed when we married that each of us would pay our own way. I wanted the house, so I paid for it. I wanted groceries in the kitchen, so I paid for them. If I'd lived in a fancy downtown apartment the way he wanted, he'd have paid half. That kind of thing. To be honest, it was a bit of a relief when he decided to be gone for work so much."

"Wow. Just wow." Cindy shook her head. "You deserve better than that."

Mel lowered her gaze to her lap. "I thought I had it." Images of Jim floated up in her mind. His sparkling blue eyes. His firm, kissable lips. His rugged, suntanned skin. Images of him hugging and kissing her, of their bodies entwined in a passionate embrace. "You know; I think I'm being passive again. We'd been going great, and out of the blue Jim wants to break up? I think he owes me an explanation, don't you?"

"At the very least," Cindy concurred fervently.

"I think I'll go right now and extract it from him."

"I'll stand by in case you need me," her friend offered.

Mel shook her head. "This might be a lengthy process. I've imposed on your time enough for one day."

"Melinda Summers, stop that right now!" Cindy shouted, shaking Mel away from thoughts of Jim and back into the moment. "You're my friend. I'm happy to return the favor for all the care and support you gave me while my husband was ill. How many times did you combine our classes, so I could go to his chemo appointments? You drove me to the hospital and waited with me during his surgery. You brought us food, not once, but every day while he was recuperating. Mindy, you've gone above and beyond the call of friendship a thousand times over. Let me do something for you, hon. Please, I want to."

Mel nodded. "You already have, and I'm not keeping score."

"Of course not, but I'll still be standing by if you need me, okay?"

"Okay."

Heart pounding, but much strengthened by her conversation with her daughter, Mel walked down the street to Jim's house. She knocked but received no reply. His car sat along the curb, a quick glance revealed, so she used the key he'd given her to unlock the door, expecting to find him doing something noisy like washing clothes or talking on the phone. The house retained the quality of silence that suggests no one is home. On a whim, she looked out the back door and saw Jim's figure, standing highlighted in the June sunshine. Rufus sat at his feet.

Mel opened the door as silently as she could and overheard Jim talking to his dog. Rufus' squashed face wore a dejected expression. He held his leash forlornly in his teeth.

"Sorry, boy, I just can't do it," Jim said. "Walking reminds me too much of Mel. And I might run into her. Then I'd have to explain, and I don't think I'm up to seeing her or having that conversation…"

Mel interrupted his monologue by grabbing Jim around the waist from behind and saying, "Sorry, Jim, but ready or not, we're having that conversation now."

Jim whirled and for a moment, he took Mel in his arms and squeezed her. Jim's bulky body filled her arms to perfection. *Yes. This feels right.* "What happened? Why did you shut me down? I was falling for you in a big way. I thought we had a future together. What went wrong?"

She looked up into his face and saw his expression tighten down with hurt and anger, and a certain desperate longing. "Come inside with me, Mel," he urged.

She shook her head. "Let's walk."

Jim nodded, retrieved Rufus' saliva-soaked leash and clipped it to the dog's collar. Rufus lumbered happily toward the gate, his flat face set in a doggy grin.

Mel slipped her hand into Jim's. He went still for a

275

moment, and then relaxed, lacing his fingers through hers as they progressed down the sidewalk.

"I'm surprised you came," he said at last.

"You shouldn't be," she replied. "You know what I feel for you, even if we didn't say it."

"Yeah," he replied. "I know. But..."

"But what? Do you think I'm wishy-washy too? I just had a long talk with my daughter. She tried and convicted me of not caring about her and tried to exile me. I didn't allow it, and I won't allow you to cut me off either. Talk, Jim. What's happening?"

"I never thought you were wishy-washy, Mel. I promise. But you can't imagine how it affected me, seeing you like that."

"Like what?" she demanded. "Sad and heartbroken? Sorry, Jim. I'm human. I have bad days. Did you think I wouldn't?"

He looked askance at her. "Sad? No, drunk and stumbling around, Mel. I can't look at that. I can't do it again. I'm sorry, but no. I can't be with someone who has a drinking problem."

Mel stopped dead and reached across Jim to grab his shoulder, turning him to face her. "Jim, I don't have a drinking problem. I wasn't drunk."

He rolled his eyes. "I've heard that before."

"Not from me you haven't," she snapped. "I don't know what's stuck in your craw, man, but you'd better spit it out. That's a huge assumption, based on two seconds of evidence. I mean, think. How much did I drink at your Memorial Day party?"

Jim pondered, leading them forward again. "A sip of my beer?"

"Exactly," she replied. "I drank tea all afternoon. And what about our last dinner date?"

"We shared a glass of wine."

"Does that sound like a problem, Jim? Really?"

"No," he admitted, his voice thoughtful. Then he fell silent, seeming to take in the beauty of a June morning.

It's well worth looking at, Mel decided. The trees in full leaf whispered in a cool breeze scented with pine and the rose bushes bloomed in wild profusion in the yard to their left. Overhead the branches interlaced, shading the sidewalk from the sun, which filtered through in irregular patches on their faces and clothing.

"I guess I need to tell you about Mandy."

Mel sighed. "I figured she was going to turn up sooner or later. What went so wrong, Jim, that you're still obsessing over it this many years later? Was she an alcoholic?"

Jim nodded. "To put it mildly. And an addict…"

"Oh no, what?" Mel exclaimed, horrified.

"Yeah, it was a really dark time in our family. Eventually, I had to divorce her, to protect myself and Drew from her addiction. The judge wouldn't let me keep Michael and Kevin, and you can't imagine how it killed me, every day, to think of them in that situation. Michael won't talk about it, but I know she lost custody and they went to foster care a few years later."

"That's terrible," Mel said, her voice soft.

"It is," he agreed. "But before we parted ways, I spent the best part of a year dealing with her addiction, coming home from work never knowing if she was going to be high, strung out, hung over or anything. It was a nightmare. What she was taking made her paranoid, and she was always prodding me, trying to prove I was cheating or trying to hurt her. I felt like I was the one losing control. And trying to protect the children… so you'll have to understand I'll be sensitized to anyone getting drunk."

"Yes, I can see that," Mel replied. "Yet you don't object to drinking."

"No, that's true. In moderation. I sure didn't like seeing you drunk, though."

"Drunk?" Mel rolled her eyes. "I wasn't drunk, Jim. I swear. Do you know how much wine I'd had that day?"

He raised his eyebrows in response.

"One glass. Okay, maybe I drank it a bit fast, but it was only one serving. I was far from drunk."

"One? The bottle was half-gone..."

"Yes. I'd had my friend Cindy over the previous weekend and we'd each had one. That's half a bottle."

"Oh."

"Jim, I rarely have more than one or two glasses of wine in a month. Does that really sound like a drinking problem to you?" she demanded.

"Not really, no," he conceded.

"That's because it isn't a problem. I'd call myself an occasional drinker rather than a moderate one."

"Sounds about right," he mumbled. "But then, why were you staggering all over? How did the glass get broken?"

"I broke the glass on purpose," she replied. "I'd just received bad news and had a momentary crazy reaction. As for the rest, well, I'm clumsy. I stepped on the glass. I was limping."

"Oh." Jim didn't say another word for the longest time, but his suntanned cheeks darkened. At last, he added, "I guess I made a lot of unfounded and silly assumptions."

"Yep," she concurred. "You did. I won't lie, Jim. It hurts. It's been a long time since I dared to trust a man. I didn't expect this."

Jim frowned. "Have I screwed this up beyond fixing? I don't like being separated from you. I had no idea, until yesterday, how vital you'd become to me. I love you, Mel. Do you think you could find a way to forgive me?"

Mel shrugged. "I don't know. I've had a lot of people

assuming negative things about me, Jim. I could have used your help. I wanted you to hug me, and instead, you dumped me. It was just about the worst thing you could have done."

He drooped in defeat.

She slipped her hand into his. "But I love you as well. And it wouldn't be much in the way of love if I couldn't forgive one mistake, now would it?"

"No, I guess not." He dared to sound hopeful.

She squeezed his hand. "But you'd better talk to me next time you don't understand something. Promise me?"

Jim nodded. "It's little enough to ask."

"Yes," she agreed. "It is."

They stopped as one and turned toward each other. Mel wrapped her arms around Jim's neck. He embraced her waist. In the dappled sunlight, on a busy public street, they kissed, trembling with relief. Though on the surface the conversation had sounded calm, almost blasé, they each felt it deep into the core of their being and both knew, even more deeply than they'd realized, that neither would be complete without the other ever again. They clung to each other as visceral relief welled up from inside them and flavored their kisses with the taste of eternity.

EPILOGUE

*J*im shivered and pulled his suit coat a little closer
to his body. *What am I doing, standing outside in
October?* But he couldn't stop smiling, because he
knew. He glanced to the side and saw Drew and Michael, in
matching black trousers and blazers, each holding one wrist in
the opposite hand.

To the other side, Alyssa and Sheridan had lined up,
wearing black velvet dresses with long sleeves. Sheridan held
her baby cradled on her hip.

He turned his gaze out over the two small sections of rented
white chairs. They'd barely managed to fit the twenty chairs
into his little yard, with enough space between the two sections
for a piece of yellow fabric to be laid over the crisp, brown grass.
Overhead, one of the two towering oak trees scattered leaves
like flower petals, the brilliant orange, scarlet and gold
providing the decoration Mel had decided was too ostentatious
to purchase. *She likes things simple, my woman. I appreciate
that.*

Movement in the vicinity of his back door snared his

attention, and he took in Mel, standing in a flowing burgundy velvet dress, arm in arm with her daughter, a golden-haired beauty in a matching outfit. They walked down the aisle to the music of a flute, harp and piano that Mel's friend Cindy and her husband were playing on a portable MP3 player and speaker.

The two women proceeded up along the yellow fabric until they reached where Jim was standing. Then Andie kissed her mother on the cheek and went to sit in the front row, beside Lucille and Julie, who were riding herd on little Dylan. The boy was squirming with boredom already, before the service had even begun.

The Justice of the Peace, a statuesque woman about Jim's age, began the ceremony, but Jim's attention remained focused on Mel. Smile lines wreathed her pretty face, making his heart beat faster. Today, the anniversary of their first walk together, had seemed the perfect date to make their relationship permanent.

"James, did you have something to say?" the judge asked, shaking Jim out of his daydream.

"Yes," he replied. "Sorry." The audience giggled. "Melinda, when I first met you, one October morning a year ago, I wasn't looking for a romance. Love and life had been hard on me, and I didn't think I would be able to trust a woman again. I tried not to. But the more time we spent together, the more I wanted to trust you. Somewhere along the line, you tiptoed into my heart when I wasn't looking. And now, I know I never want you to leave. Thank you for being patient with me while I figured all this out. Thank you for loving me when I didn't deserve it. Thank you for forgiving me for having problems and baggage, and for helping me work through them. You've earned my love, Mel, and you have it, with all my heart. From this October morning forward. For the rest of our lives."

A single tear spilled down Mel's cheek and he wiped it away with a calloused thumb, knowing he had received in this woman the blessing he'd thought he would never have. One he'd never looked for, never dared to hope existed. Love burned in her eyes. Love for him, pure, selfless and true. It touched him deeply, Melinda's love, and brought with it healing, joy and hope.

AUTHOR'S NOTE

Dear Reader,

Thank you for taking this walk through life with Drew and Alyssa. I hope you enjoyed their journey. Please be kind enough to head back over to Amazon and leave a review: short or long, positive or critical, it doesn't matter. All reviews are good reviews, and we authors need them more than you know.

As you probably already realized, this is part of a series, all of which is available for purchase. Book 1, *When the Music Ends* tells Sean and Erin's story. Book 2, *When the Words are Spoken* tells Michael and Sheridan's. There is also a fourth part, *Caroline's Choice*, which isn't about the Murphy-Burke-Peterson clan, but rather tells the story of Michael's colleague Caroline, and her desire to start a family before time runs out. Even Brandon, the career counselor, has his own story *Watching Over the Watcher*. It was my debut novel, many years ago.

In *When the Heart Heals,* Alyssa's character is a composite of many, many students I've had. The problem of childhood hunger has not yet been solved in America, and there are a shocking number of children who only eat at school, either because their families can't afford enough food, or because the parent(s) work such long hours, there is no one home to prepare it.

Discover more books by Simone Beaudelaire at https://www. nextchapter.pub/authors/simone-beaudelaire-romance-author.

Want to know when one of our books is free or discounted? Join the newsletter at http://eepurl.com/bqqB3H.

Making a difference to a family in need could be as simple as donating something appealing to the food bank, volunteering in a soup kitchen, or even just lending a sympathetic ear. Most people aren't poor because they choose to be and knowing someone realizes that can remove the stigma of needing help. Remember, no one is immune from financial disaster, so be kind, always.

Best wishes and love always,

Simone Beaudelaire

You could also like:

Caroline's Choice by Simone Beaudelaire

To read the first chapter for free, please head to:
https://www.nextchapter.pub/books/carolines-choice-
contemporary-romance.

BOOKS BY SIMONE BEAUDELAIRE

When the Music Ends (The Hearts in Winter Chronicles Book 1)

When the Words are Spoken (The Hearts in Winter Chronicles Book 2)

When the Heart Heals (The Hearts in Winter Chronicles Book 3)

Caroline's Choice (The Hearts in Winter Chronicles Book 4)

The Naphil's Kiss

Blood Fever

Polar Heat

Xaman (with Edwin Stark)

Darkness Waits (with Edwin Stark)

Watching Over the Watcher

Baylee Breaking

Amor Maldito: Romantic Tragedies from Tejano Folklore

Keeping Katerina (The Victorians Book 1)

Devin's Dilemma (The Victorians Book 2)

High Plains Holiday (Love on the High Plains Book 1)

High Plains Promise (Love on the High Plains Book 2)

High Plains Heartbreak (Love on the High Plains Book 3)

High Plains Passion (Love on the High Plains Book 4)

Devilfire (American Hauntings Book 1)

Saving Sam (The Wounded Warriors Book 1 with J.M. Northup)

Justifying Jack (The Wounded Warriors Book 2 with J.M. Northup)

Making Mike (The Wounded Warriors Book 3 with J.M Northup)

When The Heart Heals
ISBN: 978-4-86745-673-6

Published by
Next Chapter
1-60-20 Minami-Otsuka
170-0005 Toshima-Ku, Tokyo
+818035793528

7th May 2021

Ingram Content Group UK Ltd.
Milton Keynes UK
UKHW012017200423
420530UK00004B/61

9 784867 456736